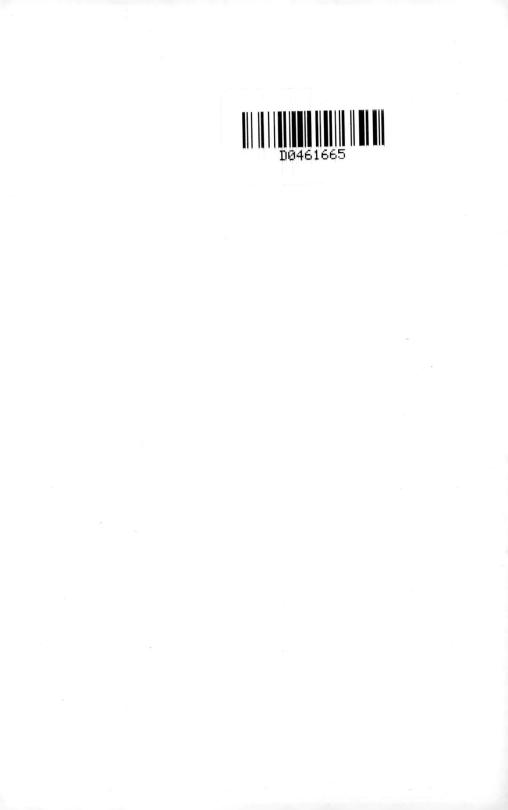

MUSEUM
PIECES

MUSEUM
PIECES

A NOVEL BY

ELIZABETH
TALLENT

ALFRED A. KNOPF

NEW YORK 1985

THIS IS A BORZOI BOOK
PUBLISHED BY ALFRED A. KNOPF, INC.

The author wishes to acknowledge the generous support
of the National Endowment for the Arts.

LIBRARY OF CONGRESS CATALOGING IN PUBLICATION DATA
Tallent, Elizabeth.
Museum pieces.
I. Title.
PS3570.A398M8   1985   813'.54   84-48497
ISBN 0-394-53928-1

Manufactured in the United States of America
First Edition

for William and Joy Tallent

When a woman lives alone, her house should be extremely dilapidated, the mud wall should be falling to pieces, and if there is a pond, it should be overgrown with water-plants. It is not essential that the garden be covered with sage-brush; but weeds should be growing through the sand in patches, for this gives the place a poignantly desolate look.

—*The Pillow Book of Sei Shōnagon*

MUSEUM
PIECES

1

"Why does the wind in New Mexico always blow from west to east?" Nat says.

"I don't know," Tara says. "I give up."

"Because Texas sucks," Nat says. She pushes the hair from her face. Strands are caught in her earring; she hooks a finger and unthreads them. There is a bandanna knotted around her ankle, its tip resting on the tongue of her basketball sneaker, which is coated with dust. It is windy in the alley, the dust lifting in knee-high whirlwinds that disappear around the corners of the houses. Tara's own hair, cut like a boy's, is too short to sting her eyes. It just whips around on her head.

"Gregory's from Texas," Nat says. Gregory is her mother's lover. "Gregory sucks."

"News flash," Tara says. She leans against the wall, pretending she can't move, trying to see into the window of the house across the alley, which is dark except for a TV left on. Reception in the pueblo isn't good; the light from the television flickers in a weak blue fan across the back of an empty chair. She doesn't know what's on TV at three o'clock in the afternoon—nothing, or "Sesame Street," or even "I Love Lucy" with its cracked satin heart under the credits. Gregory has been living with Annie, Nat's mother, since last spring, when he stopped in Santa Fe on his way to Los Angeles and spotted Annie across the self-serve island, cleaning snow from her windshield with her bare hand. Sometimes Gregory stays home watching television long after Annie has left for the office; he wears his cowboy hat even while he's in his pajamas, watching TV sleepily, spilling the ash from his cigarillo into the pale shell Annie's ex-husband brought back from the Sea of Cortez. One morning when Annie forgot to pack Nat's lunch, Gregory packed it for her—in a paper bag: five Oreos, a can of Coors Lite, and a plastic dinosaur. Tara had cut her peanut-butter sandwich in two, Smucker's grape jelly oozing out, and given half to Nat. Remembering that makes her hungry. She hasn't had anything to eat all day, unless you count the sips from Clarissa's—her mother's—coffee early this morning.

"Gregory opens other people's mail," Nat says. "He opened a letter Charles wrote to Annie." Charles is Nat's older brother, away at a military academy in the East.

"How did Gregory get it?"

"He just pulled sweat pants on over his pajama bottoms, the ones with the little giraffes on them, and walked on down to the mailbox," Nat says. "He probably looked really scabrous. I don't know what's wrong with Annie. She didn't even say anything to him about it, and it was a *private* letter, you could tell."

Tara closes her eyes. There is no feeling in her left foot; the pink bandanna she tied around her ankle this morning is thoroughly dirty and crumpled now. As far as she knows, Annie has always opened letters with an agate-handled paper knife, a souvenir from the Petrified Forest. Annie keeps things: cancelled stamps, wooden spools, and all of the old Monopoly markers—the Scottish terrier, the top hat, and the tiny iron—though the board has long since been lost. She even has one of Charles's baby teeth, in a furry velvet satin-lined box that once held a diamond ring.

"What would you do if your mother had a lover?" Nat says.

"What would I do?"

"Nothing, right?" Nat says. "You'd just pretend he wasn't there."

"She wouldn't, anyway."

"Oh, she wouldn't."

"Your mother was divorced for a long time before it happened."

"So?" Nat says. "Do you think people just get separated over nothing?"

"Sometimes," Tara says.

"*Some*times," Nat mocks.

Tara doesn't answer. She scuffs the toe of her sneaker into the dust, hoping her foot will wake up. In a minute it does—pins and needles.

She leaves a certain aloof distance between her shoulder and Nat's as they walk. Nat isn't even sweating, and Tara is, right through the thin black cotton of the old Harley Davidson T-shirt that belongs to Peter, her father. Angel wings in gold glitter sparkle across her chest, each wing ending above a nipple, though her nipples are small and don't show through the cloth, or she would have had to wear a bra. Or two Band-Aids, Charles once suggested. Two Band-Aids would do it.

"Did you know," Nat says, "that if your fingers get cut off, you're supposed to take them to the hospital? You're supposed to make sure you don't leave without them. Gregory had a friend in Lubbock that happened to. His fingers came off in the blade of a saw, and Gregory had to get down on his knees and find them, and he picked up one finger with the wedding ring still on it. Gregory gave the fingers to the guy who came in the ambulance and the guy said, 'Thank you,' and put them into this plastic bag to keep the nerves alive. At the hospital they sewed them back on, and now the guy is all right except for these hideous scars."

"Do you just believe everything Gregory tells you?" Tara says. She pinches her T-shirt and pulls the cloth away from her damp armpit. In the windows of the houses facing the alley most of the shades have been drawn, resting against the wooden sills, sometimes lifting and clapping against them in a way that suggests the houses are empty. The alley is cool after the hard, almost vertical light of the plaza, where she and Nat have been standing for an hour, watching the Corn Dance —the plaza filled with lines of dancers and closely flanked by houses whose flat roofs, one or two stories high, were dense with shifting black umbrellas. Old women sat in lawn chairs, fanning themselves or holding children in their laps, everyone staring solemnly down from the rooftops at the sweating dancers. Tourists came in chartered Greyhound buses to the dances now, but it wasn't always like that. When Tara was four, Peter and Clarissa took her to a Deer Dance at Taos Pueblo, and for the length of that winter dawn, so cold that Peter's breath had crystallized as ice in his mustache, they were the only Anglos in the pueblo—Clarissa, though she is Chinese, counting as Anglo for lack of a better category, the hood of her down jacket helmeting her face. Tara stood between her parents, leaning against Peter's leg, his jeans starched by the cold into an unfamiliar stiffness, her mitten curled over her nose and mouth so that, breathing, she melted the balls of ice in the wool into a spreading, stale wetness, half delicious, half irritating. The dancers came through the snow, bent forward, the points of their antlers held erect, the canes in their hands piercing the crust of the snow, leaving neat circles like air holes.

Their breath floated after them, and the bells on their legs rose and fell in frozen strokes. Tara couldn't see their mouths, or the expression in their eyes; she couldn't tell whether they were even aware of the cold. On the way home Peter pulled in at a truckstop he liked and ordered *migas* for them from the waitress while Clarissa did drawings of the pueblo—ladders and roofs and deep-set doorways—on the napkins she pulled from the shiny aluminum dispenser set between the salt and pepper shakers. There were wavy lines in the pink linoleum of the table, and the ghosts of coffee-cup rings. When Tara rubbed a clear space in the misted window she could see the hose leading from the gas pumps to an idling pickup truck, and a skinny boy dancing in the cold. She drew a face in the window mist: eyes, nose, mouth. When she looked up, Clarissa was smiling at her. "That's nice," Clarissa said. "A little Miró face."

Nat turns down another alley without asking Tara where she wants to go. In the shadow of a house an old man is sitting at a card table draped with a shawl, where his work is laid out—strands of white coral like the bones of some small, extinct mammal; rings of turquoise-and-jet or mother-of-pearl inlay; long silver earrings, silver rings, bracelets of braided silver, bracelets of bare polished silver; lengths of heishi so fine they could almost pass through the eye of a needle—all displayed beside a hand mirror with a plastic handle, a saucer of watermelon seeds and the rind, chiselled in wide strokes as if by buck teeth, and a transistor radio from which comes the reverent organ music of a distant baseball game. The old man's chair is rigidly upright and he wears a shirt buttoned to his Adam's apple. Except for turning the radio down, he in no way acknowledges their presence. Nat tries on one necklace after another, looking into the hand mirror each time, while Tara alternately studies the ground and the adobe bricks of the wall behind the old man—looking intently, as if they are very interesting bricks, as if there is some significance to their chipped and eroded corners, the spokes of straw in the mud, and the abandoned wasps' nest in a niche between two bricks. Diminished, the sounds of the baseball game are familiar. Peter likes to listen to baseball games. He likes to listen to them especially when he's driving at night, and for Tara, curled up in the back seat with his tweed jacket tucked around her, her chin against cloth that is scratchy as an old tennis ball and has no color in the darkness, the backs of her parents' heads would loom gradually larger and larger until they were almost like giants, talking softly together, and Peter would shush Clarissa when some crucial turn of the game demanded his attention and then say, "Way to go," or, "You missed it, how could you? You had it right in the palm of your hand, buddy." Clarissa's profile would be lit from below, when she glanced over her shoulder, by the dim, socketed constellation of the dashboard, which left her eye severely shadowed and her mouth and jaw delicately illuminated, a disappointed, mysterious face, half-frowning. Tara would look up at her and neither one of them would say anything. Neon glimmered now and then beside the highway, arching in an arrow over a truckstop whose glass had gone mirror-empty, purring in the pink oval, etched with frosty script, of a Coors sign in the window of a bar, blinking in the cuneiform VACAN Y above a motel's office door, and that was a town. In the desert a bunch of sage would show, bleached and two-dimensional at the highway's shoulder, and as the headlights swept into the knuckled roots the tail of a rabbit would flash away like a phosphorescent grounder into the dark. The baseball voices, the little clicks of excitement and periods of patient narration, were part of that, and part of her own drowsiness, because the black night in the car windows, the jacket pulled over her shoulder, and the sliding weight of the pennies Peter had forgotten to empty from his pocket combined to pull her down into sleep. Now none of that will ever happen again. If people are separated they don't go on trips together. They don't go anywhere.

Just when she is sure that Nat has offended the old man by taking so long to choose—because unless he has really good hearing he's missed about an inning of his game—Nat decides on a bracelet patterned with a crescent moon and stars. The old man counts Nat's money, five ten-dollar bills in a crumpled wad, brushing Kleenex lint from them, and when he looks up he smiles. "You girls go to school, eh?" "Yes," Nat says. "In town? In Santa Fe?" Nat nods. "That's good," he says. "All my grandkids go to school. I got one, he wants to be first Indian on the moon."

At a stand made of plywood and shadowed by sheets of thin canvas, Nat rests her elbows on the counter and scrapes a quarter around a mustard stain. The Indian woman in the booth takes an empty Coca-Cola bottle from a crate of them, pale green and dusty, reflecting a splintered quartz light into each other from the bulge of sun-heated canvas; she gives the bottle to the little boy beside her, and he squats and begins to fill it with a handful of dust, the grains ticking against glass. Nat rolls the quarter around the stain in the plywood and asks for two Sno-Cones; the woman scoops ice from a cooler into the cones and squirts them with purple ink from a glass tank that is percolating slowly in a corner. When she hands a cone to Tara, Tara can feel the gritty ice packed expertly hard inside the paper sheaf, like a crystalline snowball built around a stone; it smells wonderfully of fat grapes. "Chili dogs?" the woman says, making it sound like "chillit-dogs," and Nat says yes. The woman fishes the buns from a limp Wonder Bread bag, spears hot dogs from the sooty grill with a long curved fork, and wipes each hot dog from the fork's tines with a folded

bun. The chili she ladles from a saucepan over the buns immediately tints the paper plates to their fluted rims.

Nat and Tara find the shade of a cottonwood near the parking lot, which is really only an expanse of dusty gravel with
cars and pickups parked randomly along it. Tara holds her
paper plate carefully away from herself as she eats, peppery
meat dripping on her fingers. Then Nat sees a boy wandering
between the parked cars, and washes her chin with ice from her
Sno-Cone, rubbing the grains into her skin until they melt and
then wiping with a napkin.

"That's really gross," Tara says.

"I'm sticky, but at least I'm a little cooler."

"You smell like a huge Sno-Cone."

"He's coming over," Nat says. "Try not to look like we were
just pigging out. You've got something on your face." Nat
licks the corner of her mouth, and Tara, looking at her as if
into a mirror, licks until Nat nods. "God," Nat says. "He's
beautiful. He's so beautiful. Do you know him?"

"He's okay. I don't know him."

"Okay? Really, okay? You don't have to go to pieces."

"He's bowlegged."

"That's only because of the way he's walking," Nat says.

"It looks deformed."

"It's not deformed. His legs are straight. I've seen him playing tennis. His legs are long and straight and they've got brown
hair on them."

"Okay," Tara says. "His legs are straight. Darth Vader
doesn't breathe hard."

"I don't believe you," Nat says. "Some little imperfection
and you totally rule him out."

"Guess what?" Tara says. "He doesn't want to marry me."

"Can you be quiet? Because he's coming. He can almost hear
you."

"He can't hear me. You're wrong. He's not even looking this way."

"He's not?" Nat says, because she is staring off in another direction, turning the thin bracelet on her wrist sideways so it will slip from the bone, turning it again so that it will slip back on.

"He's not," Tara says. She waits until the boy is looking right at her, and then she crosses her eyes and stretches her tongue out as far as it will go. With her eyes crossed, the world is fuzzy, hot, and brilliant. She can just see the tip of her tongue, furred with purple from the Sno-Cone. The boy turns and walks away, disappearing around a Winnebago with Utah license plates. "He's leaving," she says. "If you look now you'll just have time to read his belt."

"Oh, Christ," Nat says, looking after him. "This is all your fault."

"You mean if you were standing here alone he would have come over."

"He would have."

"You're so arrogant," Tara says. "I suppose you think he would crawl through burning sand on his hands and knees just to talk to you."

"I'm not worried," Nat says. "I can see him when school starts. Was there really something on the back of his belt?"

"His name," Tara says. She writes the letters in the air: RICHARD.

"I didn't like the skunk-stripe in his hair," Nat says. "It didn't go with his sunburned neck."

When Annie comes, dust floating up behind the battered old Datsun as it skids to a halt near them, Tara climbs into the back seat, cautious because of the piles of *Vogues* and old Albuquerque *Journals* and the cans of diet powder on the floor, the empty box of detergent jutting from the laundry basket.

"Do you always have to drive like you're in a demolition derby?" Nat says. "They should just paint numbers on the doors of the car instead of giving you tickets."

Annie ignores her and reaches back to touch Tara's cheek. "How are you doing, sweet pea?"

"Fine."

"Fine, really?" Annie says.

"Really."

"I think that you should just believe her," Nat says.

"Should I believe you, sweet pea?" Annie says.

"Yes."

"I'm not so sure," Annie says, as if to herself. "So how was it? Were you bored?"

"The dancing goes on forever," Nat says, closing her eyes and tilting her head back. "I think I'm in love," she says.

"I think you're an idiot," Annie says. She is driving with one hand; with the other she smooths the hair from the nape of her neck, where there is a smudge of dust. "You wouldn't know love if it walked right up and looked you in the eye."

"Oh?" Nat says. "Is that how it happens to you?"

Most of the clothes in the laundry basket belong to Annie, but Tara sees some of Nat's ocelot-spotted underwear, and a ragged cowboy shirt with pearl snaps that must be Gregory's. She touches the shirt. It is not quite dry. In the front seat, Nat is twisting the bracelet around her narrow wrist. Annie looks at it sideways. "Okay," she says. "Where did that come from?"

"This very old man," Nat says. She imitates the old man's hesitant tremors, her hand extended.

"Natalie," Annie says, and catches her hand. Nat draws both their hands into her lap and rubs her mother's knuckles lightly along the seam of her Levi's. "Let go, sweetheart," Annie says. "I need my hand so I can drive."

2

Tara doesn't know who she wishes she was. In the orchard behind Nat's house, squinting down the length of her body and Nat's, side by side, she had played a game of seeing whether she could forget, for a moment, whose leg was whose, because their legs were not much different, in dirty running shorts, the brown knees puckered with scabs of various sizes and resistance to picking, the heels horny and cracked from going barefoot, especially if she viewed them through the prismatic haze of her wet, lowered eyelashes, wet because she had just drunk her fill from the cold copper nozzle of the garden hose while Nat held the arc of water steady with her thumb. Then Tara had lain on her back in the orchard grass, wishing that her soul could travel out of her body, and Nat's out of Nat's body, and the two souls, confused, would return to the wrong bodies—because it would have been a relief to live in Nat's body instead of her own, because it would have been wonderful not to go home.

Now, in the back seat of Annie's car, she simply wishes that something that happened hadn't happened. Last Saturday night Peter had taken her to Rancho de Chimayo, a restaurant she knew he couldn't afford. Lanterns were set in the shadows of the old cottonwoods, and the waiters went around lighting the lanterns with long wooden matches as it got dark. Peter ordered for her. He asked for a carafe of white wine, and when it came he spilled some into her glass, though she was sitting there shaking her head. "It's good," he said. She tasted it and made a face; he made a face back at her. The other people around them were dressed in evening clothes, as if they had all just come from the opera, but Peter was wearing a work shirt, smudged with dust, the sleeves pushed up above his elbows. He ate without saying a word, and as if he was very hungry. Once he dropped his fork, and a waiter picked up the fallen fork and immediately brought Peter another. "He thinks he's going to get a terrific tip," Peter whispered to her. Then he stopped eating and pushed back his chair, rising and saying, "Do you want to dance?" She shook her head, and he said, "C'mon, please?" She thought he might be slightly drunk. She was still shaking her head as he reached for her, his hand flat between her shoulder blades so that she was drawn in too close to him, her nose near the glint of a white button on the work shirt, his toe barely missing her own. They moved together. She was cautious not to catch the eye of anyone at the nearby tables. "Think of the separation as an experiment, okay?" he said. She knew from the way he said "experiment" that he had rehearsed it to himself, and she was frightened by that, more frightened than she had been before, even though she'd known for some time what was coming. "It's not necessarily forever," he said. "Neither one of us believes that. Your mother thought that I should be the one to tell you."

"Why?" Tara said. "Because it was your fault?"

He looked down at her. "It wasn't my fault."

"Then it was her fault."

"You don't understand," he said. "It doesn't have to be somebody's fault."

"Then whose idea was it?"

"Whoever thought of it first, then it was their fault?"

"Just whose was it?"

"Both of us," he said.

"You can't both have the same idea at the exact same time."

"Both," he insisted.

She stepped away from him so fast that his feelings were wounded—she could see the hurt line of his mouth below his mustache—and he had no choice but to follow her back to their table. They sat down, his knee knocking the table so that their wineglasses rattled. She looked over his shoulder. The lanterns threw their light into the small leaves no farther than fireflies.

"I know you don't remember this," he said, lifting his wineglass. "There's no way you could, but I taught you how to dance."

She pretended to cut into the food on her plate, her knife and fork heavy and cold, the voices around them continuing softly. She didn't tell him he was wrong, that she knew he had taught her to dance in front of the bedroom mirror, that she could remember him lifting her by her arms and waiting until her bare feet landed safely on the toes of his shoes.

3

"Now Gregory thinks he wants my mother to marry him," Nat says. She holds the tip of her braid between her teeth as she searches through her suede shoulder bag for an elastic band.

"How can he?" Tara says. "They hardly know each other."

Nat finds an elastic band and studies the link to see whether it will hold. She twists it around and around the end of her braid, smoothing the pale hair through the diminishing circle, and then she shakes her head so that the braid slips back over her shoulder. Tara is supposed to be practicing, but a couple of minutes ago Dr. Kitkov, the music teacher, was called away to the principal's office, and then Nat stopped in the doorway to see when she would be finished, and came in and sat down to study her reflection in the back of Tara's cello, which leans against the wall. Nat's face is in fragments, bits of eye and nose and chin surfacing in the fine-grained wood.

"I know," she says. "Anyway, he asked her. It was hideous."

"How did he ask her?"

" 'Annie, will you marry me?' "

"Oh, no," Tara says.

"They were out in the kitchen drinking wine. Lately the kitchen is where they have all of their really deep discussions, and they pull this huge Gallo jug out from behind the milk cartons first. They thought I was in my room watching HBO. I couldn't believe what Gregory was saying. He was so *serious*. It almost made me want to throw up." Cross-legged, Nat leans forward and pretends to retch violently. She mimics Gregory's voice: " 'I want to have children with you, Annie.' I think, What am I, a ghost? Only Annie doesn't want any more children. Can you see me writing to Charles at the military academy: 'Charles, hold on to your hat, we're going to have a little baby brother'?"

"No," Tara says.

"You know, you could've been there, except that you hardly ever come over any more. Your mother isn't exactly crying herself to sleep every night, is she? So why do you think she needs you around to watch her?"

"I'm not watching her."

"Peter, Peter, pumpkin-eater, had a wife and couldn't keep her."

"Cut it out," Tara says. "I mean it."

"Who *I* feel sorry for is Gregory," Nat says. "The suspense must be making him Looney Tunes. Last night, when they were getting ready to go to your mother's gallery opening, he ate the carnation that was supposed to go on his tuxedo lapel."

Out of curiosity, Tara makes an effort to feel sorry for Gregory; instead, she sees his rabbity mustache buried deep in the crisp white petticoat of the flower, his chipped front tooth flashing. Before he moved in, Nat's house had been one of

Tara's favorite places in the world. She could go there whenever she wanted, and through some tacit understanding that had evolved between Annie and Clarissa, no one ever wondered where she was, or called up frantic with alarm. Annie kept a spare futon rolled up in the closet in Nat's room, and though the futon was old and threadbare, smuggled out of a hotel in Tokyo by Annie's ex-husband, Tara loved it, and slept on it a cool dreamless sleep she never slept anywhere else. The house is an old adobe, thick-walled as a fortress, silent and shadowy even in summer, with the smell of rice cooking on the woodstove in the kitchen and, ranged on the windowsills, Ball jars in which mung beans are sprouting, pale shoots unkinking against glass smoky with condensation. Except for the kitchen table, which came from a monastery somewhere, there is almost no furniture in the house. They sit at the low table in the living room and eat with chopsticks. In the middle of the table there is a hummingbird's nest containing a pearl and a silver thimble. When Annie bought the house, it was completely empty and immaculate, except that in the corner of a back room the thimble was lying on the floor.

In the bathroom of that house, Nat instructed Tara in the use of kohl, the kind that comes in a clay pot from Egypt. You ground the point of the stick into the cake of pigment, brought it quite close to your eye, and the stuff rimmed your lashes in a continuous sooty line as you blinked. The kohl was good, Nat said, because of the shape of Tara's eyes. Tara's last name is the (in her ears) ugly hybrid, Wu-Barnes. She had been made to suffer for this after she transferred schools last year. Her lunch money was stolen; someone annotated her sheet music with SHIT and FUCK and WOG, a word she hadn't seen before. Much later, she had asked Annie about it, and Annie had narrowed her eyes and said, "Where exactly did you hear that, sweet pea?" "No place," Tara said. "No place?" "On a wall." "Nobody said it to you?" "No," Tara said. It wasn't quite a lie: after all, she had read it, nobody had said it to her. Annie had seemed relieved. "It's not a good word, kitten," she said, and went on to explain.

Before the first period, there had always been a gantlet to be run down the long hallway where boys leaned against lockers, one girl braiding another's hair, and a couple French-kissing by the water fountain, their jaws working as subtly as those of gazelles; so Tara became conscious of the gap between her front teeth, the wrinkles radiating from the crotch of her jeans, and the crude way her hands were attached to her wrists, which could not be disguised. Then, one lunch hour, a boy with hair like porcupine quills, only dyed a brilliant saffron, had beckoned Tara to lean across the cafeteria table, and when she did he blew a stream of smoke into her face. A girl stopped behind him, lifted the cigarette from his fingers, and ground it out in the gravy on his plate. "No smoking," she said. "Can't you read?" That was Nat. "I already know who you are," she told Tara. "We probably would've met sooner, only I've had mononucleosis. Don't kiss me. I'm Natalie Cimarron Whitman, if that doesn't make you throw up," and then, rather elegantly, she leaned forward and mimed throwing up on her lunch tray, on which there was only a pint carton of milk, a straw, and a paper bag. "You bitch, Whitman," the boy said, looking at his lunch tray. He stood up and left, tucking in his shirt tail with short chopping movements of one hand, his brown back showing under the waistband of his Levi's. Nat's motives for the rescue, if she'd had any, she kept to herself. Tara was sure that if Nat had known how desperate she'd been, how far she would have gone just to become invisible, Nat would never have intervened. Nat hates cowardice.

When Nat and Tara started going into the video arcade together, leaving their bicycles chained to the lamppost outside, the boys who stood in the cigarette dusk looked up at Tara over the flat gray panes in which spaceships and mutants floated in rows; they were reassessing her. Nat shrugged it off: boys had always looked at her. "Don't let it go to your head, okay?" she said.

By the time Saturday came around they hardly ever had any money left, but when they did they spent it on Diet Dr Peppers with crushed ice and Frito pies—tortilla chips crumbled into Velveeta cheese, sautéed onions, and refried beans, the whole mass, still smoking from the dimestore's microwave, packed into an orange Fritos bag and sold to you with a plastic spoon. Nat stole things, little things, from the back counters at Woolworth's and from shops she liked. From Woolworth's she stole a packet of dishtowels and a dying cactus, its skin shrinking away from the sheath of pale spurs. From Origins she stole a fan, from Morningbird a long velvet glove. Tara usually waits for her on a bench in the plaza, watching the Indian women descend from the pickups halted in front of the Palace of the Governors. If it is a cold morning, exhaust from the pickups hangs in the air and the women who get out are heavily laden with jewelry to sell, their shawls wrapped so that you can see no more of their faces than of the faces of surgeons. By the time Nat shows up, shaking her hair back and not deigning to look to either side, the plaza is crowded and Tara is sitting with her knees drawn up and her chin resting on them, looking down at the pigeons who stare up at her and then sulk away.

Tara watches the rest of the search through the shoulder bag without much interest, because she knows the contents almost as well as Nat does. Beneath the broken pencils, the leaky fountain pen, and the confetti of torn movie tickets, there is a flicker's wing a cat left on the windowsill, the glove Nat stole, crib notes for a history quiz, and an underexposed black-and-white photograph of Charles, standing beside Nat's ten-speed with a wrench in his hand, the collar of his leather jacket turned up. Fixing the bicycle was almost the last thing he did before they took him to the train station in Lamy, his duffel bag slung over his shoulder. In the photograph his hair has already been cropped, so that his ears stick out, and with the fingertips of his free hand he balances the bicycle by its concave leather seat, so that it does not quite touch his leg. His expression is one that Tara has seen a thousand times: it means he is about to speak, and that the intention has already cost him something, in the premonition of a stutter. His eyes are dark, a shade darker than Annie's, not as dark as Nat's. Tara thinks she will fall in love with him the next time she sees him. Nat, who knows this, has never offered the photograph to Tara. The stuttering is the only thing wrong with Charles. Nat and Tara used to lie on their stomachs in the abandoned orchard behind Nat's house while Charles called: "N-N-N-Nat, dinner. T-T-Tara." Nat would giggle, and Tara would giggle as softly, an echo. They were twinned for a moment by the feeling of being hidden from Charles, the long grass shadows passing from Tara's bare arm to Nat's in linked ellipses, and, when Nat lifted her head to study the house, the sun that was suddenly level between the rows of dying trees would light the down on her upper lip in a radiant mustache that vanished when she glanced at Tara again.

Once, looking down, she had scooted her leg against Tara's and kissed her, edging her tongue between Tara's teeth, and Tara could think of nothing to do when Nat's tongue retreated except reciprocate, stroking the point of her tongue along the enamel jewelry of her teeth and the animal silkiness of her cheek, worried that Nat wouldn't like it, worried that her mouth wouldn't taste as sweet as Nat's had, worried about what Nat would think, even though she had started it. Nat finished it, too, by turning her face away into the grass and closing her eyes, without explaining anything, and without ever referring to the kiss again. Tara didn't know whether she wished it had never happened or whether she wished it would happen again. Either way would have been all right, but that it had happened once, and never again after that—that seemed to mean that somehow she had done something wrong.

After Charles had gone away, all that Nat had had to say to cause Tara to break into deep, shamed giggles was: "T-T-T-Tara, d-d-darling." It makes Tara's stomach knot to remember the light in the orchard, the wall of grass marred here and there by the down-swinging arc of a broken stem, the smell of rotting apricots hidden in the grass and the brilliant-bodied wasps that were drawn to them, Charles holding the screen door open with his bare foot and then shrugging as if he knows where they are, really, it isn't worth his time to come after them, turning and letting the screen door slam shut behind him, the kitchen veiled again in the crisscross rustiness of the screen.

She has no reason to think Charles has ever noticed her. Okay, she has one reason. Before he left, just after he'd finished tinkering with Nat's ten-speed, he went into his room and brought out something for Tara. It was an ordinary Coca-Cola bottle, the old-fashioned kind with script on its side and a bottom quaintly thick and round as an eyeglass lens, and inside the bottle there was a perfectly formed green apple. He laughed at her amazement and then he told her how it was done. What she likes is that he has given her something. She keeps the bottle on the corner of her dresser at home, behind the music box and a wooden rhinoceros, and when she holds the bottle up, the apple still looks hard and unwrinkled. What she likes is the idea of Charles climbing the tree until he found the twig he wanted and then fitting the mouth of the Coke bottle carefully down over it, then descending the knotty branches and jumping down barefoot into a cold quilt of fallen petals.

"When I was in kindergarten," Nat says, "my mother came to pick me up one afternoon, and it was before Easter, so we'd all been sitting around a table painting Easter eggs, and I painted mine this beautiful dark purple. You know the way paint sinks into eggshell? She'd been fighting with my father—he was still living with us then—and when I didn't want to leave with her right away, because I was still working on my egg, she grabs me. When we're out in the hallway where nobody can hear her, she says, 'I hope you *break* it.'" Nat looks over her shoulder at Tara. "I knew more than you do when I was going on five years old."

"That's no reason."

"No reason for what?"

"For what you said before."

"Uh-oh," Nat says. "Peter, Peter, pumpkin-eater."

"Don't call him that."

"No?" Nat stands, easing the shoulder bag's zipper past a snag in the suede. "Next thing you know you'll be telling me you didn't know your mother has been sleeping around." She looks up just as Tara hits her, so that Tara sees the clear black of the pupil framed by the straight brow and the wing of the nostril pinched white in sudden alarm, the chapped lower lip, the seashell rim of teeth struck by her fist. Nat's head snaps back and narrowly misses the wall. There is the deep drumming resonance of the cello hitting the floor, followed by the rising plaintive hymn of the strings. Tara, realizing her hand is stinging, sucks her knuckles, and this gesture, the self-consciousness of it, frees Nat from her stiff fearful stance against the wall. She narrows her eyes and says, "Shit." The cello rocks clumsily at her feet, and Nat stops it with the toe of her shoe. "Am I bleeding?" she says, raising her chin.

"Some."

"Don't say anything to me."

"I won't."

"I mean it. Just don't."

"Okay."

"God, you're so irresponsible. You know what you fucking need? You need a fucking shrink."

Gently, Tara lifts the cello, feeling the familiar hollow weight sway into her hands, balancing it on its spike and turning it around. The scroll, the pegs, are intact, and there are no nicks or scratches that she can see. She plucks a string to feel the fine wire trembling beneath her fingertip and then she loosens that string and the others.

"So now you're crazy," Nat says.

Nat washes her face in the basin of the drinking fountain in the hall outside the music room. She doesn't want to go into one of the restrooms because there might be other girls there, who would want to know what had happened to her lip.

Tara sits in the monitor's chair beside the drinking fountain, wondering where the monitor is, afraid that he will come back and catch them—of course neither of them has a pass. She sits with her chin on her knees, her feet in the chair's seat, listening. A locker bangs distantly, but no one appears. There are words scratched into the chair's wooden armrest, incised in ball-point pen: HEALTH FOOD AND HEROIN. Below that, ANIMAL LIBERATION, and a drawing of something that looks like a maimed koala bear, dripping purple Magic Marker blood from its throat and paw. A boy's name, deeply crossed out. SUCK, in Gothic lettering. A drawing of a paramecium, its parts labelled. The initials WF inside a heart. The words HELP

ME within a comic-strip balloon, the balloon connected to nothing. MS. MARTIN IS A DYKE, printed. The word RADIANT. A large question mark blooming from the end of an exactingly drawn small penis. Tara studies her hand, which still stings: the skin is broken.

"Disgusting," Nat says. She points at the bottom of the drinking fountain, where there is a wad of bubble gum, bright pink, pitted like an apricot stone with tooth marks. "There are some true grotesques in this school."

"Does it hurt?"

"Not so much," Nat says. "It's getting numb or something." She dries her chin on the sleeve of her sweater. "Tell me the truth, would you? What does it look like?"

"It's swelling."

"Swelling?"

"Only a little."

"Oh, terrific," Nat says. "What Charles would call a fat lip." From her bag she takes out a cloisonné box no bigger than a matchbook; on its lid, a flamingo balances on one leg among lilies. "I don't drink water when I take pills," Nat says. "Maybe because I was weaned on megavitamins. Bee pollen, ginseng, garlic—anything that came along, Annie tried it out on me. The latest thing is megadoses of vitamin C." She wipes her hands down her jeans, leaving damp spots. "This morning I thought I was getting cramps," she says. "Now the pain is gone, though."

"What pain?"

"Haven't you ever had them?" When Tara shakes her head, Nat looks at her in disbelief. "You've probably had them," she says, "and just not known what they were." She takes a paper-covered wand from her bag. "See? You ought to get a tampon from your mother, because it would be hideous to have to go to the school nurse."

"You're going to be late for class."

"Christ, I totally forgot." Nat touches the cut. "This looks really hideous, doesn't it?"

"You can't even see it from here."

"You can't? It feels like a big lump underneath the skin."

"It doesn't show."

"It doesn't?" Nat says. She glances away, down the empty hall. "How am I supposed to trust you? You wouldn't tell me even if I looked like a leper."

At three-thirty they are sitting between the cement lions that flank the school's front steps. The lions have broad paws, crumbling profiles, and sloping haunches graffitied in a lace of spray-paint—girls' names, mostly, though someone has written RICKY HARPER SUCKS COCKS in telescoping print down the length of one lion's tail, which ends in a cement pinecone. Tara picks up a bubble-gum comic, reads it, and tears it into pieces, balling the pieces together and tossing the ball at the cheek of the nearer lion, in which the feathery indentations of whiskers are still visible, although the jaw has mostly fallen away and someone has painted the muzzle with a Hitler mustache.

Peter is late, but that's nothing new. Since the separation he is nearly always late. Technically, according to the temporary separation agreement, Tara is allowed to go home with him on Fridays and stay until Monday mornings, but this doesn't mean anything, because he hasn't found a place to live yet. He always says "a place to live"—not "an apartment," not "a house"— so she isn't sure what he is looking for, exactly. Meanwhile, he sleeps in the basement of the museum, on an old mattress mapped with stains. Each time Tara looks at it, the mattress is in worse shape than before, and she has the idea that something, maybe mice, is diligently disembowelling it, mining the wiry pellets of the interior. Peter's wastebasket is filled to overflowing with crumpled Big Mac wrappers and crushed Coors cans. Sometimes he digs one of the Coors cans out, straightens it, and uses it for an ashtray; he's afraid of starting a fire in the basement, though if you look around, there doesn't seem to be a lot to burn. He has one spoon, one knife, and one fork, a salt shaker stolen from a restaurant, a two-burner hot plate, and a worktable, in addition to the mattress. When he can't sleep, he works on the table, which he borrowed from someone in one of the offices upstairs. He circles ads in the "For Rent" column in the *New Mexican*—she's seen the page, heavily X'd and scratched over, when he is done. She doesn't think he calls any of the numbers.

His things occupy only one corner of the cavernous basement: the mattress is fitted into an angle formed by converging alleys of shelves that hold a large part of the museum's collection of prehistoric Southwestern pottery. Beneath the dim old fluorescent lights, in air kept cool and dry partly in the interest of conservation and partly from bureaucratic thriftiness, there is a kingdom of pear-shaped ollas, deep bowls, rare double-necked canteens, dippers shaped like halved squashes, narrow-mouthed seed jars, and fat corrugated cooking pots. Each piece shows the lines of its original breakage, and the glue, visible between imperfectly fitted fragments, gleams like pine resin in a crack. Once, left there alone while Peter conducted some business upstairs, Tara had admired an effigy jar, liking the way the small man molded into the side of the jar was crouched forward playing his flute with both hands. He had a pointed nose, made from a pinch of clay, and slits for eyes, a face like an animated electrical socket. Tara touched the flute that doubled cunningly as the handle of the jar, but it wasn't until she lifted the jar that she saw the flute was also a penis, mockingly erect. She put the jar back in the clean circle, like a spot rubbed in a misted mirror, that it had left in the grime coating the shelf.

Nat has picked the scab away from her lip; it is beginning to bleed again. "Leave it alone," Tara says. "You'll get blood poisoning."

Nat gnaws at her thumbnail a moment, then finds a Hershey bar in her bag, peels back the white wrapper, and offers some to Tara. The chocolate is slightly warm, wonderful, and it makes Tara hungry. Nat spits out an almond; it misses a lion's paw. "Late again," she says. "Who could've guessed?"

"He'll be here."

" 'He'll be here,' " Nat mimics. "Look, if he doesn't come in two minutes, I'm calling Gregory."

"Oh, Jesus, Gregory."

"Yes, Gregory. At least if I called him I know he'd get here. He's not off on another planet every time you need him for something."

"Since when do you need him for anything?"

"Look," Nat says. "If my mother is going to marry him, I have to adapt to having him around. You don't think he's just going to disappear, do you? That I'll wake up one morning and he'll be gone?" She scratches at the lion's paw with a pebble, making a chalky line down its toe. "He's not going to disappear," she says.

"You're not that lucky," Tara says.

Nat stares out into the street. Two boys pass, the taller one wearing a cowboy shirt of fringed satin and scuffed cowboy boots, the other one spinning a yo-yo from his finger and drawing it in with a quick zipping sound. The taller one looks at Nat and pats the fly of his Levi's. "Jail bait," he says. "Pervert," Nat says, halfheartedly. The boy with the yo-yo pretends to aim it at Tara's knee. She glances away quickly. "So long," the taller one says. He makes a kissing sound.

"Two minutes is up," Nat says.

"Why don't you go call Gregory?" Tara says. "I just wish you would."

"Okay."

"So?"

Nat pats her shoulder bag and shrugs. "I guess not," she says. "The smallest I've got on me is a twenty."

"You were supposed to pay your lab fee with that."

"Pay so some frog can die in a jar full of chloroform. I know."

"There he is," Tara says.

Peter honks twice in greeting, as if they might not know who it is in the pickup; not only that, but he waves eagerly. Peter leans across the bucket seat and pushes the door open. He is wearing a sweat-stained Stetson, angled to shade his eyes. She remembers finding the brown pheasant feather that is tucked below the knotted hatband. "Hey, Natalie Cimarron," he says. "Hey, Tara."

"Hey," Nat says. She slips into place between the bucket seats, straddling the stick shift. For a frightening moment Tara thinks that he is about to put his arm around Nat's shoulders, but he doesn't. The pickup's engine has a rusty high-pitched sound, idling, that it didn't have last week. Something is always wrong with it. Peter shifts, politely keeping his hand above Nat's leg, away from her knee. Tara studies her father's profile. He lights a cigarette, the last in a pack of Marlboros, and rolls his window down a couple of inches, also out of politeness, so that they will not have to breathe smoke. "How was your day?" he says.

Tara answers. "Fine."

"Fine?"

"Okay."

"Okay?"

"Just ordinary."

"Ordinary." Peter looks thoughtful. "How did Natalie get the bloody lip on this ordinary day?"

"Baseball," Nat says.

"Baseball. I thought girls only played softball."

"Not any more," Nat says haughtily. "That was the way they used to do it."

"What position?" Peter flicks ashes onto the floor; Nat moves her foot slightly away.

"Position?"

"What position do you play? What does Tara play?"

"I'm first base," Nat says. "Tara's an outfielder."

"No good," Peter says. "Haven't you ever seen Tara pitch? I taught her everything she knows."

"She was good," Nat says. "But there was somebody better. A new girl, Lisa Jimenez. She transferred from Española."

"She's really good," Tara says. If you leave Nat alone too long, she takes off on a flight of fantasy so involved that no one believes her. "She's already been in fights."

"Fights?" Peter says. "What kind of fights?"

"Fist fights," Nat says. "She's really violent. She has problems. Nobody in the whole school can stand her."

"So she beat you out as pitcher, kiddo?" Peter inhales, the spot of light rapidly dwindling down the length of ash balanced between his knuckles; he still wears his wedding ring. "I can't believe it. What a waste."

"She's at least a foot taller than me," Tara says. "Ms. Martin told me maybe next year."

"Ms. Martin?"

"The P.E. teacher."

"Of course," Peter says. "I forgot for a minute."

"Lisa's father is a heroin addict," Nat says.

"A heroin addict," Peter repeats.

"And a car thief."

"Sounds like the entire Jimenez family has its problems," Peter says.

"He was in the state penitentiary. He has a tattoo." Nat touches her narrow chest. "Jesus Christ with his arms held out and nails coming out of his wrists."

Peter glances at her. "Sounds gory."

"And her mother's a prostitute."

"She's not any more," Tara says. "She used to be."

"She still is," Nat says. "Her husband wanted her to stop but she wouldn't, no matter what."

"I see," Peter says. They are on the dirt road that leads to Nat's house. Sunflowers, complicated skeletons bearing ragged russet heads, lean against the barbed-wire fence. Some of the sunflowers have blown down; the heads of the others still incline in the direction of the setting sun. In a field, a gray horse rubs its chin against a fence post. The pickup passes a windmill. On the still water in the holding tank, cottonwood leaves drift.

"But, you know, she's pretty," Nat says. "Lisa Jimenez is so pretty."

Peter stubs out his cigarette in the dashboard ashtray. In front of the house, the Doberman pinscher is waiting, ears pricked, the tags at his throat chinking in time with the violent wriggling of his cropped tail. When Nat slides from the pickup, the dog rises on bony hind legs to sniff at her face, his paws on her shoulders, his smooth head swivelling from Peter to Tara. He knows them both. "Down," Nat says. She steps on one of his hind paws. The dog dances away from her and up on the driveway, suddenly merry, wheeling to nip at his nonexistent tail. "See you," Nat says.

"See you," Tara says.

"See you Monday," Peter says.

When Nat is gone, he starts the pickup, which lurches down the driveway and around the first rutted curve of dirt road. He looks at Tara; she doesn't look at him. "Let me see that," he says. He closes his hand over her wrist and lifts it lightly, examining her knuckles. "You didn't even wash it off," he says. "Don't you know a human bite can be as dangerous as a rattlesnake's? It's not something they teach you in school." She is silent, staring out the window. "Come on, Tar, talk to me," he says. "Don't be a child."

4

The apple is changing. First, sepia freckles condensed around the hollow for the stem. Then the vertical flecks already scattered across its sides seemed to darken, and in the line where the apple met the bottom of the bottle, a furriness appeared and spread outward. The furriness formed concentric rings; a slow-motion darkness rippled upward through the apple. Its skin grew small puckers and pouches. On one side, it seemed ready to melt into the bottle glass. It loosed into the air a rich, forlorn rottenness. Tara stoppered the bottle with a cork whittled to fit, but that stopped neither the decay nor the smell. She hid the bottle in her closet and Clarissa, walking into her room, said, "What is *that?*"

"Nothing," Tara said.

"Oh, right, nothing," Clarissa said. "It's not a dead mouse or something?"

"You think I'd keep a dead mouse in here?"

"It's hard to tell exactly what you've got in here."

"It's not a dead mouse."

"Well, whatever it is, I hope you feel like dealing with it soon, because I can't stand that." Tara burned some sandalwood incense, but she knew that she was caught: the bottle is something she can't throw away, and it is something she can't keep. One good thing, since she's had this cold, she can't smell it any more. The cold has left the wings of her nostrils reddened and raw, and she holds a dirty Kleenex balled up in her fist.

The pickup is stalled at a stoplight on Cerrillos Road. Peter moves the stick shift into neutral and works it back and forth. It has been a very bad week, beginning with Clarissa's telephoning him at the office on Monday morning to accuse him of dragging his feet. Accusations were the only time she resorted to clichés, but then she used them with relish, in unanswerable ways. "So what do you want from me?" he said. "I just want you to do your part," she said hoarsely. She had been about to go to bed with the malevolent adult version of the cold that Tara has now, and he had taken a little pleasure in that. While he talked to her, he had toyed with the fake jade replica of an Aztec bas-relief, the god Tezcatlipoca, bulbous of eye and wide of jaw, that rests on the far corner of his desk. Tezcatlipoca had liked the hearts of his sacrifices still beating. Sometimes Peter has trouble keeping the Aztec pantheon straight. Huitzilopochtli had also liked hearts, but sacrifices to Tlaloc were of children, who were drowned, and those made to Xipe Totec were flayed.

Beside the pickup, a low-slung Chevrolet inches forward until its hood ornament, a chrome swan with outspread wings, is almost touching the bumper of the UPS truck ahead of it. The Chevrolet's driver, his arm resting in the open window, raps on the car's dented roof. When he notices Tara, he calls up to her, "Hey, *muchacha*, wanna come for a ride? It's a pretty day."

She shakes her head. "Gonna break my heart," he says. "Just like that, no?" He snaps his fingers.

Tara looks past him. Tufts of turquoise angel hair obscure the dashboard, and the steering wheel is made of links of chain soldered into an arc. From the rearview mirror a naked Barbie doll is suspended inside a net sack, the kind used in supermarkets to hold onions. Someone has painted nipples on the Barbie doll's breasts in crimson fingernail polish. On the far side of the front seat a young woman is feeding a baby from a bottle. The baby's eyes are closed and the woman shades them against the late afternoon light with her free hand. Bubbles rise and pop softly against the upturned end of the bottle; the woman wipes foam from the corner of the baby's mouth with her fingertip, then licks the fingertip and smooths the baby's eyebrows. Between the man and the woman, on the dirty seat-cover, a small dog is sleeping, curled into itself.

"Who was that?" Peter says. "Was that somebody you know?"

"Not really," Tara says.

"Not really. How come you never just tell me the truth any more?"

"He was some guy talking to himself. You know."

She can see the foreheads of the calves in the truck ahead, all facing the same way, unevenly banded by the light that falls through the wooden slats. A sparrow lights on the truck bed, moving in hops down an alley framed by gigantic legs and mud-encrusted hooves. The broad curly bellies above the sparrow shift ponderously. When one calf stirs, it nudges the calf beside it until, domino-fashion, each calf in turn has made the drowsily accommodating sideways shift. The sparrow circles a tussock of manure, finds a kernel of corn, flies to the lowest slat, tips its head so that the kernel fits more snugly into its beak, and flies away. Immediately another sparrow takes its place.

The light changes and Peter treads heavily on the accelerator; there is a roar, and something on the underside of the truck rattles. "You should see," Tara says, looking back. "A cloud of smoke came out."

"Not long for this world," Peter says. "There was an old Hank Williams song that ended, 'Nothing in this world gets out of this world alive.' You've probably never heard it. You probably don't even know who Hank Williams was."

"Gregory has one of his records."

"Gregory?"

"Who's living with Annie. Annie who is Nat's mother."

"I know who Annie is." He sticks his arm out the window, signalling a left turn; the blinker is broken. "You think I don't know who Annie is? I just forgot that she was living with someone now."

When she doesn't answer, he twiddles his fingers at her, and she opens the glove compartment, taking out the flat red can with its oval portrait of the plump prince in his morning coat. She unfolds the cigarette paper on her knee, shakes out a line of tobacco from the can, scrapes the shreds into a straighter line according to some aesthetic standard of her own, and licks along the paper's edge. She furls the cigarette into a lozenge, licks and twists each end, and hands it to Peter. If she doesn't consider the cigarette sufficiently well made, she doesn't like for him to smoke it. Once or twice she's even thrown an asymmetric cigarette out the window and started from scratch before he could stop her.

"Do you remember when you were little?" he says. "You used to call the drugstore down the block and disguise your voice and say, 'Have you got Prince Albert in a can?' When they said they did, you'd say, 'Hurry up and let him out, he can't breathe.'"

"I never did that."

"You just don't remember."

"It's gross."

"You weren't so sophisticated then. You thought it was funny." He pushes in the dashboard lighter, and when it clicks, he slants the cigarette toward the fading red spiral and inhales. "You had another game, only I think you invented it."

"What other game?" She scratches her elbow, interested.

"It was called Lightly. We used to play it in your room when I would come up to tuck you in. I would sit down on your quilt and you would ask me politely, because you were polite then, if I wanted to play, and then you would wait for me to say I wanted to, exactly as if we hadn't been playing it every night of your life since you could talk. I think you must have listened for me to come up the stairs, but you used to pretend you were reading a Babar book, so that you could look up, a little bored, when I stood in the doorway, like, 'Oh, yes, you must be the Roto-Rooter man.' Do you remember that crummy apartment we had in Albuquerque? The only good thing about it was that it had two floors, so that your bedroom could be upstairs and ours could be downstairs. Christ, I must have been only in my second or third year of graduate school then."

"Sure I remember it," she says. She is annoyed by this last detail, which has distracted him from the course of his story about her, so that he can reflect on some ghostly graduate-school version of himself. The truth is that, although certain details of the apartment are clear, like a clumsy little three-pronged chandelier that hung down over the kitchen table, she can hardly remember him, except that once, during a smoky, noisy party, he had borrowed a guitar from one of the guests and played it while she squatted on the stairs in her nightgown; the spice-box smell of marijuana floated up to her hiding place, and his brown hair, beneath the kitchen light, was golden.

"There were horses and swings outside," she says. "And gangs."

"In that little park, you mean?" he says. "Those horses on

springs that would rock back and forth? And the gangs of boys wore satin jackets then. You have a pretty good memory. So when I sat down on your bed, I was supposed to close my eyes, and you would try to touch me so that I couldn't feel it, and if I could feel it I would say 'Now,' and you were caught, and then it was my turn."

"That's really banal," she says, aware, all at once, of an urgent need to distance herself from the memory, from him.

"It was not," he says. "You made it up. I always thought it was ingenious, really. You were so good at it. And I think, you know, that it stayed between us, you and me. I don't think you ever played it with your mother. But one of us could ask her."

"No, don't."

"Not if you don't want me to."

"I can't remember it."

"You're sure?"

"No. Only that at night there were cockroaches in the kitchen and I was scared to come down. If you turned on the light you could hear them running away."

He laughs. "Your mother said she knew some of them by sight. She said maybe we should hold cockroach fights and ask the neighbors in." He sounds apologetic, as if it were his fault for bringing this about—he can remember, and she can't, and it shaves another fraction of an inch from their common ground, widening the gap that opened between them, unacknowledged, when he left to live in the museum basement. "I'm taking you to see a surprise."

"What surprise?"

"You'll see."

" 'You'll see,' " she says. "I *hate* it when you say that."

"I can see you do," he says. "We have one small errand to run first. One very banal thing."

"Oh, shit."

"What?"

"For flying fuck's sake."

"Tara," he says, in the reproving voice he hasn't wanted to use since he moved out. It isn't part of his strategy with her, but sometimes he slips, having never needed a strategy before. Before, all arguments between them, however violent, had been bounded by the fact that they had awakened in the same house, within a few feet of each other, that he could listen to her bathwater running behind the bathroom door, that they had eaten—from bowls exactly alike and with the same spoons —cereal from the same box, with oval slices cut from the same banana, and that the same woman, in her kimono, her bare feet tucked behind the rungs of her chair, had mediated between them, lazily pushing her sleep-snarled hair away from her clear forehead. And it seems to him that the three of them could no more have been awkward with each other than three dragon-flies. Now there are hitches, attenuations, gaps, flaws, fallings away. Now he sees them everywhere. More than anything, he wants Tara not to see what he sees.

"If you're separated, how come you're still running errands for her?"

"Being separated doesn't mean I can't ever do a favor for her. It doesn't mean we don't still like each other."

"Oh."

"It doesn't mean we're not going to come out friends."

"Oh."

"Look under your seat." She does, and brings up a package wrapped in brown paper and tied with twine, Clarissa's hand-writing on one side. Tara looks at this. It is the address of Clarissa's gallery downtown. "I know what it is," she says. "It's that little square painting she doesn't like."

"She doesn't like any of them, once she's finished them."

"Where are we taking it?"

"The woman who bought it wanted someone from the gallery to drop it off."

"You're not from the gallery."

"Close enough for government work."

"What's that mean?"

"It's a saying. I guess I picked it up while I was doing that environmental-impact work. It means 'Good enough, it'll have to do.' And in a way it means your heart isn't in it."

They have left the highway and turned onto a dirt road, and from there onto a second dirt road, its ruts stretching away across the plain like tire tracks on the moon, straight except for sudden quizzical sideways loops, which curve around a boulder or a rise of earth no different from a hundred others and then return to the original direction. There are mesas in the distance. The furred tips of the grass in the mound between the ruts, hissing along the pickup's underside, spring up again behind, a slow-motion khaki wake, and Peter can see, in the bare spots between clumps of grass, small barrel cacti green as pears. Sometimes one of the ruts is deeper than the other and then the pickup's cab slants, Peter on the downhill side, Tara bracing herself against her door. There hasn't been a house since the old Airstream trailer a quarter-mile behind, but that can't have been what they're looking for. Balanced on creosote-darkened railroad ties, its windows sealed with cardboard, a pyramid of beer cans beside its cement block stairs, the trailer would have seemed abandoned if its door had not been swinging back and forth, loosely banging the corrugated aluminum. On the inside of the door was a painting of the Virgin of Guadalupe, surrounded by a hundred spikes of light, her bare feet, below the hem of her gown, pointing at the ground as helplessly as a parachutist's. A goat grazed untethered beyond the cans, its long, rabbity ears flopping against its slowly grinding jaws. The dirt road winds down the arroyo in a negligent curve that bottoms out in mud. Peter downshifts. The arroyo is wide here, the mud so pockmarked with cattle tracks that it has the brittle, engineered look of a honeycomb, each track holding two chips of dark water divided by a delicate dam. Peter changes gears again and the pickup bucks across the arroyo, printing over the cattle tracks with parallel herringbone lines, veering past a campfire of charred driftwood in a hollow and up the other side, where the road levels out again among straggling piñons.

"This must be hell when it rains," Peter says.

"She lives out here?"

"The woman who bought the painting? She'd better. If she doesn't, someone's in serious trouble." Tara turns the painting over and over between her knees. "Be a little careful with that," he says.

"I was."

"All right."

"I really was."

"I said all right, didn't I?"

"You act as if I don't know anything about anything," she says, at almost the same instant that he breathes "Ah" and stops the pickup by a mailbox with a rusty flag, the flag still up, although it is late in the afternoon. The side of the mailbox is painted with a name, WARREN, in crooked orange letters. The N is smudged at the bottom, as if the paint had run and someone had had to stop it with a finger. Above it there is another name, SCHOFIELD, but it has been painted through with a wavering blue line.

"Should I see if she got any mail?" Peter says, and Tara looks at him in disgust.

* * *

The woman scratches a fingernail down the screen door, trying to dislodge a moth wing, stuck to the outside, from the inside. "Who?" she says, without looking at him.

"My wife's gallery gave me the directions," Peter says. He feels a slight prompting toward greater truthfulness—well, greater precision—as the woman's first cool glance lengthens into an inspection. What does he look like to her, a rapist? It's true that he skipped shaving this morning, that when the racket of the alarm, seeming to echo along the basement's dim walls, woke him from a dream in which he had been left alone in a warehouse filled with confiscated goods to sort through a table filled with women's belongings, many of them vaguely familiar, he had turned on his side on the mattress, irritated to find that it was damp with sweat, although he had not been aware, in the dream, of having been frightened. When he couldn't find the pack of Marlboros he was sure he'd left near his elbow before falling asleep, he fished a butt from the Campbell's Soup can he was using as an ashtray, straightened it, lit it, and inhaled, feeling suddenly alert and depressed, rather alarmingly alert and too depressed to face the bathroom cubicle where he would have to shave.

What can he say that is true, though? *My estranged wife?*
My wife, who really wants to divorce me?
He doesn't amend it. *My wife.*

The moth wing, which she has succeeded in brushing from the screen, flutters through the air and lands on the toe of his Adidas. Peter bends and brushes it away; it is insubstantial, and though he sees his fingers touching it, he can't feel it. He is oddly embarrassed by this. When he straightens, the three of them allow a courteous interval of silence around the moment, as if at a little death.

He realizes too late that Tara is carefully weighing the words *my wife*. He has the abrupt insight that the woman who bought the painting also wishes he had not confessed to a wife, but all she does is unlatch the screen door and push it open with her foot. Her extended leg is graceful, her knee, in a ragged hole in the jeans leg, pale and freckled, asymmetrically, cleverly freckled, as if for camouflage, like a meadowlark's egg; he is aroused. She's barefoot. She has long, crooked toes, the second toe crossed over the big one, the small unpainted nails showing, along the inner edge, a starchy trace of cuticle. He feels relieved to have noticed the small, unattractive detail. She follows his look. "I know," she says. "They're horrible. I'm a dancer. At least, I was a dancer until last year. I have a bad knee." But she says "bad knee" with indulgent affection.

"I'm sorry," he says, absurdly.

"I'm Mia," the woman says.

Tara laughs. Peter looks at her quickly. "This is my daughter," he says. "Ugly, isn't she?" He doesn't know why he said that. He feels he is getting in deeper.

"No," the woman, Mia, says. "She's lovely."

But there is a moment when the three of them admire her chickens, feeding in the dry acequia that borders her front yard, separating it from the dirt road where the mailbox leans, when Peter feels unexpectedly at ease. It is not even properly buried in the ground, that odd Howard Johnson's mailbox; instead, it is anchored in a cement-filled coffee can, somebody's bright idea that didn't work out well. Schofield's idea, maybe. In the corner of the yard nearest the house there is an old Russian olive, wide-trunked, luxuriant, and there are geraniums in pots the size of barrels. Mia has just let the chickens out. She explains that they were given to her by a friend who got tired of them, and she hasn't really established any rapport with them yet. The chickens move in a slowly dispersing cluster down the acequia, between glimmers of bottle glass and patches of weeds still flattened by the ditch's last flooding. There is a wreath of barbed wire on the near bank, and the chickens pick their way through it daintily, one by one, as if assigned to follow an obstacle course. Across the road there is a field, bare except for groves of cholla, blackened and old, edged with elongated pincushion buds. There is something mechanical and oppressive about the way cholla grows, Peter thinks, though in the spring its compacted blooms are brilliant as radishes on these skeletal branches.

Tara follows him up the steps and they stand in the narrow kitchen. There is the smell of woodsmoke. Peter looks at the stalks of garlic hanging from the *vigas*, peeled wooden beams that run the length of the ceiling. There are also several copper-bottomed pots, badly tarnished, hung from nails. On the mantel of the corner fireplace he notices letters and a coffee cup and several cookbooks. A red-tail hawk feather, tied with string to a *viga*, twirls in the draft through the screen door. It is a sweet, spare room. He remembers the gloom of the basement at dawn, the expanse of unswept floor, the lumpy raft of the mattress, the cigarette smoke he drew hungrily into his lungs; his chest hurts. "What's the neighborhood like?" he says.

He meant to tease her—there is no neighborhood—but she answers seriously, "Not so bad."

"Not so good, either?"

"Even out here you get low-riders," she says. "It seems impossible, because of the road, but they come. You can't tell whether they know you live alone or not. Sometimes I want to hire one of my friends—one of my men friends—to drive out here every evening at five-thirty, nicely dressed, a jacket and a tie, and walk through the door carrying a briefcase. The nearest neighbors are—well, you saw."

"Way back on the other side of the arroyo." *Men friends.*

"They're nice, but their kids have all gone away to Albuquerque or Cincinnati, and they're quite old. Mr. Archibald Ramirez and Mrs. Ramirez. They're always giving me things, I practically have to fight them off. Mr. Ramirez wants me to take one of his goats, the next time his doe has kids. He's really trying to talk me into it, but I'm not sure I want one."

"Why wouldn't you?" Peter rubs his hand across the kitchen table. A chip of paint breaks away and catches below his thumbnail. He looks up; she hasn't noticed. He feels he has stolen a sliver of the quiet in the room.

"Because I'm usually gone all day." She pauses, looking over her shoulder before taking three unmatched cups from the shelf above the sink. "Would you like some tea? You had a long drive. That road."

"Do you have any coffee?" he says.

"No, but this is Lapsang Souchong. It's very good."

"Sure," he says.

"You see, I have to start for work about seven-thirty, and I get back not long after six, if I'm lucky and the road isn't bad. Goats need more domestic regularity than that. But I should show you something." She sets the cups on the table, and reaches into a closet by the door, standing on her toes to reach the highest shelf. When a broom falls, Tara catches it and hands it to her. "Thanks," she says. She is holding something light and wrinkled, a mask with an old woman's hooked nose and pleated upper lip, slits for eyes, an aureole of hair the no-color of dandelion fluff, and as bristlingly dry. Mia slides the mask on and hunches forward so that her back acquires a widow's hump. The mask's lips are shaped in a severe smile, heavily lipsticked, and she wobbles so helplessly, reaching for a teacup, that Peter almost forgets himself and reaches for her elbow to steady her.

"What is that for?" Tara says.

"If someone knocks at my door in the middle of the night to tell me that their car has broken down in the road, I put on the mask, see, and a torn sweater over my nightgown, the way an old woman would, and I hobble across the kitchen and open the door." She turns to Peter. "Do you think they would leave me alone?"

"Why answer the door at all?"

"Because if they think there's really nobody home, they break into the house. I think it's better if you let them know that you're here, and that way you don't catch them off guard. That's the worst thing you can do."

"I think you're a little paranoid," Tara says.

"Tara."

"Oh, no, she's right. I am, a little." She lifts the mask from her head, slipping it over the back of one of the chairs, where it seems to stare vacantly, possessively, through the arched doorway into the other room. "You think it's a stupid idea, don't you?" she says to Peter.

"No," he says. "I just wouldn't want it to be the only thing you have to rely on."

"I never wanted to live with a guard dog. And they cost two or three hundred dollars now, trained."

"I'm going to tell my mother about it," Tara says. "She lives alone, too."

"She lives with you," Peter says. "How is that living alone?"

Mia sets a blue enamel kettle on a burner of the gas stove, moving the dial until the flame grazes the bottom of the teapot. "We're separated," Peter says. She looks over her shoulder at him. "So how can you afford to buy paintings?" he says.

"Only one, so far," she says. She laughs.

"No one wants them, lately," he says. "Because of the recession. Although a painting can be a good investment."

"I wanted this picture as soon as I saw it," she says. "Have you seen it? It's beautiful."

"She'll be glad you think that."

"What?"

"My wife," he says. "She likes to know that whoever the painting ends up with cares for it."

"Of course I do," she says, as if he had suggested some atrocity—letting a child go hungry, say, or clipping a hummingbird's wings. "How couldn't I care for it? I wanted it, didn't I?" She reaches for the package, and Tara hands it over, Peter thinks, somewhat reluctantly. The woman scratches at the twine, tears the paper open, slides the canvas out. It is a small painting—the corner of a room, a single uplifted spray of bamboo, leaves lit on their upper sides, the tips of the leaves settled against each other, the rest of the plant hidden behind the back of the white-linen sofa, and a cat asleep in the corner formed by the arm of the sofa and its back. Peter recognizes the painting, after all. It is one of very few of Clarissa's paintings that has a living creature in it: two living creatures, if you count the bamboo. The cat's cheek shows a watery dark sheen, almost a rainbow, but very faint, almost imperceptible, triangulated by the outer corner of the closed eye and the burr of chin. "Oh, lovely," Mia says. "Isn't it a lovely thing?"

"It's not a new picture," Tara says. "She painted it a long time ago."

"How do you know, kiddo?"

"That was Laura Murphy's cat. It got hit by a motorcycle, and the guy on the motorcycle didn't even look down. The cat used to come into our house in the afternoons and sleep on the sofa like that."

"Did your mother do the painting before the cat was hit, or after?"

"After," Tara says. "Why?"

"Because there's an elegiac quality."

"Elegiac," Peter says to Tara. "A quality of grief."

The kettle whistles and Peter, who is nearest, lifts it from the burner. The enamel handle is cool, and the steam teases the fine hairs of his wrist and mists the face of his watch.

"What's wrong?" Mia says.

"Nothing."

"You have to put the kettle down to put the tea in," she says.

He pries open the lid of the Lapsang Souchong box with the handle of a spoon, and packs a strainer with dry crumbs of fragrant tea. He lowers the strainer into the kettle, and the water darkens in a cloud. Tara is watching him, and when he looks at her she makes a gentle mocking gesture of applause. He notices, with irritated tenderness, the gap between her front teeth, which he can't yet afford to have fixed. But he will: he will put money away each week, find a sympathetic orthodontist, one who will agree to modest payments. It will just mean a little scrimping, a little foresight. There is too much sloppiness around, too many new-age parents who don't even get their kids vaccinated against polio, believing, or pretending to believe, that brown rice is sufficient protection. He can remember his own father lifting him up so that he could look down the long line of heads, children his own age and younger, mothers in housedresses, fathers in coats and ties, and the table at the end where the doctor waited, the chevrons of his tie tucked silkily into the acute whiteness of his doctor's coat, to hand you the white paper cup containing the white sugar cube that you rattled experimentally and then tipped onto your tongue, the sugar cube dissolving so fast it seemed hollow, the sweetness that was *vaccine* riding down your tongue to remain inside you forever, the school auditorium echoing with the cries of children who had somehow got frightened.

That kind of care, that kind of expectant attention, seems so much rarer now, and Peter is aware of this as a diminishing. He will look up orthodontists in the yellow pages tomorrow. He smiles to himself. At this, his daughter bends forward from the waist, her brief hair stirring on the crown of her head, and touches the floor, yawning.

*   *   *

The coffee table is an old steamer trunk with brass latches on straps of decaying leather. Tara puts her cup down on a page from *The New York Times* financial section. David Stockman, his expression guarded, gazes at the ceiling through boyishly round spectacles. Tara wonders why someone who is as clearly poor as Mia is would read *The New York Times* financial section, where they would even get it. She looks at the paper again. It is two weeks old.

"Some toast?" Mia says. "Or maybe an English muffin?" She has kinky pale-red hair drawn tightly away from her small face; it is as if the willfulness of her hair is so formidable, its shiny knottiness so painful to its owner, that it must be disciplined by numerous tortoiseshell clips and half-hidden pins. Her eyebrows are straight and severe, a shade lighter than her hair, her eyes gray; her cheekbones, the bridge of her nose, and even her eyelids when she lowers them, pouring more tea, show constellations of freckles. She is wearing a black sweatshirt, far too big, and old Levi's, the knee worn through to reveal an arch of bone light as clamshell. The balls of her feet are glossily callused, and her hands look too strong for the raku cup. "There's blackberry jam in the refrigerator," she tells Tara. "Homemade."

"If you're hungry," Peter says.

"All right," Tara says. "I'm going."

"I didn't give you any orders, kiddo."

Tara shrugs. In the kitchen she pours out the tea, which was too sweet, and runs water from the tap into her cup. Tea is supposed to be good for colds, but that couldn't mean such awful tea. Near the toaster she finds an ellipse of mouse droppings, tiny, desiccated, like shavings from a pencil lead. She opens the English muffin and pushes the halves into the toaster's slots, which are crusty with singed crumbs. The toaster gives off a pleasant smell of charring. Tara spreads the muffin thickly with butter and jam. Even though they can't see her from the other room, it feels funny to be in the woman's kitchen. Clarissa would never allow a fan of mouse droppings to accumulate around her toaster. Tara looks through the refrigerator, but there isn't anything good; in the freezer a package of frozen peas rests on a drift of ice. She digs into her shoulder bag, finds a Kleenex, blows her nose, sticks the Kleenex away, and takes out a book. She opens the book on the table. At the margin of the page, CHARLES is written in green ink. She fills in the loops of the A and R with neat parallel pencil strokes. The diagram, of an isosceles triangle, bores her, so she colors it in too, and pushes the book away. She tears a sheet of paper from the back of her spiral-ring notebook, where the paper still has a fresh, brand-new feel, and on the first line she begins, in her best handwriting:

Dear Charles,
    I know you don't remember me, but I was thinking yesterday how <u>exquisite</u> it was to see you play soccer before you left. I had no idea soccer was so interesting. I mean I <u>have</u> seen it on TV but then it was boring. I don't know if you knew we were watching, it was sort of in a crowd, sitting on the grass, but I was with Annie and Nat

She sucks the end of the Bic pen until the plastic stopper comes out stickily, and she rolls it with her tongue against the back of her front teeth, careful not to get any saliva down into the pen because that causes the ink to come out blurred. She reads the letter again. The first line is not true—she would probably die if he didn't remember her—but it seems more polite not to assume too much, as an acknowledgment of the distance he has travelled. Still, she doesn't really want to begin by lying, and in the words a new danger takes shape: that, written down, they will cause what she doesn't believe to come true, and he will actually not remember her. She tears the page into bits, and begins again, on a fresh piece.

Dear Charles,
Do you remember me? Hopefully!! I am wondering about life in a military academy. Write me a letter with all the details like what you eat, is it gross, and are your classes hard. And do you like anyone. I hope this is not too boring to ask you. I was remembering yesterday the exquisite afternoon that you were playing soccer, your shirt that had purple stripes

This last detail is good, because it will make him remember, but after it she is stuck, and chews the pen stopper into a gummy plastic pellet, waiting for inspiration. The sudden conviction that this letter will go unanswered oppresses her, and she tears it up, noticing that she has torn both pieces of paper the same way, with one lengthwise tear, one down, and many small scrapping tears, increasingly fast. Lately she always seems to be tearing things up or hiding them; she might as well be a spy. She tries to hear what Peter is saying in the other room, but she can't quite distinguish the words. Mia must be bored stiff by now, listening to him. She's hardly said anything at all.

The bathroom opens off the kitchen; its door resembles the door of a stable, except that the two halves have been screwed together. Tara goes in. There is a pair of opaque tights, wrinkled like crepe paper, draped over the shower rod, and on top of the toilet tank, several bottles of shampoo and an abalone shell containing a single green marble. She opens the medicine cabinet and examines the shelves: a pair of rusty tweezers, a bottle of Mercurochrome, a pink bottle of contact-lens wetting solution, a white contact-lens case, a box of tampons, a colored eyeshadow stick, nicely sharpened. Tara reads the lettering on the stick: Smokey Amethyst. She draws a fine line of Smokey

Amethyst around each eye. There is a good mascara, too—the woman needs it, with those pale, curiously straight lashes. Tara uses the mascara generously, looking down to apply the first coat, then looking up, sweeping the mascara brush through her lashes from below. Her eyes look darker, exotic, bloodshot. The tampon box is open. She takes a tampon and fits it down into the pocket of her jeans. The bump will show, but no one will notice if she keeps her hand in her pocket. She flushes the toilet to cover the squeaking of the medicine cabinet's hinges. On the wall above the toilet there is a taped poster:

PLAGUE

is passed to Man by WILD RODENTS,
Rabbits, and by their FLEAS

an EASILY CAUGHT Wild Animal
is probably SICK

NEVER HANDLE THEM!

Restrain your pets
they can carry infected fleas to you
USE flea powder
on each pet

DO NOT

Pitch tents or lay
Bedrolls on or near nests or burrows

Use insect repellents

SEE YOUR DOCTOR

About ANY unexplained illness

PLAGUE is CURABLE
When treated in time

In the kitchen Tara shifts the tampon from her pocket into her shoulder bag. There is a dying geranium on the windowsill, its knotted stems bearing parched leaves and unevenly petalled flowers. Tara sticks her finger into the soil—dry as dust. She waters it carefully and when water seeps out from the bottom of the pot, running along the windowsill, she wipes it up with a dishcloth. She can't hear them at all now, in the other room. They seem to have lowered their voices. Maybe Peter has done something truly grotesque, like asking her out. Tara opens the refrigerator door and, this time, finds a jar of olives hidden behind a jar of Territorial House green-chili salsa. She unscrews the lid and eats several olives, spitting the pits into her hand, then going over to the windowsill and burying them in the freshly damp soil of the geranium. That would surprise the woman: a little row of olive trees. When she hears Peter coming into the kitchen, she slides the last olive into her cheek and turns around guiltily.

"Kiddo?" he says. "Are you about ready to go?" As if there is any reason she would want to stay. She takes her book from the table and fits it into her bag along with her notebook and the scraps of the letters to Charles.

"You're not leaving?" The woman has followed Peter into the kitchen. She pulls a thread from the cuff of her sweatshirt without looking at him. In her hair, the parting is crooked and radiantly white. "I thought I could cook some dinner for us," she says; it is almost a question.

"We can't," Peter says. "Though it's really a nice offer, Mia." He uses her name self-consciously.

"Then take me up on it?"

"I wish we could, but we really had something planned. Thank you, though."

"Don't thank me," Mia says.

"Thank you," Tara says.

"*De nada*," Mia says. "It was nothing."

* * *

Peter puts his arm along the back of Tara's seat as he backs the pickup down the curving ruts, the driveway too narrow for him to turn around. The pickup's fender almost grazes the mailbox.

"Didn't you think she's nice?" Peter says.

"Sure."

"What are you smirking about?" he says. "And what's that you're sucking on?"

"See?" She shows him the olive pit between her teeth. "A rabbit turd."

5

Once they have gone, Mia stands for a moment in the kitchen, wondering why she said so many stupid things. It comes from hanging around dancers. She even had to tell him that she'd been a dancer, and she'd had to sound bewildered by the loss, not even a recent loss, a year-old loss, when the truth is that she's lucky to have gotten the job she has, assistant art director for a small dance company downtown. The truth is that she's lucky. She likes it, and she does okay. She got in trouble because he was attractive, was that it? That straight brown hair almost in his eyes. If you were accurate you would say more Tom Sawyer than Huck Finn, because in spite of his ragged haircut and apparent need for a good night's sleep, he had not seemed lost. She recalls his voice when he said, "My wife." It was so much surer than when he said, "We're separated." So, he was probably the victim rather than the instigator. Separation, meaning it will be more complicated and fragile than divorce, but with divorce looming inevitably at the end, no clean wounds to lick, not for a long time yet. That injurious little possibility of reconciliation. And, oddly, she had thought that he liked her. He had *looked* at her. Sure he had looked at her. He had looked at her the way a man who's just had a heart attack notices a sliver under his thumbnail. Fat chance, she tells herself. She tries to remember a joke one of the dancers in the corps told her last week, an anorectic little Giselle with eyes so huge they seemed crossed below her painted brows:

How many unmarried heterosexual men does it take to change a light bulb in Santa Fe?

I give up, how many?

Both of them.

Mia lifts her heel to the top of the table, bends her forehead to her knee, arches her back, and sighs. Her cat is mewing at the kitchen door, and when she doesn't respond right away, he rises on his hind legs and swats mechanically at the rusting screen, pinning a moth between the mesh and his paw. She opens a can of cat food, dishes it into his bowl, holds the screen door open for him, and watches him crouch over the bowl. Then she wanders through the house, trying the painting on various walls.

6

Peter turns off the highway at the exit for Cañoncito. By now
he has driven this road so often he could probably find the exit
in his sleep. Last New Year's Eve he drove into the canyon,
only half-listening to the warnings that spliced together the
country songs on the radio—"Stand by Your Man" followed
by a traveller's advisory—the snow falling lightly at first and
then, as prophesied, more and more steadily, so that the last
junipers visible in the early dusk were suddenly hooded in snow.
When one of the pickup's headlights burned out, the remaining
light cut a narrow channel above the increasingly slick surface
of the highway, and gradually that channel filled with snow
until Peter was looking into a flat white moon with snowflakes
sketched on it in dazzling Brownian motion. He turned the
radio off. He knew that section of highway well, and it was
flat and straight enough, with no dangerous curves to be negotiated blind, but adrenaline dried the back of his throat and

caused his palms to sweat against the wheel. A truck made its way toward him. It carried a line of lights like burning coals on its uppermost flat edge. Its headlights briefly meshed with his. Peter did not see how there could possibly be enough room on the road for them to pass, but they did, the truck gliding by with a honk of benediction, and then he could see its tracks shining black and clear, and he followed those, though the snow was filling them in almost as fast as he drove, its continuous white pelt rolling from one side of the road to the other. After he made the turn into the canyon, he knew he was safe: nothing could happen to him there. It is not rational to believe that a configuration of canyon wall, ancient strata of sandstone, a stretch of level ground, can protect you—nonetheless Peter believes it, he believes it beyond the shadow of a doubt. The next morning he had his wish, waking with his feet pushed down into the coldest depth of his sleeping bag, where the down was still crisp and unflattened, pushing himself up to rub a clear space in the camper's window and look out on his land, deep in snow, flawless and untracked, with the canyon wall framing it like a halted glacier. Once he had dressed and started the Coleman stove purring below the coffee pot, Peter paced his name out in enormous straggling letters, PETER in knee-deep snow.

Cañoncito itself is nearly bare of signs of life. A dozen undershirts hang from a clothesline behind an adobe house whose roof has grown a crop of heavy-headed thistles. There are empty corrals of upright branches bound by wire, the dirty salt blocks still holding tender hollows. A rusting real-estate sign is propped against a wheelbarrow, and in the grass around an abandoned chicken coop a burned bicycle rests upside-down beside the rib cage of a horse. The church, its narrow front facing the highway, is an oblong of adobe, its tin roof painted a garish rustproof red that stands out sharply against the thousand dry variations of fawn and ochre in the sandstone slope behind, so that the roof always seems precariously lodged there, less inevitable than the goat trails winding upward through blue-chalk shadows and pinpoint mica lights. The church's front doors have been bolted by a single narrow plank, fastened with a lock like the one you would use on a bicycle, and spare crosses for the *camposanto* lean against the wall on one side of the door. The wall of the *camposanto* is built of old Lamy sandstone, exactly the shade of the earth it divides into grave-yard and highway embankment. The crosses inside the wall are close together, leaning at different angles, and the effect is mildly claustrophobic and domestic, like that of a rickety picket fence. The twiggy ground between the graves shows ricegrass and clumps of iris and the severely pruned trunks of old lilacs.

On the other side of the highway overpass, the road con-tinues for several crumbling yards of asphalt, as if there were asphalt left over from the building job, and then changes to dirt again before jolting over a cattle guard. There are stones locked within the rectangles of the metal grid; in the ditch below, water gleams briefly. Here, in the most accessible part of the canyon, there are already a few houses, one or two windows that are lit this long before dark, signifying—in Peter's eyes—an invasion. He would prefer the canyon to be deeply empty, purely his own, lit, if it has to be lit, by moonlight.

The dirt road divides and Peter takes the left fork, which curves away, its shoulder crumbling into a ditch that is partially filled by bullet-riddled tin cans and tumbleweeds blown to-gether and compacted between the dirt walls into a screen of interlocking dry twigs, thorny as rosebushes. The ditch deepens and leads into the arroyo, where the walls, much steeper, are also crumbling, and there is nothing to halt the widening ver-tical folds of erosion except the occasional spindly cottonwood saplings and, once every half-mile or so, a dam of cobblestones braced by a bulging sheet of chickenwire, the hexagons of the wire a fine mosaic of rubbish, dead leaves, bits of rubber peeled from abandoned tires, rags and string and deer ribs. Each time Peter drives this road, the arroyo seems almost visibly wider, eating away at the level ground of the canyon's bottom, where there is piñon and juniper, nothing big enough for firewood, and the curious bleached mauve circles of ring muhly, the center of each grass circle either as bare as if recently swept or occupied by a red ant hill. Chamisa grows by the road in stiff bunches, each bunch shaped like the wide edge of a well-worn broom, and among the bunches there is prickly pear, its flat pads held at right angles to the ground.

He glances into the rearview mirror. In the dust of the road behind the pickup, a dead skunk lies on its side, its tail blowing forward over the pointed head with the loop of white between the snub ears. That smell, tarry and bittersweet, which vanished just before you got used to it. On either side of the road there is cholla, the long stems packed with small buds. Cholla likes to grow where the earth has been disturbed. In aerial photographs a dense growth of cholla sometimes indicates an archaeological site—a ruin with elegant masonry of sandstone wafers fitted together without benefit of mortar, the ruin shadowed, when you saw it from above, by the whaleback of its own garbage mound rising from the desert floor, a hump composed of bones and detritus and thousands of potsherds crushed together. The most meager and remote pueblo could yield a treasure of potsherds that crunched beneath your sneakers as you climbed the dusty slope. Peter is in the habit of attributing character to each sherd. Kana'a Gray has a workmanlike air, Cibola White is graceful and accomplished, Jeddito Yellow is humble. In southern New Mexico, in Hidalgo and Catron counties, exotic with heat, there are the Mimbres bowls buried with the dead, a neat hole drilled in the bottom of each bowl to ensure that it will accompany the departing soul, and the sherds have a Picassoesque mimesis of fishes or quail or even, though rarely, the topknotted hunters carrying their frail bows. His favorites, far and away, are the sherds of unassuming utilitarian gray that, pieced together, resurrect someone's fat, sooty-bottomed cooking pot. He doesn't even like the sherds to be corrugated, which means that a cord was pressed into the clay while it was wet to leave a braided impression circling the pot from rim to bottom. There's an argument that corrugation, by increasing the surface area of the pot, makes it more fuel-efficient, but Peter can't help it. He likes the smooth sherds, unadorned.

Many of the ruins, when you wheeled over them in the old two-engine Cessna buffeted by the desert updraft, were marked with intersecting ditches and deeper shafts where pot-hunters had come at night, illegally and furtively, to dig by the light of the moon or the headlights of a Jeep aimed at the side of the garbage mound, the dust that floated up clouding the beams to an underwater smokiness. His rapid assessment of the pot-hunters' damage was accompanied by the shaking of the plane and the smell of the pilot's aftershave. The interior of the plane was not much different from that of his pickup: it had worn seats that grew sticky beneath his Levi's in the summer heat, gum wrappers scattered across its floor, and one of its doors was held shut with wire. Once they stayed out too long and flew home late, the pilot fretting over the fuel gauge, and below them, following the zigzags of a steep-walled gorge, there was another plane that the pilot assured Peter was smugglers, up from Mexico, heading for a rendezvous north of Tierra Amarilla. The shadows of the planes overlapped in the moonlight in the bottom of the gorge and then they drifted apart and the smugglers' plane vanished and the pilot flew Peter safely home.

Tara leans her face against her hand, her hand against the window. Peter thinks she looks tired, but maybe it is only her cold. He is watching the side of the road for a particular reef of sandstone that marks his turn. When he sees it, he brakes and turns onto a road even narrower and more rutted. Chamisa closes in around them, leaning above the road which is, here, more deeply cut, the bushes stroking the pickup's sides like those great soft brushes you drive between in a car wash, but more brittle, twigs snapping in sudden whispers. Where the road crosses the arroyo, the banks on either side are too steep, so that the roots of the chamisa are exposed in a dry latticework above the soil, which bleeds away each time it rains and renders the road impassable. There aren't supposed to be any cattle grazing in this part of the canyon, but Peter sees their tracks in the bottom of the arroyo, mostly along the side that is shady all afternoon long. The pickup rocks across the arroyo, and Peter is furious. Old Man Salazar gets away with murder. After another quarter-mile he stops the pickup in front of his gate, really only some strands of wire within a sagging rectangle of iron pipes soldered together, and opens his door. "Slide over behind the wheel, will you?" he says.

"You want me to drive the truck through?" Tara says.

"You can manage that, can't you?"

He unlocks the gate and drags it open, the pipe ends swinging in the hollows they've already gouged in the road. Tara stalls the pickup, sticks it into reverse, gets it right, and passes him slowly, but close enough so that he has to back a little way up the bank. She grins at him. "That was great," he says, climbing back into the truck.

"Is this your land?"

"How did you know about my land?"

"She told me." *She* means Clarissa.

"She did, damn it," he says. "It was supposed to be a surprise."

"It still counts. I've never seen it before. How come you waited so long to bring me here?"

"I wasn't sure what was going to happen with it. I didn't know for a long time whether I could afford to keep up the payments or not, and it was no use letting you get to like it and then having to sell it."

"And could you?"

"So far."

"You should live out here."

"There isn't any water."

"So? You could use the bathroom in the museum when you went into work. I could get a horse and keep it here."

"See what I mean?" Peter says.

There's a platter of cow dung in the middle of the road, grass green as algae embedded in the flattened coil, drawing flies. Salazar gets away with whatever you let him. Peter knows he should do something about his fences, which are in sorry shape, but that would take money and, he calculates, two weekends, possibly three, though it would be worth it just to achieve a sort of demilitarized zone in his war with the old man. He doesn't know why he dislikes Salazar so intensely, because this sort of trespassing is fairly common, especially if the cattle belong to someone Spanish and the land to an Anglo who lives in town. Salazar is blind in one eye, and his good eye blinks faster than normal in a forced, oddly shy rhythm, that of a butterfly drying its wings on a grass blade. Peter believes that the blind eye, its lid sagely lowered, also garners impressions, passing a more covert and intuitive kind of judgment, and that with his blind eye Salazar long ago decided that Peter is weak and should be taken advantage of, as a corollary to natural law. Furthermore, the old man has the irritating habit of pouring salt into the palm of his hand and licking it up as he speaks. He keeps miniature Morton salt shakers, the kind designed for picnics, tucked with his bandanna in the pocket of his bleach-stiffened jeans, and whenever he's talking to Peter, and Peter pauses to light a cigarette, the old man slips the salt shaker from his pocket and muses a moment before dusting the palm of his hand. His hand is permanently cupped because of arthritis, the knuckles locked and wooden, the thumb twisted across the palm, and Peter sometimes wonders whether the arthritis had done its damage after the salt habit began, or whether the salt-licking was a response of some kind to the immobilized begging of the hand. Peter has rarely heard Salazar discuss anything more abstract than the mean temperament of Brahma bulls, the duration of saddle sores on his favorite workhorse, the worthlessness of the pig-nosed heifers belonging to a neighbor, the efficacy of various coyote poisons, and the damage barbed-wire spurs could do to a cow's udder. Once Peter saw him pick up an owl that had died on a power line and cradle it in his arm, his bad hand with its cocked thumb tracing the owl's round skull and smoothing the dappled brown spears of the feathers around the eyes; he had knocked it down from the power line with a single expertly thrown stone.

Peter has cautiously implied, now and then, when he thought they were on good terms, that his land is looking a little used. Salazar has graciously ignored this, his blind eye getting a faraway look. Peter then tried commenting on the unusual abundance of locoweed he's been finding on his land, but the possibility that he might lose one or two calves that way doesn't daunt Salazar. His calves are wild, and he demonstrates little more concern for their well-being than he would for a herd of deer. There is actually little more that Peter can do, short of risking real hostility, and that would be unwise because he plans to live on the land eventually, and a house is simply too vulnerable a possession—windows can get broken while you're gone, things stolen. Not that Salazar himself would ever sanction such actions—he would not—but word would get out that the Anglo wasn't getting along with the one-eyed old man, and such a breach in diplomatic relations would surely be taken advantage of. In effect, Salazar has grazing rights on Peter's land, and they cost him nothing but a little graciousness, which is second nature to him anyway.

"Are we there yet?" Tara says.

"Not yet," Peter says, "in a minute," and when the pickup rounds the last curve of the road and he can see the slope of his land he is relieved, as he always is, by the first sight of it. Long shadows stretch away from the well house and its lean-to shed. He studies the well house and the lean-to to see that the lock has not been tampered with, nothing lost, nothing stolen. On the side of the lean-to there is a cord of wood, mostly cedar, dry and neatly stacked, beneath a tarp. Swallows have built a jug-shaped mud nest below the corrugated tin eaves of the lean-to and he points it out to Tara.

"You've got to be careful when you go near them," he says. "Because it would be bad luck to scare them away." Then he wonders why he said it like that. He could as easily have told her that it was considered good luck to have them there at all. He could have said that much, and she would have understood.

7

The house site consists of strands of string between wooden stakes in a clearing in the brush. Peter likes the shape of the house, laid out with the help of his friend Adam, who designs passive-solar houses for a company in town. They had christened the spot with lukewarm tequila and smoked a joint, walking down as far as the arroyo, and then climbing back to the house site to polish off the bottle, Adam arguing all the while for a hogan, or perhaps a modified pit house, its windows at ground level, its doorway facing east, Peter resisting. "God, you're straight," Adam said finally. "But this place is so beautiful you could live here in a chicken coop and be happy. I just hope nobody comes and builds an A-frame across from you on the canyon wall." "Nobody will," Peter said. He had known from the first time he saw the land what he wanted. He wanted a house with a flat roof, long pine *vigas* on the ceilings inside, corner fireplaces, hand-plastered walls, tile floors, and the classic virtue of adobes, that of remaining cool all summer and frugal with costly warmth in winter, when he plans to rely on wood-stoves, a large one in the kitchen and a smaller shepherd stove in the corner of the bedroom.

A deer trail curves past the house site and up the slope between clumps of brush, through a grove of dying cotton-woods, to a concavity at the base of the canyon wall where there was once a spring. Peter has found the hollows between the cottonwoods where deer slept, leaving tufts of fur and their gray-green bulletlike droppings in the dry leaves. He supposes that the deer have found another drinking place by now, prob-ably a windmill tank that they share peaceably enough with Salazar's cattle, deer muzzles dipping through the scum on the water. The old man can remember watering his father's horses at the spring when he was a boy, or says he can, and that the water of the spring was cold and clear. Downhill, Peter found a tin cup, a filigree of rust with half a handle, and a bird point of white quartz no longer than his thumbnail. He could see that the quartz had been chosen for the splintered line of black that divides and balances the shape of the point, buried within the prismatic quartz like the thread of mercury in a ther-mometer. The flakes along its edges had been taken away in small, even strokes. He wondered how long whoever lost it had looked for it. These two things have, for Peter, talismanic significance; he means to keep them in the house, once it is built, maybe on the mantel of one of the corner fireplaces.

Where the canyon widens, the view is over level ground, occasional tilted boulders, dusty grass, and the arroyo's yellow yawn; beyond that, more level ground, the ribbon of road, a talus slope, and the far wall of the canyon. In spring, once the ground has thawed, Peter will have a backhoe operator come in and dig the trenches for the foundation. A single young cottonwood, its leaves shivering, flutters beside a strand of the string. He will have to remember to warn the backhoe operator to be careful of the tree, because he wants to keep it for the shade it already casts, in his mind's eye, against the wall of the house, and because it is a descendant of the massive long-suffering grove below the dry spring. Someone had carved a heart into the tree with a pocketknife, and when the real-estate woman first brought Peter out here, careening over the wash-boarding in the dirt road in a black Cadillac with Willie Nelson on the radio, the bark was peeling away from the wound in ribbons, and Peter thought that there was always something like that that could ruin a place for you if you let it—you could climb Truchas and find FUCK carved on the last quivering aspen at the tree line.

Now the young cottonwood has hemmed the central scar in lumps of swollen bark, and the trunk is thick enough so that his hands barely fit around it, his thumbs touching on one side, forefingers on the other, the way that his father used to measure his mother's waist before zipping her dress for her. Peter remembers the patient, freckled triangle of his mother's back. He wonders if Tara can even remember her: she died when Tara was three, and his father is in Florida now, re-married, and, hardest of all to get used to, a born-again Christian. Each year Peter gets a Christmas card with a Biblical quotation and a photograph, and each year he is shocked that the woman within his father's arm is not his mother. He really ought to go to Florida to see his father, but Florida, especially at Christmas time, discourages him. His father likes to walk along the beach behind their trailer park, picking things up and dropping them, bending to examine a dead crab, sometimes keeping a driftwood branch in which he imagines a face, a nose, a mouth, eyes.

No matter how long the tree lives, the scar will remain at eye level. Peter thinks of the old cottonwoods along the Rio Grande near Otowi Crossing, so old that they hang swaybacked above the river, the points of their lowest leaves skating the surface, anchored in the bank by huge, humped roots, the saddles of bone-white wood whittled out by beavers in the dead of winter. Or the cottonwoods at the campground in Canyon de Chelly, where you pitched the tent on a bed of fallen leaves among the widely spaced trunks and the shadows of leaves dappled the tent's wall until dusk, and in the morning you washed your face with the iron-tasting water from the pump at the edge of the grove. The cottonwoods in the wash at Chaco gave shade deep in summer, when even the walls of the ruins were hot to the touch, and if you followed the arroyo past the unexcavated pueblo of Wijiji there were spindly young trees, bearing their leaves in long uplifted shafts rather than tipping layers, several trees together along the arroyo's wall, where there were eroded holes, no bigger than a pool table's pockets and crowded with twigs, where mourning doves nested. Peter rubs the bark of the young tree, watching a red ant circumnavigate a knot. It will be a beautiful tree. He is glad that it is on his land, where he can protect it.

He has begun to think in terms of his house, and things for his house, more and more often. In an antiques store last month he came across a panel of stained glass that threw flat spots of color across the cluttered tables of clocks and dolls when the salesgirl held it into the light. It had come from an old house in Las Vegas, she told him, and he didn't know whether to believe her or not; there were air bubbles trapped in the glass, and the panes were wafer-thin, so he supposed that she was telling the truth. He had paid too much for it, and the salesgirl, who had seen that phenomenon before, had taken his check and slipped it under the coin tray in the cash register without asking for any other I.D. He had wanted a slight feeling of being cheated to take the edge off possession of something so beautiful. A year ago, even six months ago, he wouldn't have kept the stained glass for himself; he would have given it to Clarissa without thinking, because she liked beautiful objects and it had not yet occurred to him that he had any use for them.

He just didn't acquire things, and she did. Once, after a surveying trip along the Colorado, he had brought her a black river stone. She had said it was the best gift he had ever given her, a perfect stone, *the* perfect stone, and after that her drawing table was cleared each evening of India-ink bottles and paintbrushes and X-Acto knives, boxes of charcoals and the stubs of well-used pastels, until only the stone was left. He knew that she loved it, but the gift had been so casual, so nearly an afterthought, that he was wary about taking credit for it. In fact, he had walked several feet past the stone, his boots squeaking wet, before he blinked and somehow saw it again, and retraced his own bootprints and picked it up, a single dark stone among a thousand pale river-rounded stones, and felt its thoroughly cold, algae-smudged, heavy black perfection in his hand. It almost seemed he had understood her better on the spur of the moment than for the years they had lived together.

Buying her a birthday or Christmas present—that was an ordeal. She would have said she was precise, but what she was was hard to please. In supermarkets she went through the slanting tier of fisted and furled green peppers as if she were Edward Weston. She had broken a dozen wineglasses they had got as a wedding gift from one of his professors—broken them deliberately, Peter thought, even though the breakages were widely spaced throughout the years—because she thought the shapes were wrong and it bothered her to pour wine into them. This is what it is: she doesn't trust human beings, she trusts the shapes of things. Once she had painted the kitchen sink, one of her more beautiful paintings, and it was clear to Peter that she had been interested in the gloss of light on aluminum, but the art critic for the *New Mexican* had noted the yellow bottle of dishwashing liquid labelled JOY, claiming that, for the painter, happiness lay in domestic things, and even a kind of exultation. Peter hadn't believed it for a moment. She had wanted the hourglass of primary color provided by the bottle to balance all her shades of trompe-l'oeil gray. It was wrong to read anything more into it than that.

Still, in spite of the difficulty, he had sometimes managed to give her something that she liked. He thought that as far as giving gifts went, he had been a good, even an ingenious, husband. There was the time he had caught a zebra-tailed skink on the garden wall and carried it into the house in his cupped hands, the lizard keeping the length of its body above his palm as if it could not bear that contact, riding along in its feather-weight stance of alarm with its tail, acting as a kind of counter-balance, flicking the pads of his curled fingers. He had let the skink out in the bathtub and gone to get Clarissa, who was working in her room. The skink was scouring the bathtub's sides on its hind legs, like a dog trying to get out over a fence, and when it could find no way out, it settled in the bottom of the tub into a series of convulsive pumping movements that comically resembled push-ups. "I think you'd better let it out into the garden again," Clarissa said. "You can keep it for a minute or two," he said. "It won't do it any harm." So she sat down on the closed lid of the toilet and drew the skink, a series of drawings, one of which she had given him. (She had given him remarkably few drawings, throughout the years; sometimes she even turned him down, when he asked for one, saying, "It's not good enough," and shaking her head stubbornly if he persisted.) He had also given her a condor's feather as long as her arm, handsome and light and faintly embroidered by feather lice, the central quill waxen yellow, aerodynamically flattened on the underside, ringed with smoky lines. In one of her shows there had been two walls of condor-feather paintings, the feather floating on a different shade of gray in each canvas. When there had been a teachers' strike, and she hadn't sold anything for a long while, he had made several payments on her car. He had bought her some expensive handmade drawing paper and a scrap of true Egyptian papyrus. He had bought her a sand-cast silver belt buckle and a grape-colored beret that she wore jauntily, over one eye. He had given her *The Complete Brothers Grimm Fairy Tales*, illustrated. He had given her the first pomegranate she had ever seen, and she kept it until it was withered and dry. Once he had found a small, used portable typewriter and bought that for her, and she learned to type on it. Sometimes in the spring he parked the pickup by the side of the road and gathered wildflowers and brought them home to her. For Christmas one year he had given her a tweed jacket that fit her precisely, even to the anxious hunch of her shoulders, which are surprisingly wide. He used to tease her that she could be a halfback if she wanted to, and she wouldn't even need shoulder pads. He doesn't know exactly when this ceased being funny, when the muscular little pulse of nicknames and endearments and private catchwords between them dwindled and died: it was one of those losses that slipped through the cracks between the other losses.

Tara scoops up a handful of dirt, throws a clod his way, and wanders up the deer trail. Her cropped head still occasionally troubles him. She had cut it herself, when he left her alone one afternoon in the basement of the museum, thinking he wouldn't have to be gone long, and it was the first time her motives were truly obscure to him, as opaque as those of another adult. In one corner of the basement there is an improvised bathroom, not much more than a converted broom closet, with a chipped sink with one faucet that works, and a light bulb that hangs from a string. Peter had propped a mirror above the sink so he could shave; it was that mirror that Tara used, if she looked at herself at all. The metallic snipping had sounded strange to Peter as he came down the stairs, and entering the bathroom behind her he had seen the last handful as it fell. The floor showed a flattened ellipse of hair, such a shiny black that it held the dusty imprint of his Adidas when he accidentally stepped on it. When he first told Clarissa how it had happened, he said, "I could have cried when I saw that," and she regarded him coldly. "So?" she said. "Why didn't you?"

She had taken Tara downtown to get her hair properly cut and undo as much of the damage as could be undone, and now it didn't look so bad, really, just slightly punkish, not even very odd. Still, Clarissa had wanted to take Tara for a session with her analyst, Sasha Peabody. Peter had hated the idea, and he vetoed it. Why would he let someone he barely knew, and didn't greatly trust, do away with the last traces of his daughter's innocence? He wouldn't. That was all: he would not.

"Sasha doesn't destroy innocence," Clarissa said. "That's the guy that drives up in the long black Cadillac and says, 'Come for a ride, little girl, and I'll give you some candy.' "

"You know what I mean," Peter said.

"Sasha's very good with children."

"Let her be good with somebody else's children," Peter said. "Not with mine."

"Tara isn't so innocent. We never kept our problems from her, did we? We never went into the bedroom and closed the door before our fights, or anything?"

"No," he said; he wishes now that they had.

"She's almost thirteen, Peter. That's old enough to understand a lot of things. She's clearly troubled by the situation."

"I really don't see what Sasha could do. The situation exists, and we're each troubled by it, that's the natural response. There's nothing odd about that."

"No, and nothing odd about cutting off your hair in the basement of the place where your father spends almost all of his waking hours."

"Is that how you see it?" he said.

"Isn't that how you see it?"

"I knew if I got into this with you I'd end up having to defend myself."

"I just wish you were better at it."

"I get a lot of practice, don't I? Every time I see you."

"Look," she said. "Could we stick to talking about Tara? I understand that you have her best interests at heart."

"You say that as if you memorized it. That's a Sasha tactic. That's exactly the kind of exquisitely dishonest shit I don't want Tara to learn."

Then she laughed, throwing her head back and really laughing, and he liked her for that, that in the middle of a fight she could still stop and laugh. "God, Peter," she said. "Exquisitely dishonest shit, huh?" He liked her again, and as soon as he liked her he felt sorrow. She could always surprise him—for as long as they'd been together, that had been their saving grace. One of their saving graces. She looked at him gravely. "Peter, I won't do anything you would really hate, okay? I won't do anything that you don't think you could live with."

Not long after they were married, Peter had gone to Berkeley with her to visit her parents. She visited them often, in part because her mother was on dialysis, and in fragile health. Her father was a biochemist researching the behavior of starch in frozen foods, and her mother was a linguist, rather widely known, who taught at the university. A collection of her essays on problems in pronoun reference had been published by a Midwestern university press in a handsome clothbound volume with yellow endpapers. Clarissa, who had done the diagrams and illustrations for her, was thanked discreetly in the acknowledgments. Her mother had dedicated the book to her cat, who was buried in the garden. Peter sat with Clarissa's father in the long living room, listening to Vivaldi's *Four Seasons*. Each time "Spring" had finished and "Summer" was about to begin, her father rose from his chair and lifted the stereo needle and replaced it at the beginning of "Spring." In the garden outside the picture window two small cherry trees, bandaged and staked, bent in the wind, shedding petals that stuck to the wet gravel and the glistening stucco of the garden wall. A newspaper flopped over the wall, into the gravel, and when Clarissa's father went out to get it, it was covered with cherry petals. He shared the sports pages with Peter and when he put on his glasses before reading, the lenses magnified his eyes until they were all pupil, pitch dark, framed by engraved scallop-shells of wrinkles that extended back as far as the first crease in front of his ear, where the clipped sideburn was feathery white. His English was a precise monotone, and he spoke very kindly to Peter, asking him where his parents lived and looking concerned when Peter said that his mother had recently been sick with the flu. "That must have been very hard for your father," he said. "You must make certain sickness draws you together"—he lifted a hand and clasped it tightly with the other, so tightly the bones stood out in the back of his hand—"instead of forcing you apart." Peter regretted having mentioned it; it hadn't been that serious. Clarissa's father redoubled his efforts to make Peter feel at ease. They talked about baseball.

Clarissa's mother, however, clearly believed that Peter's uneasiness was appropriate. She had an alert narrow-jawed face, framed by beautifully cut dark hair which fell into a thick arrow at the nape of her slender neck. The strands of gray at her temples seemed somehow to extend her already long eyes. She wore pearl earrings and a plain gold wedding band and her black skirt creased once, across her lap, when she sat down opposite Peter, a critical and monochromatic presence in that pale room. Her legs were long and very fine and Peter admired them, being very well acquainted with those legs in a younger version. Her high heels had open toes and he thought that that was, possibly, a lone concession to vanity, an inch of tawny silk exposed there, binding the dovetailed toes. He knew from

Clarissa's stories that she had been a strict mother, sometimes remote, thorough and watchful. Clarissa had told him about stealing comic books from the dentist's waiting room because her parents had forbidden her to buy them—her mother considered them a degradation of literature. Her father had taken the training wheels from her bike one Saturday morning and taught her to ride down a shallow incline—Berkeley was full of gentle hills, and she could see the Bay at the end of the street, and the sails moving slowly across the water. She had done her first painting in a Saturday morning art class and her mother had it still. She had kissed a boy for the first time in the shadows of her own porch and later he had given her his letter jacket, which she wore with the leather sleeves pushed up above her elbows. She had smoked marijuana for the first and last time in her own room, with the bedspread patterned with ballerinas drawn up over her knees because the dope had made her cold, and when she had gone into the kitchen to make a chicken sandwich, her father was there, making notes to himself on a legal pad, and he had drawn her into his lap and sniffed gently and told her that she needed to wash her hair. She had found the cat, a stray, in an alley near the campus, and carried it home inside her sweater. The cat and her mother had fallen in love. It was a long-haired orange cat with serious round eyes and it had had a habit of sleeping curled up on the back tire of her father's car, inside the wheel well, when it was cold, and one morning her father had come out to start the car and had backed down the driveway, forgetting to look into the wheel well first for the cat. Peter had the feeling that neither Clarissa nor her mother had ever quite forgiven him.

In dialysis, Clarissa's mother seemed to dislike most keenly the loss of privacy, for in the dialysis center men and women, some of them in their bathrobes, lay on plastic couches, their arms extended and taped, the machine beside each couch pumping and purifying blood while a nurse on a television soap opera cornered a doctor in a supply room and told him that she loved him, she had loved him for years. The television was left on all the time, detergent commercials and love affairs the monotonous background to monotony. Clarissa's mother invariably went for treatment wearing a black linen skirt and a crisp white silk shirt. Peter saw that as defiance: white silk to a dialysis treatment; she had lost three shirts because blood had splattered on them. Peter bought a small tape recorder, thinking that Clarissa's mother could drown out the soap operas with Vivaldi or Pachelbel or Erik Satie, and though she accepted the gift with a pleased, almost flirtatious gaiety, he never saw her use it. He guessed she believed it would set her too much apart from the other patients, who were like bored and curiously pallid sunbathers on their couches, shifting restlessly while a technician paused at each couch, checking dials and the hard lengths of amber tubing, relaying the odds and ends of gossip, coaxing, cajoling. Though some of the other patients came late, or went off their diets, or found other means of sabotaging dialysis, she remained punctual, strict, and uncomplaining. She didn't mind the constant self-discipline; she understood the necessity for it. But often she must have wished she could have spent those hours alone, exactly as she chose, in one of the reading rooms in the library, beneath the vaulted gold-leaf ceiling, students coming and going between the long oak tables, their hair young, their skin young, their eyes young, none of them, no none of them, sick.

Clarissa had wanted to stay in Berkeley for the summer, to be near her mother and keep house for her father. Peter agreed that she should; he knew he would only be in the way, however much they pretended that he was now part of the family. When someone was seriously ill there were no parts of the family, there was only *family*. Anticipating her decision, he had already decided to go to Texas, to an archaeological site where there had once been found, lodged between a mammoth's ribs, a laurel-leaf shaped point, a single chip flaked from its base to expedite the flow of blood.

Once at the site, Peter worked on excavating a Pleistocene antelope, lying on its back, its vertebrae still linked in a slight arch. He knelt by the antelope's rib cage and cleaned the atlas vertebra with a toothbrush, the bristles, splayed from use on his own teeth, now burnishing ancient bone, and fattening with fine dust as they did so. He had been happy then, in spite of what he knew Clarissa was going through in Berkeley. The locusts hissed all day long in the dry grass, and sometimes while he was digging in one of the upper levels he sliced through a cicada larva with the blade of his trowel. Peter kept a clipboard by his knee and on it he drew, in pencil on graph paper, the forehead and oval eye sockets of the antelope as they surfaced, and a pebble that appeared late one morning, a few inches from the antelope's cheek, looming as large on the graph paper as a boulder exposed by receding tide. Peter did a new drawing for each five centimeters that he dug. Every twenty centimeters, the camp cook, doubling as photographer, came and took a series of black-and-white photographs. The dirt Peter had dug away was carried off in canvas bags, sifted through a window screen for chips of stone or any fragments of bone or ash he might have missed; then samples for pollen were taken, the samples made into microscope slides, the remainder of the dirt sifted again, packed once more into the same canvas bag, and stored in the laboratory tent. The pebble was probably nothing, just that, an unworked pebble, but once it had been completely excavated it would be examined for signs of use. Peter hoped for the sliver of stone that would turn into a flaked edge, the flaked edge emerging as an elegant concave point, but none appeared. Except for the antelope and the pebble the soil remained fine, dry as curry powder, and uninhabited. Each dusk the trench was covered with a sheet of black plastic weighted with stones. The sheet fell in an arc from the rim of the trench,

dipped into the trench, and was anchored on the yet unexcavated, brushy ground below with stones that Peter placed
himself. Each night, like clockwork, he dreamed that the antelope came alive. It was alive, and still partially buried, and
Peter must calm it before he could begin to work, and the same
rules for excavation applied: he must go down by centimeters.
The dream was short, and Peter woke from it sweating on his
Army cot, the four other sleepers in the tent breathing evenly,
and fireflies moving in the dark beyond the mosquito netting.
He would watch them for a while before falling back to sleep.
In the morning after breakfast when the mail was handed
around there was nearly always a letter from Clarissa, often
written from the room where she sat with her mother, and he
wrote back as often as he could manage, on a legal pad he kept
beside his plate at dinner; sometimes he also wrote to her
mother—short, shy letters that he hoped she would like. He
told her about the camp and the land around Lubbock and the
clouds. He called Clarissa as often as he could afford to, from
the pay telephone on the wall of the kitchen, the only real
building at the site—cement block, with a tar-paper roof.
Clarissa's voice on the telephone was not familiar, though it
asked familiar questions. She loved him; did he love her? Was
he still sure? As he listened to her he kept his legs away from
the wall, where scorpions and children of the earth scuttled up
and down in the dark, making quick skeletal noises, like dice
rattled in a cupped hand.

Then, after dinner on a particularly long, hot day, he noticed
one of the girls in the crew coming back from the showers—
her wet hair had soaked the shoulders of her T-shirt, her nipples
pushed at the sodden cloth, and as she picked her way through
the thorny grass he could see that her shaved ankles were clean
but the soles of her bare feet were caked with dust. He courted
her briefly until she slept with him. He liked her, but she didn't
move him much. She wore a kind of perfume called L'Air du

Temps that drew the stunned mosquitos from the evening air, and lying beside her in the grass he would sometimes watch a mosquito alight and feel too lazy and sated to slap it. She scratched in long delicious self-pitying scratches, and, as if his back in sex were simply an extension of her own, she scratched him too. That embarrassed him, because he had gotten into the habit of wearing only a pair of running shorts while he worked, and the T-shirt he had to put on seemed to him like a white flag of sex. Still, when she ran out of the perfume, Peter went into Lubbock one Saturday morning with some of the others and looked around for it, but they didn't have it in the drugstore, so he bought her a sweatshirt with TEXAS PRINCESS on the front and a pair of plastic barrettes. She was a Christian, and when she wanted to read him some passages from the Song of Solomon one night, he listened unwillingly, liking her less for it. It wasn't hard to avoid her after that; it even seemed possible that she was beginning to avoid him too. She must have seen that she had no future with him, a married man and an unbeliever.

Years later, in the heat of argument, Clarissa would some-times remind him that he had not been with her when her mother died, and he would wonder if this was not, in some way, an oblique accusation of infidelity, that she had somehow caught him out. He had flown in from Lubbock for the funeral, accept-ing the Christian girl's offer of a ride to the airport, carefully keeping his leg away from hers on the Chevrolet's front seat, and sweating into his suit coat until he felt he fairly reeked of Ban. The kindness of her offer, in the heat of the day, was almost overwhelming. He couldn't tell—maybe she thought she was turning the other cheek. In the airport in Lubbock she waited with him and he saw how more than one middle-aged executive in a lightweight summer suit and scuffed cowboy boots turned to follow her patched denim skirt and skinny sunburned shoulders; he realized, a little bitterly, that her desirability was not a function of his desire. In the camp she was not regarded as one of the more attractive girls—because of her beliefs, which had a gentle barbarism, as if she'd worn a gold stud through the wing of one nostril, and because she did not intend to go to Harvard or Crete or Olduvai Gorge but only back to the small teachers' college in Iowa from which she'd come. The consensus was that she was ineffectual, out of her depth, not really serious, and it was seriousness that was attractive. Peter had accepted this view too easily; sleeping with her had not changed it. Now he wished he had been more thoughtful, more aware of what had been happening to him. She bought him a magazine, he bought her a frozen yoghurt, and then his plane's departure was announced.

In the airport in Oakland, Clarissa was a stranger. Her father actually looked, to Peter, slightly more familiar than she did. They shook hands and Peter could feel the bones in his wife's father's hand: he felt grief at that moment more clearly than he had ever felt it in his life. He also felt obscurely resentful, as if he should have been warned that he was about to walk into the middle of so much sorrow. Outside the terminal, when the humidity struck him, the smell of exhaust and the glittering roofs of the cars in the parking lot, he felt flooded with nostalgia for the life of the dig. It had been his until that morning, and he had not valued it properly. The clannish joking of the crew members, the nicknames and pranks and derogatory tenderness, had provided a sort of family life more intimate than this one, of the stricken elderly scientist and his grieving daughter, who both gave him wary backward looks, as if unsure what he might do next, this gloomy and oddly overdressed hitchhiker, when he lit a cigarette in the rear seat of his father-in-law's car. The Wus' neighbors had left an array of heavy, lidded casseroles on the front doorstep. The next morning the bronze-trimmed casket was lowered lightly down into the grave and Peter put his hand on Clarissa's shoulder and closed his eyes and inhaled the smell of spaded earth.

Clarissa went back to Albuquerque with him, and for months everything was difficult and strained between them. They didn't sleep together for so many weeks that he lost track. They went to movies. Movies, in fact, got to be a habit between them, a sort of surrogate conversation—even, it occurred to Peter, surrogate lovemaking, because in a movie theater you were in the dark and your attention was directed at the same thing. As soon as she got up in the morning, she paged through the newspaper and called him at the university, at his office, to tell him what she had found, pleased if there was something really good, and later in the day she visited the grocery store and bought chocolate, Hershey bars and M&M's, which they could smuggle in instead of buying the much more expensive stuff in the lobby concession stand, although sometimes they gave in to a desire for a giant buttered popcorn, since they could see it spitting against the walls of its brilliantly lit glass box, and its keen stale smell was all around. Once or twice Peter tried grading papers in the lobby while Clarissa went into the movie, but then it wasn't the same. Cashiers knew them, and made jokes about any movie they happened to miss. Slowly Clarissa grew less edgy, less evasive, and he watched, not wanting to press her, to interfere with the process of recovery she seemed to have devised for herself. Finally, after Dollar Night in a theater downtown and a Japanese monster movie featuring an enormous moth, whose wings clapped in flight with the baffled delicacy of marionette's hands, caught in a web of spotlights above the city, they went back to the apartment and made love, clumsily at first, she seating herself above him and leaning forward so that he saw the goosefleshed undersides of her nipples and the smoothness of her throat and the dark almond-shaped nostrils, her knees wedged alongside his rib cage as she rocked, her hands on his chest, and then to his surprise she slid off him and stripped the condom from his penis as if she were peeling a Band-Aid from a child's skin, and dropped it over the side of the bed; she wanted to be beneath him then, and when he moved back into her he could feel more clearly the strength of her body and its complicity, her breasts flattening beneath his chest, her lip caught between her teeth. Afterward she turned away from him, drawing her knees up, and the shape of her long back was so beautiful that he traced the crack between her buttocks with one finger, then with two, feeling the little clenched starfish below the final knob of coccyx accept his fingertip, and maybe because he hadn't wanted anything, he had only wanted to look at her, she closed her eyes, and it seemed to him that she nodded, and he moved above her and through his slitted eyes he could see certain things, the face of the clock and the corner of the room and the back of her head, and they moved together softly and for a long while, and as they moved the night air came through the window screens and blew across the bed.

Tara has gone exploring. She comes back with treasure: a fossilized shell, white as a fox's tooth within its sandstone matrix; a chip of mica; and a length of snakeskin, which she'd found near the stone the snake had used to slough it off, the outer part braided and flaking, the inner dryly iridescent. Peter admires these things, and she goes to put them away. He knows that she will show them to her mother in the morning, and his feelings are hurt, a little, because that is the point in having found them.

He strikes a match and lights the camp stove, which stutters until the front coil is ringed with flame, and then he sets the coffee pot on the coil. The stove, his Army green Coleman, rests on a hearth of stones, the grass below them singed and powdered with ash. He always begins his evenings here with a cup of strong coffee, and now he wants it badly. He had wanted it, he remembers, even in Mia's kitchen. What kind of woman doesn't even keep coffee in her house? Since he has been living in the basement of the museum he drinks coffee all day and doesn't notice any ill effect. Maybe coffee no longer makes him anxious. Either that, or he is already so anxious he can't feel the difference. His hand sometimes shakes when he's signing a check, but he thinks that is purely psychological—as a result of the separation, he's feeling impoverished. He should indulge himself, grant himself luxuries occasionally, but except for the stained-glass panel there hasn't been anything he can think of that he wanted. He could get his life in order, and then need would arise quite naturally, and he would want things again. What did she have, that tinny casket thing you put the crumbs of tea inside? A man who lived alone wouldn't have something like that, not unless he was a faggot. Peter nudges the coffee pot with a stick, and Tara squats down beside him. "It's not even big enough for two people," she says. "Did you ever think of that?" She means his house, the string diagram.

"It's big enough," he says. He feels oddly defensive.

"I want to come here and live."

"Oh, you do, do you?"

"I want to live here with you, once you get the house finished."

"Why?" He opens a can and dumps beans into the saucepan. She holds out the salt shaker to him. He shakes salt over the beans.

"Because," she says. "You could get me, couldn't you, if you wanted?"

"Of course I could get you," he says, rising. She backs away from the stove, then takes off up the slope in a clatter of stones, looking down at him. He drops the stick. "But would I want you?" he calls. "That's the question. Would I want you?"

"You'd want me," she calls. She tears some grass stems from the ground and twists them around her wrist in a bracelet.

"You're very sure of yourself."

"You'd want me," she calls, but this time her voice is hollow. She slides the bracelet up her arm and looks at it. Suddenly he can't stand it, any of it. He sprints up the slope and catches her around the knees, seeing as he tackles her the dust on the seat of her Levi's, surprised to find—in the middle of the fall, her hair against his chin, his chest bearing her down while his extended arm shields her from the ground—that she weighs almost nothing at all.

"Was I too rough?" he says, and she looks at him sideways before wriggling out of his arms, holding out her elbow to inspect it for cuts, not answering.

The beans are hot and have an ashy taste because he forgot where he had dropped the wooden spoon and stirred them with the stick, which had fallen partly into the fire and was charred. There were eggs, too, sunny-side up, the way Tara likes them, with the yolks left runny. He doesn't know when he's seen her eat so hungrily, firelight dancing around the aluminum rim of her plate, wrinkling her nose against the smoke. "Smoke follows beauty," he tells her. She's never heard it before. "Don't we have any chocolate?" she says. "How come you never remember chocolate?"

"I just forgot."

"Will you remember next time?"

"I'll remember next time."

He says he's going to stay awake a while longer and she finds her sleeping bag in the camper and drags it, along with the moth-eaten Mexican blanket, up the slope. She arranges the sleeping bag in one corner of the string house and takes off her shoes and puts them, resting toe by toe, on a stone.

When he walks up the slope to kiss her good night she is sitting up in her sleeping bag, rubbing Chapstick along her lower lip. "I think my cold is almost gone," she says.

"That's good," he says, nuzzling her hair, which has a clean, still childlike, scent of shampoo. "You won't get chilly?" She shakes her head.

Peter walks back down the slope and sits for a long while feeding cottonwood twigs one by one into the fire. That night, the first night that Clarissa had really been there again, he hadn't been sure of what she had done until the morning after, when he looked down into one of his sneakers and saw the condom crumpled there. It hadn't surprised her at all to learn she had gotten pregnant. In fact, she was delighted. Peter was the more reluctant one. In the obstetrician's office she had held the stethoscope, like a small cymbal, to the curve of her belly. Her sweater was tugged up casually, one breast dipping down, one hidden. The long amber plastic stems framed her face, the earpieces resting in her ears. She was listening to the baby's heart. "Boom," she said softly, to Peter. "Boom."

8

Clarissa has a splinter in her finger—it must be from this morning, when she was stretching canvases. She looks at the splinter instead of watching Sasha, who is across from her in the hot tub. Sasha's elbows rest on the tile rim, her breasts just above the level of the water. Her nipples, puckered from the cold air, are nonetheless the size of half dollars, and of a ripe rose shade that Clarissa envies. She studies her own small breasts. Peter used to accuse her of narcissism, because, when he was standing beside the rumpled bed, already dressed, she would sit up and kiss her own knee. He hadn't been able to see that it wasn't narcissism, it was simply an extension of all the half-completed gestures between them, their whispers and touches still vanishing into thin air. Sometimes, in a motion that screened the length of her raised thigh in falling hair, she had even licked her knee, tasting the sweat in the fine-grained skin above the jut of bone. He had misunderstood. The narcissism that didn't exist had aroused him.

Peter, Peter. Isn't there a point when all of his stubborn opinions, all traces of argument between them, will drift away from her like so much smoke?

Their last fight had been particularly vicious. It was the fight they would have had about Sonny, if Peter had known about Sonny, but he hadn't—he had kept himself from knowing like a kind of Sherlock Holmes in reverse. It wasn't as if she had left matchbooks lying around, or talked in her sleep, because she hadn't, but she was sure that she had changed, that the quality of her skin was finer from lovemaking, the enamel of her teeth frostier, her hair shinier; she had examined herself nightly in her bedroom mirror for bruises, barefoot on her Persian rug, turning like a cat with a burr on its back. When, in bed, Peter slid his hand along her thigh, and she was wet at his first touch after months of difficult, reluctant sex, she was sure that he would see through her, and read, in her willingness, a lover; in the morning, when she slid her hand across his side to his penis, enfolding it, she was sure he would guess that she was remembering the springy erection Sonny always woke with. She let the head of Peter's penis peep from her fist and saw that it was grainier, darker, distinctly older than Sonny's, and she felt guilty and homesick for Sonny's narrow bed. As far as she could tell, though, Peter had not understood a thing. He hadn't even done the simple marital arithmetic of realizing that, for the first time in a very long time, they'd made love the morning after a night when they'd made love, and therefore twice within twenty-four hours, remarkable after such a drought. She began to see that she was safe. Safe, she began to be contemptuous.

In their last fight she had counted out his flaws for him: he could not seem to balance a checkbook; he never remembered to do the grocery shopping, and when he did remember, he forgot certain items—milk or bread, the *basics*. What had really, truly angered her was that he had walked into the kitchen wearing only an old baseball shirt, long-legged, his hair damp from the shower, his penis hanging gray and sorrowful as a rag doll's arm, and she'd thought *I can't live with him*. He did exactly what he wanted, she said. But that's not true, he said; he had been amazed, rubbing at his wet hair with a towel. He had dropped the towel on the kitchen table. She had picked it up and thrown it at him, and when the towel caught on his hip and started to slide down, he looked as if he were about to laugh, and she pitched a coffee cup at the wall near his shoulder. The cup was delicate and old, printed with small roses, and she had often kept it near her while she worked. As soon as it broke, she understood her deep fondness for the cup. She shouted at Peter, "Why don't you ever act as if you're *married?*"

She saw that he couldn't move. He was barefoot, surrounded by shards. He was going to stand there until she did something.

She found the broom and dustpan and swept carefully, looking at his long toes and the fan of dark hairs over his neat male ankle. She scooped up the largest pieces of the cup and dropped them into the wastebasket. All the while she was watching him for a sign. He didn't move. Something happened between them at that moment: she knew that their accumulated weariness with each other was going to bring them down, that it really was going to be as simple as that.

Clarissa lets herself slide farther down into the water, tilting her head back so that her hair is a submerged waterlily weight that drags, not unpleasurably, at her skull. She can see the moon rising above the *latilla* fence that screens their private pool. The third woman in the tub, whose name is Meg, is another client of Sasha's—*client* is Sasha's word; Clarissa doesn't know when *patient* became pejorative, but that is a good way to annoy Sasha, by using it. Meg is dying of cancer. She has feathery short hair and protuberant amber eyes of great beauty. Around her head she wears a band of twisted black cloth wound in strands of red and yellow metallic thread, slightly crooked. Sasha carries the conversation. You can always count on Sasha for talk. She tells the story of how her ex-husband, Richard, had recently fallen in love—with an Israeli woman, a kibbutznik, no less, and a correspondent for UPI.

Sasha says that UPI was bad enough, but the woman had been handling a very difficult transcontinental affair with a married war correspondent who was about to leave his wife for her, on the very *brink*, when he was killed in El Salvador. It was bad luck. That was before El Salvador even was El Salvador. No one could have predicted it.

"A very difficult affair," Clarissa says gently, mockingly.

"What?" Sasha says. Irony is often lost on Sasha. Clarissa sometimes thinks that this is why she is such a wonderful analyst.

"Nothing. Go on."

Sasha ticks it off on her fingers: the woman had had a tragic love affair; a heroic recovery from the tragic love affair; roots (Israel was roots); education (Cambridge was education); good in bed (according to Richard); *macha* (she had been in the Israeli army, and they all agreed that that was *macha*); glamour; guts; self-sufficiency.

"I hate her," Sasha says. "You don't believe me. I really hate her."

"Of course Richard would say that," Meg observes.

"Say what?"

"Say that she was good in bed," Meg says. "It can only reflect credit on him."

"God knows he needs it," Sasha says. "But how do you figure?"

"Well," Meg says, "he's the one making this commando, this G.I. Joe, orgasmic."

"But that's just it," Sasha says. "She's beautiful. Really beautiful. She's turning heads all over town. You don't think she's just saving herself for that big dope, Richard, do you? She's cutting a swath, a wide swath. Is 'swath' the word? Hearts all over Santa Fe. She has it all, so how am I supposed to compete? You know the kind of shoes you see in the windows when you're walking up Madison Avenue in New York, and all of a sudden you find yourself wanting something like a pair of two-hundred-dollar leopard-skin high heels? And you sublimate and buy a hot dog from a street vendor? Well, she bought them. She bought those shoes. A foot-fetishist's dream." Sasha drinks some champagne. "When we were first married, Richard used to like me to wear those wooden Japanese clogs, and walk around in them naked, *clip clop clip clop*. I forget why I did it. Why doesn't she have athlete's foot from showering after the Foreign Legion? That's what I want to know. It isn't fair. After twenty minutes in those wooden clogs I had to rub Tiger Balm into my back before I could bend down to change Nicholas's diapers."

"The tough get tougher," Meg says. "The weak get squashed." She slaps the water, splashing.

"There's room for vulnerability, isn't there?" Sasha feels compelled to switch into her therapist's mode, and Meg looks at her and smiles. Clarissa is surprised that her smile is so dazzling. Sometimes she almost believes she can see what men see in women. There is a slight, charming crookedness to Meg's front teeth.

"There must be," Meg says. "I'm still alive."

So far, Clarissa thinks. She is astonished at herself. It must be the wine. The guilt at having thought this is immediate and complex: she almost feels that Meg had been about to add that, herself, and had deferred at the last moment to Sasha. If that was true, it had cost Meg something; she had a face that had been conscripted for honesty.

"But why does Richard tell you that she's good in bed?" Clarissa asks Sasha.

"Oh," Sasha says. "We still talk."

Clarissa thinks that it is more than that. One afternoon after a session in the back room of Sasha's house, she had gone into the bathroom and there was a message scrawled in soap on the mirror: BABY, YOU KNOW YOU'RE STILL A 10. It was Richard's handwriting. Clarissa knows Richard's handwriting because he is the lawyer for her gallery. Actually, Richard is the lawyer for half of the galleries in town, though he isn't her lawyer. He likes painters and paintings, and if he has to make his living by practicing law he would like it to be something to do with painters. Once, covertly, he asked Clarissa to lunch and she refused as tactfully as she knew how. It would have gotten complicated. Peter used to refer to Richard as "artsy-craftsy" but that was irrational, part of his general dislike of Sasha, and of all lawyers.

"Good old Richard," Clarissa says drunkenly, surprising herself.

"Clarissa likes Richard," Meg says. "Good old big dope Richard. To Richard."

"That's old hat," Sasha says. "They've been flirting with each other for years."

"That's not true."

"You have to admit he has a nice body," Meg says.

"I don't have to admit anything of the sort." Sasha grins. "Love handles and a three-day stubble."

"I always thought he had such nice thick curly hair," Clarissa says.

"All over," Meg says.

"And a violent temper," Sasha says.

"I don't mind that."

"She doesn't mind about his temper, Sasha," Meg explains. "She doesn't mind at all."

"No," Sasha says. "Clarissa likes men who have obvious flaws."

"Well," Meg says. "That doesn't narrow it down too much."

"How's your jazz musician?" Sasha asks.

"My jazz musician, yes. My Joey. He left for San Francisco. Would you like to know the reason he gave me, for leaving for San Francisco?"

"Yes."

"My refrigerator was too loud," Meg says. "It makes a rumbling digestive sound in the night, not a loud or particularly bothersome sound, really. In fact, a sound I find rather comforting, myself. You know, a house sound. You get used to them. But the sound of the refrigerator didn't please Joey at all. He said wasn't there something I could do? What did he have in mind? I asked. I said I had accommodated enough. It was my house, my kitchen, my Frigidaire, and if he wasn't so neurotic it wouldn't bother him at all. If he just jogged, or something, he'd sleep like a baby. Enough of his whims and his long hours and his high-strung demanding musician's temperament. Was he going to offer to pay for the new refrigerator?" She shakes her head. "And his hours, to tell you the truth, were getting stranger and stranger. Stay out late, sleep late in the morning, wake up looking like a zombie, go for a little walk to get the paper, head over to the bar after I pressed his shirt for him. Not a bad life, really. But I didn't want to buy a new refrigerator, not even a fine and absolutely soundless one that could make ice cubes by itself. I didn't want to go refrigerator-looking. I couldn't find it in my heart." Meg circles the rim of her wineglass with a badly bitten fingernail. "So okay, the funny thing is that now the sound of this refrigerator, which I have lived with for years, now it wakes me up in the middle of the night and I can't get back to sleep." She looks at them triumphantly.

"So," Sasha says. "You stuck by your guns."

"That's me." Meg laughs. "A pillar of decisiveness."

"Maybe he'll come back," Clarissa says. "San Francisco is cold."

"And full of raucous refrigerators," Sasha says.

"Maybe he will come back," Meg says. "It could happen like that. Am I crazy to think so?"

"You're not crazy."

"Am I going crazy?"

"You're just grieving. Grieving can feel so crazy."

"But I'm clinging to this void."

"Absence isn't a void," Sasha says.

Clarissa decides that she likes Meg. When Meg had first lowered herself into the smoking water, she'd frowned downward, the scrolls of her pinkish-blond pubic hair softening into a cloud beneath the sharp angles of her pelvic bones: her stomach was hollow. Now she paddles with her bony feet while Sasha pours for each of them. "Formal toast," Sasha says. "To vulnerability." She lifts her glass.

Meg takes her glass from the tiles. "To vulnerability," she says. She tips her head as she drinks.

"To vulnerability," Clarissa says. She doesn't want to drink to it. Bubbles break against her teeth and a dry, clean taste unfurls along her tongue. When she was still in college, she won a commission to paint a wall, one wall of an enormous auditorium, newly constructed; it was a prize, and the entire art department had fought over it. Above the detritus of construction, buckets dripping with paint and canvas painters' cloths crumpled around the feet of the scaffolding, the wall she was to paint was huge, pristine, an expanse of white quartz sand on the most beautiful beach in the world. She had turned to the older painter, a professor, who had come with her to examine the painting surface. "I'm scared," she told him. "Oh, honey," he said. "We're all scared. We're all scared to death, all the time. Don't let them fool you." And she had seen that he intended nothing by it, not reassurance and certainly not commiseration, because she had gotten something he wanted, and he could not help wanting it even while he stood there beside her. Very simply, he was telling her the truth. She had painted on the wall the bones in a hummingbird's wing, many thousands of times magnified, poised against a background of blue that was, in the painting, so intense and light-filled that when she leaned away from it, on her haunches in the scaffolding, she felt the sparks in her stomach that signalled her old fear of falling.

That was a long time ago: before Peter. Or maybe she had only just begun seeing Peter. Really, the strangest part of being separated from him is that she has to remember these things by herself. If she said, "Remember when I painted the wall?" he would know instantly what she meant, how long the painting had taken her and what the people who had stood around watching her had said about it, and what she and Peter had done together in the evenings when the light had gone and she couldn't work any longer. Of course, without his memories overlapping her own, she is clearer. Clearer-eyed, she sometimes says to herself, as if the change were truly a physiological one. Since she has stopped seeing Sonny, the benefits of being apart from Peter are much sharper. They occur in a vacuum.

Sasha's explanation of Sonny is that Clarissa picked the unlikeliest of lovers in order not to threaten her marriage. "But I did threaten it," Clarissa said. "What do you think separation is?"

"I think separation is a way of extending the status quo until you can sort things out," Sasha said. "I don't think it's the end, exactly. Do you?" Clarissa shook her head, no. "And as for endangering the marriage," Sasha continued, "who's more important to you, Peter or Sonny?"

Peter is. Of course, Peter is. He always was. Sasha knows this very well.

"You see," Sasha said, not unkindly.

But Clarissa thought that nothing, really, had been proved. Pitting a relationship of fourteen years against one of a few months wasn't a fair way of appraising either one. She knows which of Peter's teeth show commas of gold when he yawns and you happen to be lying with your cheek on his belly, looking up into his mouth; she still wears his soft old sweatshirt, the hooded one, UNIVERSITY OF NEW MEXICO across her chest, when she does yoga; when she cleans her brushes, she wipes them dry with rags torn from his discarded shirts. When she puts on her mascara she studies, through the calligraphic strokes of her own eyelashes, a picture tucked between the mirror and its carved wooden frame: a six-month-old Peter, naked and demurely bald, gazing into the camera lens from the bubble-shaped fender of his parents' new car, one fat knee on either side of the round, deeply glassy headlight. Their entire history is as dense as a rain forest: it lets very little light down to the bottom.

Because of this, Sonny had had to edge his way into her life. Sonny's father is Anglo, his mother is Spanish, and his older brother once made a pilgrimage to Santuario de Chimayo, walking barefoot along the shoulder of the highway, when his daughter was found to have diabetes; Sonny's own knowledge of Spanish seems to consist mostly of endearments and an ability to translate the titles of jukebox songs in dark bars. He makes his living by odd jobs—caretaking, carpentry, or restoring old adobes. He has groomed quarter horses at Santa Fe Downs, bussed tables in Tia Sophia's, and waxed floors in the labs at Los Alamos. Roofing tar obscures the moons in his fingernails, and his clothes often have the sweet smell of wood shavings. His skin is a handsome sunburned brown, glossy on the shoulders and back, and at night, lying beside him, bored and at ease, she would peel away the sunburned flakes, leaving dime-sized spots of new skin. His hair is ragged and has that silveriness, beneath the blond, of boys who spend a lot of time in swimming pools. She could not believe he was so young— twenty-two, eleven years younger than she. He chewed bubble gum while he drove, and then combed the pink collapsed strands from his mustache. He found hints and nuances in her conversation where she had intended nothing of the kind, and when he told her that he had dreamed of flying the night before they met, she could see she was supposed to take this seriously, as some kind of omen. Sonny believed that she was important enough to have premonitions about; he claimed that meeting her had changed his life. She didn't know how to explain that she liked his life the way it was, that she didn't want it changed by her—she couldn't shoulder such a responsibility. In his narrow apartment the most prized object was an R. C. Gorman poster—one of those pear-shaped Navajo women, the fringe of her shawl draped across her rudimentary bare feet, in Crayola crayon colors. Clarissa had made him take the poster down and put it away in a closet before she would make love with him. His bed was the bottom half of a child's bunk bed, bright Sears Roebuck maple, sturdy and far too small for the two of them. His television set had an antenna fashioned of clothes hangers and tin foil, and they stayed up late, watching "M*A*S*H" reruns and eating organic goat cheese that Sonny cut into slivers with his pocket knife. Making love, he was self-conscious and splendid. She thought of those Chinese acrobats who smoke a cigarette held between the toes, of dramatic contortions that proved, in the end, very little. When they went to the movies he put his arm around her shoulders, and that uncomprehending tenderness so exhausted her that she fell asleep with her head in the crook of his arm, smelling his russet skin, woodsmoke and sawdust and sun against the dirty schoolroom scent of the theater, and afterward he had assumed that it was his lovemaking that had worn her out, and he promised to be gentler. When she finally found her nerve, and brought up the subject of their inevitable parting, he'd said, astonished, "You mean breaking up?"

"Jesus, Sonny," she'd said, annoyed. "Do you think we're going steady?"

So she had not exactly left him. She simply found it increasingly hard to wedge her times with him into the choreography of her separation from Peter. She had been alarmed at the complexities of child custody, in which the entire city of Santa Fe now seemed caught up: it was like when you first discovered sex, and understood that everyone was sleeping with everyone. Custody was like a secret society that should have a code of its own—rings, insignia, some special handshake. Indeed there were numerous handshakes, some formal, some consoling, once she had entered into the conspiracy. These people surrendered their children to each other, for the most part, gracefully enough, following old lines of fracture, expensively negotiated—ex-husbands and ex-wives maneuvering over cups of espresso for the safety of the hostages, all of them apparently believing themselves to be on the thinnest of ice. Clarissa began to be convinced that she, too, was walking on some fragile surface, that she could fall through; she couldn't risk a lover's added weight.

Sasha wipes champagne from her chin and dips her glass into the water until its stem is submerged. Then she lowers her head to it and drinks, her hair falling into the water around the glass.

"The moon," Meg says. "Look up!" The moon is round and

white. They look up silently. It is possible that Sasha has another, ulterior motive for the evening—that seeing the way Meg has been able to make a sort of peace with coming death, Clarissa would begin to believe that something similar, some parallel recognition, had been possible for her mother. If her mother had been granted such an epiphany, she, Clarissa, had remained in ignorance of it. Her mother had proved only that you are alive until you die. Clarissa remembers herself leaning over her mother's hospital bed, the tray in her lap, the spoon in her hand. Her mother's eyes followed the course of the spoon with wariness. The food on the tray, small puddles divided by plastic partitions, had an innocuous sweet lumpiness. Clarissa had tasted it. Tasting, she had found herself cooing, "Mmmmm." A dull subterfuge, beneath contempt, but it was as if some ancient pattern of coaxing and refusal existed, and she had been drawn into it. She could not for the life of her have thought of anything intelligent to say about that food.

"Try to eat." The daughter had smoothed the edge from her voice.

"I can't eat." The mother had turned her head away on the pillow, suddenly peevish.

"You can eat, darling. If you want to, you can." She had begun to call her mother "darling." It had crept in, the way terms of endearment sometimes do, to pad out awkward silences; it occupied the place that the word STOP occupies in a desperate telegram. It had even found its way into Clarissa's thinking: *The darling is trying to eat*, she thought, or *The darling has gotten the sleeve of her nightgown dirty*, and in this way she continued to believe that she was thinking about her mother with tenderness, even under these circumstances. In actuality, she had been quite harsh with the dying woman, out of fearfulness; she sees that now. She had had a discipline: she thought of one thing at a time, the world reduced to the diameter of a bent spoon, salvation in an ounce of oatmeal. Her father, perhaps out of some courtesy deeper than her own, had refused to watch these exchanges. It had seemed to Clarissa that he was still infatuated with her mother. He brought her flowers. Often when Clarissa came into the room, she found him speaking to her mother in Chinese, leaning forward, clasping her hand, but as soon as he caught sight of his daughter, he abandoned Chinese for English; Clarissa was left with the sensation of having jarred him from one language into another, of having forced him, almost physically, into a realm where he was uneasy. This discontinuity troubled her. She felt sure that the conversation in English never quite took up where the Chinese had left off, and that in these gaps lay her parents' true understanding of each other. When the nurse appeared in the doorway, holding the dinner tray, it was understood that Clarissa would try to convince her mother to eat. Her father would stand and kiss her dryly on the cheek before leaving the room.

"You eat for me," her mother said, wearily.

"One for me, one for you, is that fair?"

"That works with babies. You should see how it works."

Clarissa licked the grainy oatmeal from the spoon—it was sweetened with saccharin, she thought—an expression of delight, or what she imagined was delight, fixed on her face.

"You little fraud," her mother said.

"This is your spoonful."

"You should have a baby."

"Do you think so? Don't try to talk your way out of it."

"A house, a husband, and a baby."

"Did you like having me?"

"I can't remember that I *liked* it. 'Like' isn't the word. You were so different from what I had expected. You weren't a Gerber baby, soft and pink. You'd scratched yourself in the womb."

"I had fingernails?"

"You had little claws," her mother said. The spoon clicked

against her mother's teeth, and her mother closed her eyes, swallowing painfully.

"Nice," Clarissa said. She tasted her own spoonful. She swallowed.

"How is Peter?"

"I don't know." Clarissa hadn't called him for nearly a week. It pleased her to think of him on his hands and knees in the harsh west Texas heat; it was a properly penitential position for him. Before leaving, he had told her, "I don't think your mother even likes me very much. I think she would much rather be alone with you," and Clarissa, though she believed that that was probably true, had insisted that he was wrong, and that he should stay in Berkeley in case she needed him. "You don't think you're going to need me," he had said. "I'm sorry, but there's no way you really think that's a possibility."

Her mother waved a hand, forcing Clarissa to lower the spoon. "I know you don't like to look at this," she said, and pinched the angle of her own thin arm. "In here, there is a Teflon-and-Silastic shunt, Clarissa, U-shaped, consisting of a surgically implanted tube connected to an artery and another tube connected to a nearby vein. And I am grateful that the shunt is there. Do you want to know why I am grateful?"

"Why are you?" Clarissa said. She hated looking at her mother's arm.

"Because the shunt can be slipped off, and one end of the tube connected to the kidney machine's inlet port, and the other end to the outlet port, and blood flows through the machine—my blood. You've seen that. And without the shunt, each time I was scheduled for dialysis, and you're aware how tediously often that would be, they would need to do surgery to link me to the machine. Do you see?"

Clarissa nodded. She had preferred to remain ignorant of the details; except for having read a booklet that her father had handed her in the early months of her mother's illness, entitled "This Machine Could Save YOUR Life," she really knew very little. It seemed safer that way. She could trust what she did not understand, and, magically, it would work to protect her mother. Her mother had always seemed a woman without vanity. When Clarissa was a child, she had searched for clothes to play dress-up in, veils and shawls and necklaces like those that the other girls found far back in their mothers' closets, but she had found nothing except the plain black skirts, linen for warm weather and virgin wool for cold, the white blouses, silk stockings with the doubled tawniness that would rim the thigh, thick glossy girdles with the rubbery garters that left deep pained dimples in her mother's skin. So when her mother insisted that there was not a great deal of pain, had Clarissa been wrong, a fool, to believe her? Her mother's face was locked around some central alertness, with something aloof in the arch of the lid, something hollowed and flattened in the cheek; only near the end had this alertness, usually directed toward some intricacy of language, begun to be focussed inward, on the failings of her own body. As her face, whose covert architecture had never been meant to expose what Clarissa had wanted to see, shed its burden of personality—for personality can exist only where there is not mortal pain—the bones flared toward the skin, centimeter by centimeter, in almost perceptible relief. Clarissa held her mother's hand with intensity, as if she was in private communion with the hand and it was no longer simply a hand to her, a once-nimble thing of skin and bone; it was the furthest extension of her mother's body and the most intimate part of her that Clarissa could bring herself to touch.

Her mother's doctor told Clarissa that he wondered if, in some way, her mother was not on strike against dialysis, against the endlessness and the fatigue and the dependency of it, to which he had never once heard her object. One night, he came to wake Clarissa in the waiting room. Exhausted, she had been

paging through an old magazine, and stopped at a photograph
of some men wrestling with a bull. The bull's forehead was
crowned in paper flowers, and his eyes were covered by a man's
hands, the way a child will come up behind you and cover your
eyes and ask, "Guess who?" The bull's nose was slick and
grainy, its long tongue red, and it seemed to be panting; the
men were pushing it down to its knees. The caption read:
"Tribesmen struggle to subdue a buffalo during a Toda funeral
ceremony for an elder clansman. They will sacrifice the animal,
and it will accompany the dead man to Amnodr, the Toda
afterworld." *The bull doesn't look as if it wants to go*, Clarissa
thought before falling asleep.

When the doctor woke her, he had a Styrofoam cup in his
hand. In the cup, which he handed her as she sat up and
shook her hair back over her shoulders, there was pitch-black
coffee. This small courtesy moved her immeasurably. She told
herself that she would always remember it. She was so tired
that everything, even the simplest thoughts, occurred to her in
terms of the most heroic sentiments. She finished the coffee and
looked up into the doctor's eyes. It was as if she could do only
one thing at a time: put the cup down; now look up.

He took her hand and, weirdly, he began to play with her
engagement ring, squinting down at the diamond chip, drawing
it to her knuckle, pushing it back down into the web of skin
between her fourth and little fingers. It was curiously painful.
She didn't resist, or withdraw her hand from his, because in
the fraction of an instant she had developed a superstition; if
she moved her hand, if even so much as a finger lifted in apprehension, he would tell her that her mother had died.

He cleared his throat, and she began shaking her head.

"Your mother," he said.

"My mother what?"

"Your mother has, ah, lapsed into coma."

For a moment she thought, *Is that all?* She could see by his face that this was a wrong, an inadequate, response. "You mean while I was sleeping?"

"It's all right," he said. "She wouldn't have known you."

Several blurred days and vigilant nights later, the doctor took her hands again, in the hallway outside her mother's room; this time her father was with her. She could feel the impulse to cover her face rise and pass away, because the doctor held her hands tightly, and it would have meant something to pull them away; it would have been an almost social affront, and who was she to offend him, someone her mother might need? "I'm very deeply sorry," the doctor said. "But Mrs. Wu failed to regain consciousness, although we did everything we could. We lost her perhaps ten minutes ago. There was no pain at the end—none at all. I want you to know that." Her father made a fist and placed his fist against the wall and then began, softly, to pound on the wall, like a man killing flies in slow motion. Clarissa leaned against the wall, shaking her head slightly, rapidly, *no*. Her mother, failing? If it was a question of will-power, determination, presence of mind—her mother could not have failed, it was impossible; it wasn't like her. *Failed to regain consciousness?* When consciousness was, from the doctor's tone of voice, the Nobel Prize, the brass ring, the light at the end of the tunnel? She wanted to ridicule him for having made such an obvious mistake. Her mother had long ago ruled out failure. She would never, never, never let something important slip through her fingers like that.

How could she explain to the doctor, who stood watching her, her hands held by his own, ten surgically clean fingernails resting against her tired skin, touching her lightly, not a caress, not a caress because a caress meant that something was moving and the only thing that was moving in that hallway was the minute hand on the doctor's watch, and she wished he was holding her hands for any other reason, she wished he was trying to seduce her, she deserved it, she had flirted with him, she had tried to draw him to her and now here he was. She hated his hands. She wished Peter was here. Peter—she could have pounded on Peter's shoulders, struck his chest with her fists, and he would have understood. You couldn't hit a stranger, not unless he had stolen something from you.

She stood still, with the doctor in front of her, and her father beside her, saying nothing, and she was breathing. She was still breathing. Her father was breathing. The doctor was breathing. They were all breathing. They would go on breathing. They still had their lives.

A plaintive beeping rises from the kimono crumpled on the tiles near the tub's rim. "Damn," Sasha says. She boosts herself from the water, leaving a wide scoop in the surface of the pool. "My answering service," she says. "I suppose I should have known. It's a full moon."

She dries herself hurriedly, tousling her hair so that fine drops spray from her fingertips, dashing against the tiles. She wraps herself in the kimono. "I've got to find a telephone," she says.

"I'll come with you," Meg says. She looks scrawny as she emerges from the tub; her small wet head is sleek as a seal's, which makes her eyes seem huge. They look down at Clarissa in the water.

"You want to stay?" Sasha says. "There's no reason why you should come, but you'll have to call a cab or something, for yourself."

"What does the beeper mean?"

"An emergency."

"You run," Clarissa says. "I'll come in a minute. Before you're done telephoning. I'll meet you in the parking lot."

"Can you get the glasses, please?"

"Yes." Clarissa says, but Sasha has already opened the gate and disappeared down the path. Meg tugs on her robe and slips out after her, looking back briefly at Clarissa and lifting one shoulder playfully, as if there were something comic about an emergency, or at least about Sasha's vivid apprehension. The night around them is clear and quiet.

When she is gone, Clarissa lifts herself onto the rim of the pool. Water from her hair slides down her back. She draws the hair around her waist, a black sash, and squeezes the water from it. She will have to face the empty house alone. That's the part she hates. The rooms that darkness alters slightly, the clutter of Tara's room, the spokes of her bicycle in the hall-way, the dusty spines of Peter's books unclaimed on the shelves. Where are they now? Peter had had some idea about taking Tara into the canyon where he has a couple of acres of bare land, and camping out. Well, they have a pretty night for it. What would he have made for supper? Something smoky, greasy, cooked in oil—beans and bacon in a skillet, maybe. Tor-tillas. Rich in carcinogens. He would give Tara a taste of his coffee. Letting her sip at adulthood. Her down bag would be warm enough, probably, although there might be a little wind in the canyon. Clarissa looks up at the moon and wonders how cold it will get. The plains and seas are very clear. Who were the Toda, and how did they, live? Where is the afterworld?

9

Peter stops the pickup in the road about a quarter of a mile away from the house, and gazes through the windshield at the empty yard. A hen is bathing in the dust, scooting along the sun-warmed rut of an old tire track, fluttering her wings. When she pauses to rest, her breast feathers are fluffed by the accumulation of dust. It is a cold clear morning in October.

A dog rounds the corner of the small adobe house and begins barking violently. It must belong to the neighbors; she had said she didn't want to live with a dog. Peter sees that the dog has lost one paw. It holds the stump cleverly away from the ground. The barking does not disturb the hen that is basking in the tire track.

Mia kicks the door open with her foot, paying no attention to the dog, an ax in her hand. The screen door slams; this quiets the dog, which trots away, looking once or twice over its shoulder at Peter. Mia still hasn't noticed the pickup, and he is balked from opening the door and approaching her because she is wearing only a man's U-necked undershirt and a pair of black lace panties. She lifts a chunk of wood from the stack alongside the house, examines it (for spiders, he guesses), sets it on the chopping block, an old cedar stump surrounded by a halo of pale chips. She swings gracefully and the chunk splits in two. She quarters each of these halves with increasingly quick small blows of the ax. Her hair, which he remembers as a coppery tangle, has been subdued into a polished coronet of braid that makes her head seem smaller, more fragile. She has, he sees, biceps like a boy's. Still, he doesn't move; it's likely that she would be embarrassed at having been seen. Her profile has the unself-conscious quality of someone who is sure of being unobserved.

When she is finished with the wood, she scratches her arm (he guesses a mosquito bite), drives the blade of the ax into the cedar stump, and gathers her kindling. The dog trots back around the corner of the house and she kicks at it, narrowly missing.

For four weeks he has tried to think of an excuse to call her; it occurred to him that, since she offered him a rain check, he could suggest dinner, but that seemed too crude a way to begin. And he just didn't feel like calling first. He tried, but he couldn't bring himself to dial her number. He doesn't know why, but it has something to do with the fear that she would refuse him, and even the mildest hesitation would have daunted him considerably. He would feel it as a rebuke, and things would end right there. He wants some perfect imaginary freedom to exist between them, and so far it does: they don't even know each other. He wants an unequivocal welcoming eagerness from her, because of what he's already extended to her, in spite of himself. Any demurral would collapse his longing completely, exposing him and making him absurd. He knows it is not a real feeling and that it can't bear the polite weight of common sense. He doesn't know exactly what is happening, but he is more than willing to protect it.

He knows it's odd to have founded so much on so little—he's even started running again, each morning before the back roads near the museum are clogged with Winnebagos and station wagons, running with his head held high, elbows in, cool morning air striking the bottoms of his cigarette-tormented lungs. He is working up to three miles, and after that he imagines five miles, eight, his stride the definite, economical stride of the long-distance runner, and maybe eventually a marathon, not New York, possibly Boston. He takes long, scrupulous warm-ups in the basement of the museum, waking his muscles from their long sluggishness, stretching to touch his feet, which have a horribly white and unloved look. He runs to the track at St. John's College, where there are weeds growing up through the cinders and stray dogs who sometimes follow at his heels for a lap or two; sometimes he leaves the track and lopes along the rutted ground to the street and follows Camino Cabra the long way around to Canyon Road and down Canyon Road in the thin morning light, past the lost-cat posters stapled to the telephone poles and the paintings in the gallery windows, the menu in the window box of an expensive restaurant he has never been to; the screen door of Gormley's, the old grocery store, already ajar, the clock glowing green within, the elderly clerk with his newspaper propped against the cash register; and then the smell of coffee coming from the next restaurant he passes, so that he feels hungry and clean, rising on the balls of his feet to run faster past the new pueblo condominiums at the bottom of the hill, so new that a bulldozer is parked in the muddy open space that will be a parking lot, and the sidewalk is red with dirt that has washed downhill from the construction; he runs past the Cathedral with the old women going in to Mass with their pocketbooks held close to the sides of their coats; he runs past La Fonda, listening to the clatter from the Pastry Shop and thinking of *pain chocolat*; in the plaza he sits on one of the benches and watches the clerks opening the first stores along San Francisco Street, fitting their keys into the locks that will silence the burglar alarms.

Yet he is painfully aware that his belly still isn't flat enough to please her. She's used to dancers, to men much younger than he is, to an ideal male beauty. *L'après-midi d'un faune.* And what would she make of the mattress with its stains and craters, its homely lumpishness, and the paperback thrillers he's begun to read, lying with broken spines on the cement floor? He crumpled all his Coors cans together, collected them in a paper bag—which they filled to the brim—and carried them to the trash dumpster in the parking lot behind the building. Then he made an effort to sweep, but it was mostly futile— the dust balls skipped away from the broom and disappeared deep under the metal shelves. When he studied the pots with a critical eye, trying to see them as she might, they seemed only grim and old and ominous. There were too many of them to be beautiful, and the place had a funny smell. It smelled of dust and ancient clay and glue, workmanlike smells that are, in a way, dear to him, but are not exactly comforting. He's thinking again about finding a decent place to live. It would have windows and a bed.

He will have to ask around, because that's how you're really likely to find a good place in Santa Fe—through the people, instead of through the *New Mexican.* He has known this all along. Who can he think of who knows a lot of people? Sasha, maybe. Or Annie, Nat's mother. Annie always seemed to know a lot of people. When he considers his own situation, he seems to know no one at all.

Mia, finished collecting the wood, pries open the screen door and vanishes into her house. Peter hates it that she can come and go from his sight as easily as that. It seems careless of her. His retina is still stamped with that crown of tightly braided hair, as if he had looked hard into the sun. He decides he should make his presence known. It would be logical to get out of the pickup, walk up to the house, knock on the door, and call out, "Is anybody home?" as if he hadn't seen her. He has only to wait a little longer, and this will be plausible. But he already knows he's going to release the clutch, back the pickup into the overgrown field, and turn around and drive away. He accuses himself of cowardice, but the accusation is defused by some deep certainty that this is not cowardice. This is something else.

Once he read in *Newsweek* that visual images leave shadows in the retina of the eye for less than a second, but when he closes his eyes, he can still see her. When he opens his eyes, smoke is rising from the chimney of the house.

10

Mia is alone in the room with the King of the Rats and his ragged Lieutenant. The light in the room is thin and wintry. The Lieutenant stands before the barre, his ankle cradled in his hand; his mask's curved whiskers brush the glass of the mirror as he cocks his head, studying his uplifted foot.

"Something is wrong here," he says.

"Something is wrong where?" It is the King of the Rats, running his fingers appraisingly down the line of his papier-mâché jaw. He discovers a loose tooth. He wriggles it gently between thumb and forefinger.

"In my ankle," the Lieutenant says. "Something is terribly, terribly wrong."

"I wonder what it could possibly be?"

Oh, Rats, Mia thinks. Please don't start. Please don't start now, not when I'm so tired I can hardly see straight. She is sitting in a corner of the room with her back against the wall, closer to the Lieutenant than to the King.

"You don't wonder," the Lieutenant says. "That's the point." He crosses to the window, hopping to keep the sole of his left foot from touching the floor. He rests his hands flat against the panes of glass—dust on the inside, frost crystals on the outside—staring out. "If they took an X-ray, they wouldn't find one bone in your body capable of wonder."

"Has anything ever happened to that ankle before?" The King scratches his bristled chin. "You're nearly twenty-four, you know. That's not so young any more."

"You think this is funny?" The glass in the window rattles as a truck jolts over the railroad crossing in the darkening street below. The Lieutenant shivers. He strokes his whiskers, and they flatten along his cheek. The hollow of his throat is shadowed, although light glosses the knobs of his collarbones. He was sweating all through the long series of *entrechats*. He ate too much at Thanksgiving and, although this is a week later, he hasn't recovered. "Do you think I have weak ankles or something? Bones so frail they'd snap between your fingers?" He snaps his fingers.

"Well, what sort of pain is it, steady or coming and going?" The King strips the glove from his hand and inspects the pearl button. He pulls a stray thread from the fabric and blows it away.

"Don't ever get on his bad side, Mia," the Lieutenant says. "Just don't ever let it happen."

"I'll try not to," she says.

"I was being *sympathetic*," the King says.

"Sympathetic," the Lieutenant says. He lifts his mask. His hair seems very blond; in the parting, straight as a schoolboy's, there are strands of silver.

"My career is hanging by a thread," the Lieutenant says. "And my lover and my best friend keep giving me blank stares. Are blank stares supposed to calm me down?"

Mia, sitting cross-legged, shakes her head. She looks down at the knees of her blue jeans, printed with oblongs of dust from the floor of the studio where she has been kneeling all afternoon, mending a ragged tear in the backdrop for *Swan Lake*. The director—whose assistant she is, officially—never lets her forget for a minute that she's lucky to have a job, that in his eyes she was barely qualified for it, that he considered her two years of art school in New York a fluke, due more to her bad knee than to any real commitment. At the same time he has a way of implying that he likes her, personally, and would only let her go with some regret. As she was working earlier he came into the studio and looked over her shoulder. He dropped his cigarette and ground it out beneath the heel of his cowboy boot; she felt he was disappointed in her. "I'll be at the Barretts' soiree, trying to ease some more money out of the old bitch," he said. "That's one silk purse I could relish as a sow's ear. God, if I never had to listen to her discourse on Reaganomics again, I could die a happy man. Well, maybe there will be a few K in it for our little darlings. Oh, the rich. The rich rich rich. If she'd just spend on us what she pisses away on caviar." He studied Mia's bent head a moment longer. "You could come, if you'd like," he said. "No? Then I'll bring you some caviar on a stale Saltine."

He lit another cigarette, dropping the match into a coffee can that holds drying paintbrushes. "I'm off to the ball, kid," he said. "Give my regards to your two ugly sisters." After he was gone, she had fished the burnt match from the bottom of the can. The floor of the loft is splattered with old varnish and spilled paint, all of it, in her eyes, dangerously inflammable.

* * *

In winter, the vast studio is nearly always overheated, the air clear and so resonant that a dancer swearing at a knotted toe-shoe, or a pianist turning a page of Chopin, can be heard fifty yards away. This is the least fashionable part of Santa Fe; the building was once a brewery, and even in this—its High-Tech incarnation, with the girders above stripped bare, the skylights cleaned of soot and pigeon droppings, and the walls sand-blasted and painted white—there is occasionally a remote, bittersweet whiff of malt. Sangre de Cristo beer: it had lasted less than a year. The amber bottles were now acquiring a certain cachet among the tourists who browsed the curiosity shops on San Francisco and Guadalupe streets. Previously, the dance company had been housed in an abandoned airplane hangar, but everyone got tired of driving all the way out to the airport. The hangar was always drafty; the pianist was drowned out by airplanes. Several of the dancers had developed hacking coughs. Compared to the hangar, the converted brewery is luxurious—heat, excellent lighting, and, from the loft where Mia does most of her work, a view of dirty roofs and a peeling billboard that shows a woman reclining against a black panther. The woman is clasping a flat bottle of colorless vodka; the panther's eyes are golden, its gaze abstracted. Mia often daydreams, looking at the panther's blunt paws below the curve of the woman's bare shoulder. Above the roofs, to the northwest, the horizon is flat except for a distant butte, quite steep, weathered into a triangle long on one side, steep on the other. Someone, she's forgotten who, once told her that the butte was an ancient volcanic cone. View or not, the director warns, the company cannot yet count itself secure. The mirrors alone cost a small fortune, and a small fortune was all he'd had.

The steadiness of the Lieutenant's stare is beginning to un-nerve Mia. What if he's serious? What if he thinks of her as his best friend, and she can't even tell if he means it or if this is more sarcasm? And *best friend*—are those even the terms they should be thinking in? She's almost thirty. *Best friend.*

"Don't turn on Mia, please." The King stretches, twisting a whisker. "Take it out on me, if you have to."

"Why should I?"

"Because I'm familiar with your little spells of apprehension. I can take it."

"Oh, you can take it. I suppose she can't."

"No doubt she can, ordinarily," the King says. "But the details of her life grow ever more perplexing and *triste*, as is common among heterosexuals of a certain age."

"What are you talking about?" The Lieutenant looks at Mia. In order to confront him, the King lifts his mask from his head and holds it for a moment, looking down at the threadbare fur of its forehead. He is wearing a red tunic with a small black velvet heart sewn in the center.

"Mia's in danger of losing her job," he announces.

"That's only a rumor," the Lieutenant says. "I've been hearing that for months."

"Well, something's in the air," the King says. Now that they are both unmasked, Mia reverts to thinking of them by their names: the Lieutenant is Theodore, or Theo, and the King is Edmund. When she first met them, she was still in the corps, and they were more in love with each other than anyone she had ever seen. That was five years ago.

"Nobody knows anything for sure, do they?" Theo says.

Edmund is not in a mood to give, or accept, half-baked reassurances. "Some psychologist drew up a scale," he says. "And on the scale the worst thing that can happen to you is that someone you love dies. After death, the worst thing is divorce. After divorce, it's losing your job. After that I forget."

"You're cheering her right up, Edmund. Look at those circles below her eyes."

"I was lost after my divorce," Edmund says.

"Look," Theo says. "She's depressed enough. She doesn't want to hear the sordid details of your divorce."

"Andrea," Edmund says.

"Andrea," Theo says. "Oh, God. Andrea."

"I left her for him," Edmund says, nodding at Theo.

"We've all heard that story a million times."

"That's not true. I haven't told it a million times."

"Whenever you get started on your divorce, it comes out sounding like a parable. You think your shitty divorce equals the changing of the water into wine, or something." Theo tips his profile into the window light. He lifts a white towel and dries the hollow between his collarbones, lifting his chin so that he can pat the sweat from the length of his throat. That's a pretty gesture, Mia thinks. "It didn't happen," he says. "You didn't change anything into anything. You were wine all along. It was just that nobody had looked in the jar."

"Cut it out, can't you?" Edmund turns to Mia. "He can't stand it that I have an ex-wife."

"I can stand that," Theo says. "I can stand that, all right. I can stand it that you leave your wet toothbrush any old place around the house when you're done brushing your teeth. I can stand it that your mother is in the habit of calling at six o'clock Saturday mornings and that you've never once discouraged her. I can stand it when you lose your Visa card, and it's somehow acquired by a motorcycle gang in Arizona. I can stand it when you forget to buy wine for a dinner party. What I can't stand is pretending to like *The Nutcracker* so that you'll be happy. I hate *The Nutcracker*, and you don't. That's an irreconcilable difference, my love. Sometimes I look at the Sugar-Plum Fairy and I want to run my sword right through her. Change the plot. Little kids going *Oh no*."

"We've been through this," Edmund says. "*Nutcracker* is like money in the bank."

"So they tell me."

"There's nothing wrong with that, even if you think you're above it. Every company needs a warhorse. Something to fall back on."

"What if we didn't fall back on anything? What if we just didn't fall?" Theo drapes his towel around his neck. "We'd be better dancers for it."

"Art, art, art."

"Money, money, money."

"If only you lived in the real world."

"Oh," Theo says. "If only you didn't."

"I hate winter," Mia says softly. "We always fight in winter."

"We do?" Theo says.

"Remember last winter?" Edmund says. So the King of the Rats, pulling on a sweatshirt, is willing to be conciliatory. It's usually him, Mia thinks. Why, in relationships, is there always one person who gives in first? And why should it always be Edmund?

"I remember," she says. "We fought all winter. We used to shout at each other until we were hoarse. I was trying to get the costumes right, and you two weren't much help. God, I was bone-tired."

"*I* wasn't much help?" Theo says.

"No, you weren't," Mia says.

"I suppose."

"You act as if you doubt it," Edmund says.

"I remember it clearly," Theo says. "I hated every minute of last winter."

"Well," Edmund says. "I wonder if there's ever been *anyone* who ever loved winter."

Theo turns from the window. His left foot touches the wooden floor daintily. His mouth is fixed in a thin line, his eyes almost closed, as if in relief at the pain he has been expecting all along.

"You don't wonder," he says bitterly. "I'm the one who wonders."

There are puddles in the worn asphalt of the parking lot. The puddles hold embers that are really the last few lit windows of the building behind Mia, reflections reduced to the size of matchbooks, the light squared off in panes and floating in the cold water. Usually Mia loves coming out late from the building, but not tonight. Her Mustang is the only car left in the parking lot. Suddenly she is really frightened, although she knows the Rats will appear at any moment, wearing their matching motorcycle jackets, Theo's hand tucked into Edmund's pocket, because after a fight they are always twice as charming, to each other and to whomever they happen to come across. The long black gas tank and the shallow leather saddle of their BMW motorcycle gleam beneath a streetlight. Mia thinks she sees something move, just behind the motorcycle; she sucks in her breath and waits. "Fire!" you're supposed to scream, "Fire!" Even if you're about to be raped, because that makes people come more quickly—"Fire!" A quick, economical lie. People come. Everyone states that as if it were a fact; when she thinks about it, she's heard it all her life. She lets out her breath and tries to breathe deeply, evenly, a dancer's breathing. Christ, she thinks. I've been getting jumpy lately. Living alone can ruin your life.

Come on, Rats, she thinks. Come on. She has seen this landscape, the deserted parking lot and the rear end of the Mustang, a thousand times, and it has never terrified her before. She looks at the motorcycle and tries to will the Rats into appearing. The director is appalled that two of his dancers would risk their slight bodies—the oval kneecaps sharply outlined by the velvet of old blue jeans; the twin spines visible, in summer, beneath flapping T-shirts—to the mercy of "that monster," as he calls the motorcycle. Mia has seen them, on a rainy Monday morning, weaving in and out of traffic on Cerrillos Road, Theo's chin resting on Edmund's shoulder, his knees drawn up, while businessmen gazed after them through tinted glass and wearily flogging windshield wipers. The Rats used to like to go dancing in the Senate before the Senate was torn down and they used to take her with them, sometimes. The Senate was an improbably ugly bar with an equally improbable, rather good, dance floor of polished wood that was sunk several feet lower than the shag carpeting and surrounded by an ugly iron fence, and drinkers arranged themselves along the bar or the fence and watched, and Theo would dance by not moving at all, only cocking his head or lifting his chin a little and looking at Edmund, but when he danced with Mia he would take her right into his arms, and she liked that. Above them a mirrored ball revolved slowly, bits of lunar light skating along the dirty walls of the bar and sliding through Theo's hair. He whispered that boys made love in the graffitied men's room, leaning against the wall below the paper-towel dispenser, and was pleased to have shocked her. If they came out of the Senate very late, there were low-riders cruising slowly down the street, their tail-finned Chevrolets sleepless as sharks, and she held tightly to Theo's hand on one side and Edmund's on the other.

Now she is holding cold small keys, all alike. One of them fits the Mustang, but she can't remember which.

"Here," Edmund says, close to her ear. "Let me do that." He peers more closely at her face. "What's wrong?"

"Nothing," she says.

"Nothing," Edmund says. "I *hate* that answer."

"Now, now, children," Theo says. "Now, now."

11

Mia nurses her hangover with tea sweetened by spoonfuls of honey from bees who live somewhere in the Sangre de Cristos and feed only in wildflowers. At least, that's according to the label on the jar. During her marriage Mia acquired skepticism the way other wives acquire cold sores, political beliefs, a taste for California wines. She had thought it was a concession to Cody; she had thought it wouldn't really take. Nonetheless, the label on the jar, which would once have left her with an impression of a meadow full of larkspur and Indian paintbrush, now arouses suspicion. Her head aches. The mousetrap on the counter snapped sometime during the night, but there is no mouse; a ragged spot recently dawned in the plaster ceiling above her bed, which may mean the roof is leaking; the plaster is flaking away from the kitchen walls, exposing the uneven adobe surface, the clean dirt that is sifting lightly down along the counters. The landlady, an elderly woman who lives most of the year in Italy and visits New Mexico only once or twice each summer, has been evasive whenever Mia raises the issue of repairs, promising nothing. That was New Mexico: you rented a crumbling adobe ruin from a rich woman, and the rich woman suspected you of trying to cheat her. Mia studies the jar of honey. The bees probably clamber into the mouths of nettles on an overgrown radioactive-waste dump near Los Alamos.

She breaks two brown eggs into a bowl and beats them with a fork, then feels nauseated. For some reason she has been imagining a true breakfast: eggs scrambled with green chilis, diced tomatoes, and sautéed onions, a pinch of her carefully hoarded sage from Chaco Canyon—the breakfast a healthy person, someone undaunted by living alone, would indulge in on a Saturday morning like this. Forget it.

The eggs slide from the bowl into Pancho Villa's dish, and the cat runs in from the bedroom, mewing, and squeezes between her legs, his ringed tail held straight up. The egg yolks are a deep rose-yellow, like ripe apricots; that's the color you get when your chickens are doing a lot of foraging. Chickens will eat anything, she's found. Pancho makes small pleased sounds while he laps, his rather broad front paws placed precisely together, his tail curved closely alongside his body. "Yes," Mia says to him; she runs her bare foot across his back. "It's so lovely, being a tomcat."

She searches through her cabinets: no vitamin C, which is what she really wants, but lots of B-complex, and some E's in translucent amber capsules. She takes a couple of each, chasing them with more tea. There is a distinct soreness in her throat, making it difficult to swallow. There's probably some inescapable logic at work here—she's about to lose her job, so of course she's going to come down with the flu. She imagines herself, a pitiful invalid in a severe, sexless nightgown, attended by the Rats. If the Rats are still together by the time she's on her deathbed. It's curious that until now she'd never really considered the possibility of their splitting up, but she hadn't. They seem so permanent. Last night, after she got home and bathed, Theo came over alone, on the motorcycle, and they both drank too much, and before Theo left he dragged her out into the yard to watch the first snow of the year, stray flakes, thinned out by the wind, that made little perceptible earthward progress. Great spaces of dark air seemed to press down above the scattered, drifting snowflakes, and it was this— a massed and intelligent darkness—that she seemed to feel as the snow, rather than the spare flakes. Pancho had awakened her early by beginning his licking routine. He saw that she was awake, lifted his hind legs into a splayed V, grabbing one hock with a front paw and holding it in place, his tongue moving vigorously through the dirty-orange fur. She shoved him over with her foot, briefly interrupting his toilet, and he began to purr. "Beggar," she said. "Sado-masochist." She pulled the down comforter higher and curled up, closing her eyes against the light that fell through the bamboo shade, trying to fall back asleep. She heard the radiator clank, finally coming on, and then she was thinking about Cody, Cody in New York. The last time Cody was in New York he had been followed by a pair of dogs, a vicious-looking, mostly black German shepherd and a mongrel that resembled a hyena, its ribs showing through its spotted fur. In Santa Fe you only have to bend and pick up a stone, and the dog, which has been stoned many times before, tucks its tail between its legs and flees, or trots away looking nonchalant, according to its character. In fact, the dogs know the gesture so well that you have only to bend down and pretend to pick up a stone and the dog will run. Cody, in the Manhattan alley, bent and pretended to choose a sizable stone from among the shards of glass on the asphalt, and when he stood up the two dogs were still watching him, baffled and full of malice, edging a little closer. Cody realized then, looking down, that there were no real stones in the alley, none at all. That was what was wrong: the dogs hadn't known what he was pretending to pick up.

He had gotten away all right, but he said he felt less secure walking around Manhattan in the evening, after that.

The truth is that she still misses Cody. By now they have been apart longer than they were married. She still hates opening a closet and finding nothing male in it, nothing that is not, to the very creases in its sleeves and its scent of many-times-washed-out perfume, absolutely hers. She hates sleeping alone. When they were married she used to fall asleep by holding his penis inside her hand, stroking for a while and then simply cupping it, the slim weight against her palm like a rabbit's foot without the little polished bones of the claws. She had known she was lucky. What she had not known was how to keep on being lucky.

Once, not long after they were married, they had been awakened while it was still dark by the clock radio, and the newscaster's voice, grained with static, announced that it had snowed during the night, an unexpectedly severe storm, and a light airplane had gone down in the mountains north of Taos. Then Mia heard quite clearly: "Angels waded through the snow to the flaming wreckage to rescue the survivors." She kicked Cody under the bedclothes. "Did you hear that?"

"Did I hear what? Stop kicking me."

"Angels," she said. "Angels waded through the snow to the flaming—"

"No," he said. "Rangers, park *rangers* waded through the snow." He sat up, naked, shivering, and kissed her bare shoulder. "You're so funny," he said. "I was right to marry you."

She was amazed that he'd ever had the slightest doubt. She had wanted to marry him all along. Right after they met he had taken her to a cheap motel in Albuquerque, advertised in bill-boards all along Highway 85, where there were mirrors on the ceiling and blue movies on the closed-circuit TV channels and, in the bathroom, something called the Roman Bath, with a bar of mink-oil soap inside a plastic swan, and limp ferns dripping despondently from the ceiling. Cody thought that she should spend at least one night of her life doing something really sleazy. In the mirrors they had looked comically alone, stranded on the broad round bed, isolated by an expanse of tattered shag carpeting from the padded walls. They luxuriated in Road Runner cartoons all Saturday morning amid the rumpled satin sheets. She had never really watched Road Runner cartoons before. The landscape in the cartoons was a pastel desert broken by a ribbon of highway. Bugs Bunny was substituting for the Road Runner—who, Bugs Bunny explained, was on vacation. Everybody needed a break sometime. Wile E. Coyote was trying to trick Bugs by fishing with a carrot dangling above a chasm. If Bugs went for the carrot, he would surely fall. Instead, as Wile E. Coyote snickered in anticipation, a shark shot up from the chasm and snatched the bait, and fell back, dragging the coyote over the edge after him. Cody began kissing between Mia's legs and she pushed his head away. She hadn't ever liked that. He licked the hollow behind her knee and licked along the inside of her thigh, cupping one foot in his hand, and kissed upward to the arch of bone that rose, lightly furred, fore-shortened, below the curve of her stomach, and she lifted her buttocks so that he could slip a pillow underneath. She closed her eyes and when she looked down at him again his mustache was as wet as if he'd been drinking from a foamy cup. "Oh, you are sweet," he said, and they could hear the maid knocking at the door and talking to herself, rather quietly, with the radio on in her cart behind her, knocking with dignity but persistently until Cody called out, "Please come back later," and the maid said, *"Bueno,"* and went away, the wheels of her cart squealing in protest.

Sometimes she would find, on one of the windowsills or in the far corner of the kitchen shelf, a wishbone that Cody had saved and left to dry. It was a small habit, almost feral, the way, if you live with a cat, you sometimes come across a wetted sparrow's feather, the tapering shaft licked clean, beneath a chair. Mia's mother had taught her that the object of house-keeping was to leave no trace of the possibility that domestic life can ever falter, moth and corruption creep in, or dust accumulate in balls beneath the beds. Her instincts were for white roses, Oriental rugs, and needlepoint; her marriage to Mia's father lasted thirty-two years, until he died of a heart attack. Mia's instincts are different and her marriage—even from the beginning—was far more tentative. Yet, in those first months, it alarmed her to find those small, still mildly greasy, matchstick bones on the windowsills. When she told this to Cody, he nodded, as if to imply that it would stop. Instead, he began to hide the bones more carefully, though she would still come across them from time to time, when she was in a really thorough housekeeping mood. Cody was thrifty with things like nails and screws and bolts; he kept jars of them in the basement, ranged along wooden shelves built by the previous owner of the house. The jars were clean, though occasionally there was a dead spider between two of them, and the nails inside them were matched by size. Mia liked those jars. They were proof that Cody was a husband, after all. Husbands hammered things into the walls with the exact nail required. But apparently the laws of husbandry do not apply to wishbones. One afternoon, be-tween a pair of chipped pots that held leggy geraniums, so dispirited that they lost their petals at even the slightest touch, Mia found several wishbones, each a shade paler, slightly more desiccated, a little more bonelike than the others. The driest must have been there, in the chink of light that was all the curved sides of the pots permitted to fall on the windowsill, for months. It wasn't a habit Cody could break, after all. It was the wish residing in those delicate unbroken bones that he could not throw away, and which he had ended up hiding from her.

After the divorce was final, Cody bought a trailer on low monthly installments. ("No children and no money," Mia's mother said. "Isn't it funny that the problems in your marriage turn out to be the strengths in your divorce?") He keeps it in La Cienega, not far from the river, in a grove of cottonwoods, and Mia would go there from time to time, not exactly to sleep with him, not exactly not to. He is funny, and he knows her very well, and often that was enough and with a little effort of will she could ignore the box of Kotex in his bathroom closet and the pair of dirty wineglasses in the sink. Sometimes, with the morning-after blues, she would question herself severely: Was it too strange, some sort of psychological aberration, for her to still be sleeping with Cody? Did she do it only because she felt he was safe? He would make an excellent breakfast for the two of them, moving rapidly around his small kitchen, while she sat at the table wan and uncombed, watching, through the open door, his neighbor's horses grazing. The horses moved through the tall grass, and feathery seed tufts from the old cottonwoods collected in their manes and along their wide backs like snow. Cody would tell her about his work. He had never minded telling her about his poetry, though she got the impression that he was extremely reticent about it with other people. She had even asked him about it once and he'd said, "That's you, Mia. The beautiful exception." After she had stayed overnight with him several times she found that her feelings were far from violent, either way: sleeping with him wasn't a terrible thing to do, but it wasn't what they had once had, either. In this way she had faltered to a stop. It no longer really occurred to her to drive to La Cienega when she was lonely, and the last time she tried, there was a shabby Volkswagen parked near the trailer, and she turned around and drove back into town. Now, if she runs into him, he hardly ever suggests that she come back out to La Cienega with him. Instead they go for coffee and afterward, in a friendly fashion, he walks her outside and kisses her on a street corner, tilting her head back in the old way, so that he can see, he always used to say, into the bottom of her eyes, and the steady flow of tourists parts and passes around them, and sometimes it goes on just a moment too long and they both laugh, helplessly.

The most serious problem, after they stopped sleeping together for good, was that Cody began falling in love with other women. Mia was astonished by his ability to do this; she was equally astonished that she hadn't seen it coming. "I'm going away with Renata this weekend," he would tell Mia, as her introduction to a lanky woman whose hand rested confidently on the sleeve of his satin cowboy shirt. (Cody always had good clothes; he was a little vain.) Renata would look at Mia warily, trying to determine if she and Cody had ever been lovers, ready to fall back on the established method for dealing with a new lover's ex-lovers: keep your distance, because in each scrapped affair, no matter how well healed it appears, there lies the possibility of rapprochement, withered but intact, like those thousand-year-old grains of wheat discovered in the Pyramids—which, when planted, began to send up slender shoots. Mia doesn't know how to make it clear that she's not an ex-lover, she's an ex-wife. The two are qualitatively different, at least in the eyes of Cody's women, and an ex-wife does not seem to arouse the same degree of apprehension. It was as if you could safely assume that the divorced couple had passed through the varying stages of bitterness into bitterness's aftermath, indifference; in any case there had been a divorce, and divorces were not interesting. Affairs that had been interrupted in some phase of tension or complexity were still interesting and sometimes became even more so, through the combined pressures of sexual nostalgia and selective memory, but this was not likely to be true of a marriage.

For quite a long time Mia could not be introduced to one of Cody's lovers without giving a mild involuntary shake of her head, *no*. At first she thought this was some sort of subliminal refusal to recognize their existence, but finally she figured out that she was simply trying to give a clear answer: *no*, she was no longer interested in him. Because wasn't the question, in its way, fair enough? Mia believed in self-protection and was willing to make accommodations for it in others and, often enough, she simply liked the women Cody had fallen in love with. They were, as a rule, soft-spoken and attractively evasive. They knew about ex-lovers, and about ex-husbands, through having acquired a number of their own, mostly in the extreme southern states but sometimes, as if to be on the safe side, in foreign countries.

For a time there had been an Israeli UPI correspondent with golden bracelets and hair as kinky as Mia's own, only black, and the irritably self-contained expression of an independent and well-travelled woman. Mia had feared that it was serious. She often wonders how she would cope if the obvious occurred, and another woman thought to ask Cody to marry her, but this has not happened. The Israeli woman vanished, leaving no more trace on the surface of Cody's life than a stone dropped into a well. Cody accused the Israeli woman of having been promiscuous, and when Mia laughed, he only looked puzzled. She had tried to explain, and he'd shrugged. "Well, Jesus, a journalist," he had said. "What do they know about language?"

So this morning, over her third cup of tea, it occurs to Mia that she could call Cody and cry on his shoulder. It would be one small step in the direction of straightening out their gnarled, intricate karma, for how many times has he cried on hers?

Whenever he gets into trouble, he always comes to her, because he knows that nothing, however fleeting or casual the affair had actually been, would ever strike Mia as something to be taken lightly. She was very vulnerable in those years following their divorce, and the only vulnerability she felt free to ridicule was her own. Cody, who after all knows her very well, relies on that. He often assures her that she could count on him, too, if she were ever in trouble. Sometimes she believes him.

Pancho rubs against her knee, a slow burnishing, backed by the solidity of his scarred tomcat's body; it is an attention she values. Pancho brings a deep skepticism about human beings to even the slightest caress. Mia wraps her robe more tightly about herself and digs the top of her spoon into the honey, stirring it into the coffee. Maybe Cody would take her out to dinner. At the thought of food, her stomach lurches. Okay, not dinner, just some company. Cody would be good for that. Not exactly good, but he would do.

When she calls he says, "Sure. I know what. I'll take you to the Periscope, okay? You've never been to the Periscope, have you?"

"No," she says. "Why?"

"Why?" he says. He seems to think for a moment. "I just want to do something you've never done."

Cody hands Mia a poem. Its title is "Sleeping Out in Tsegi Canyon." "Where's Tsegi Canyon?" she says. They are in a taxi, going to the Periscope. All traces of last night's snow have vanished; now there is only a softly falling rain.

In his poems there are no women; there are only landscapes. The landscapes are Western, and bare—he told Mia once he couldn't write a poem about New York City to save his life (and added, knocking on wood, "God bless Frank O'Hara"). Cody's terrain begins at the Mississippi River and extends south to Big Bend, north to the Black Hills, down along the coast of California until it tapers out at the chiselled tip of Baja. He once tried to explain it to Mia: while he was in high school, he had worked summers in a hotel, part of a chain, and in the manager's office there had been a map of North America. When you pushed a button, clusters of tiny lights representing hotels went on all across the map. Cody knew that he wanted to live in one of the places that was bare of the tiny lights. Now, he sometimes imagines the places he has written poems about as a different sort of light—dainty, bright, scattered across the big bare flank of the country, a Reclining Maja with the Rocky Mountains as the hipbone.

"Navajo reservation," he says. "I was out there for a while, last summer. The best thing about it was driving out to Hubbel's Trading Post—you remember?"

"I remember," she says. "We stayed there for an hour, sharing one can of Coca-Cola. It was July."

"Well, this time the trading post was closed, and there was a sign on the door, a big sheet of cardboard with crooked lettering in Magic Marker. It said, 'The Navajo Nation is on Daylight Saving Time.' "

"That's nice," she says.

"Isn't that great? As if the Navajo Nation ever did anything except on Navajo time."

"Cody," she says. "If you ever get married again and start staying home, your work will probably fall apart." She means it playfully.

"It didn't fall apart before."

"We weren't married long enough for there to be any real impact."

"So I'll stick to short marriages," he says. "*No problema.*" When Cody is annoyed he sometimes switches to Spanish, of which he knows only a few words; it is an affectation shared by many people in Santa Fe. She smells beer on his breath and feels disloyal. "Tell me why you just can't take it seriously and read it," he says.

"Because it's dark in here."

"There's enough light, if you wanted to."

"Can't I just keep it for a while, and read it later?"

"Sure," he says, because she has cornered him. At least she remembers how to do that.

She folds the poem and slips it into the pocket of her coat. In a way, he is wrong: it would have been difficult to read with the huge square-shouldered bulk of the driver blocking the faint glow from the dashboard. The driver is a Jamaican and has a Band-Aid across the bridge of his nose, and he doesn't seem to know his way around Santa Fe. More than once he has glanced back at Cody, asking shyly for directions. Mia wishes that the driver would talk, so Cody could be entranced by his almost impenetrable depression and his blithe singsong accent. When they'd first ducked into the cab, the driver had made a long speech, so flawless it seemed almost memorized: he sends all of his money to his mother at home on the island, he told Cody, because he has eight little sisters. He grinned to show that eight was an absurd number of sisters for anyone. His mother had had all daughters except for him, the only son, and she deeply feared that he would catch cancer from the dangerous things that existed in the air and water of America. He did not know how to allay her fears, although he wrote to her regularly, and in a cheerful tone. She was a very old woman, and there were things she did not understand, he said, sighing. That seemed to be the end of the story.

"Look," Cody says. "Don't worry about me, Mia. I'm just not thinking straight at the moment."

"You do seem depressed," she says. "What's the matter?"

"Oh, I don't know."

"Of course you know."

"Nothing," he says. "Nothing's the matter."

"There must be something." She settles back, her cheek to the taxi's worn leather; she could go on this way all evening, if necessary. "Come on," she coaxes. "I can tell there's something wrong."

"Nothing's wrong, really. I had a vasectomy this afternoon."

For an instant she feels the foolish desire to laugh, because this is so sudden; then she could bite her tongue for having had the desire.

"No," she says.

"What do you mean, no?"

"You couldn't have, Cody. You couldn't."

"Why in hell couldn't I?"

"Cody," she says. "Is this really true, you've really gone and done it without talking to me?"

"Don't do that, Mia," he says. "Don't cry. Just don't do that to me tonight."

"All right. Look. I'm not crying."

"Just don't do that. I'm asking you."

"But how did it happen?"

"It only takes about half an hour now," he says. He is looking away from her, down the street. They pass an alley in which ash cans shine, glossy aluminum, bright and wet in the taxi's headlights. A cat is crouched on the lid of one of the cans. "You're in and out of the office in less than thirty minutes. They've really got it down to an art."

"It happened this afternoon, and they let you walk around tonight?"

"Mia," he says. "It isn't as if it hurts."

"Was this just a spur of the moment thing, or what?"

"Don't be a fool," he says. "I've been thinking about it for a long time."

The cab stops and she climbs out into the street. She is astonished to see that the lights of the restaurant are on, shining on the sidewalk, slate-colored between rows of neat bushes, exactly as if nothing is wrong, as if nothing in the world were different. She fingers the silk of her shirtsleeve as if she is about to tear it into rags. Her hair, absorbing the damp, curls away from her forehead, those strict knots and whorls, impossible to work a comb through. She had wanted to look so good for him. She looks at him, and at the idling taxi, wondering what they are waiting for. Why does he always ignore her, why is she still standing in the rain? He is leaning into the cab's window with his hand held out while the driver sorts through a money holder with shadowy gestures. It takes her a moment longer to understand that Cody is only waiting for his change.

12

Clarissa rinses her face with distilled water. She rubs a cream made of aloe vera, sassafras, extract of lemongrass, and wheat-germ oil (she knows there is soybean oil in it too, but she chooses to ignore this) along each cheekbone with swift upward strokes, from the corner of each eye outward to the hairline, and into the space between her eyebrows. She frowns at herself in the mirror. *Vogue* now advises women not to pluck their gray hairs—they are supposed to lend a certain lightness and poignancy to the shape of the head. She pulls her hair forward over her shoulders and sorts through the strands: no new gray ones. She fastens a gold stud in each earlobe. In the living room a cartoon character pleads in an awed voice, "But you don't understand, Rocket Man. This planet could go up in smoke at any moment."

She wraps herself in an old linen shirt of Peter's and pushes the cuffs up above her elbows. "Vanity, vanity, saith the preacher," she tells her reflection. Her father would quote Ecclesiastes to her when he thought she had been in the bathroom long enough. Now her idea of what is long enough for Tara to stay in the bathroom corresponds exactly to the ideal he instilled in her; would that please him or not?

In Berkeley, the last time she saw him, he had suddenly seemed an old man, his heavy overcoat smelling of camphor, his Woolworth's gloves snapped to his cuffs. She had feared her mother's death would disfigure him, but she saw that he was only more himself, perhaps slightly quieter, a shade more weary. They had gone to the library to return some overdue books of his and then they had driven to the pier, and she had rested her hand in the crook of his elbow as they walked. Her chin was level with the crown of his head, and his bald spot made her feel that she was a protective American giantess: it had once been a dime of smooth new-minted skin, hidden among his bristling black hair, that she had loved to search out with her fingertips, to his great irritation. On the fishing pier, the smell of salt-encrusted, slowly rotting wood was very strong. Disembowelled minnows and chipped mussel shells lay where they'd been swept into heaps on the cement, and seagulls slept on the pilings, their heads below their wings. At the railings, the fishermen worked by flashlight, handling the big triple hooks and the indigo-blue lines with care, and in the big sinks near shore an old black woman, her bare arms glittering with scales, was cleaning fish: slitting each one along the belly, cupping her hand for the knot of bowels, letting this slide down the rusty drain; then nicking the coral tendons behind the gills, which she pushed open with a thumb, and tossing the head to the nearest gull, which caught it in mid-air and swallowed with an upward twist of the head and a brief fiddling of the throat. She had wedged a portable television set on the back of the sink. Its antenna dipped when the wind hit it, and the picture flicked up, causing the old woman to snort in disgust.

When the picture was finally still again, there was a glossy tarantula crouched on Johnny Carson's sleeve and he was stroking its abdomen with the eraser of a yellow pencil.

"I've begun to dream in Chinese again," Clarissa's father said. "That hasn't happened in years."

"When was the last time?"

"When your mother was in the hospital."

"What do you think it means?"

"Means?" he said. "It means I'm getting old. That's what it means. I had not hoped to outlive your mother, and now look at me. I cling to life like a drowning man to a straw."

Am I a straw? she wanted to ask. Don't I matter? Doesn't your granddaughter? But she hadn't asked; she hadn't wanted him to feel cornered, just when he was beginning to confide in her. She had always counted on their closeness, believing it to be extraordinary, but it was rituals and small tasks that bound them together, and not words. When she was a child, he had sometimes taken her to the beach near the mouth of the Russian River, where there were black stones far out in the sea; she had loved being alone with him. He would unfold a scratchy dark Army blanket, soon to grow unbearably hot in the sun, and set his shoes precisely side-by-side near the blanket's hem, and his wedding ring, in case he should decide to go in wading, in his left shoe, and while he read the *Journal of American Biochemists*, she would lie on her stomach and watch the neat brown shore birds patter across sand that was exhaling tiny, silky bubbles. Other Saturdays, he had taken her to the lab with him, and she had liked the narrow hallways, the linoleum floors waxed to an anthracite gleam, the fire extinguishers, and the big gloomy women's room, empty except for her. Down one of those hallways, a frosted glass door held his name, DR. WU, within a faint grid pattern that resembled chickenwire, and it seemed both mysterious and fitting that his name should be printed across glass. She had sat at his secretary's desk until, in the inner office, he had finished his paperwork and was ready to take her down the flights of stairs to the room where the electron microscope glimmered awake at his touch. He had showed her a dragonfly's eye—a fuzzy lunar surface that looked quite blind—and the thorny cells in a housefly's wing. Years later, after her mother died, Clarissa's father, in cleaning out her mother's closet, had discovered a strand of hair wrapped around the button of a blouse he had been about to pack in a box of things for Goodwill. He had asked Clarissa to come with him to the lab, and once again he had led her down flights of stairs, their rubber treads grooved so that technicians carrying flasks wouldn't trip, around a corner, down another hallway, and to the door of the microscopy room, which he unlocked. Inside, he flicked a series of switches, and the lights on the vertical panel went on, green and amber, to a barely audible purr. He had ignored her, and she sat in a corner while he prepared the strand in the old-fashioned, costly way, by positioning it within a bell jar, where it was sprayed with a minute jet of gold. "Now you can look," he told her, and the strand of her mother's hair was illumined, hugely magnified, foreign as the dragonfly's eye had once been, thorny as the housefly's wing. She had studied it for a long while. At that magnification, there was no longer anything human about the hair; it had nothing to do with her mother. It was a dazzling line of fracture in the dark viewing screen.

And so, that night on the pier, she had not bothered to argue with her father. He had his reasons for treating himself as an old man, she supposed, and in any conflict between the two of them, mild though he seemed, he would always prove to be the subtler, the stronger. At bottom, she had seen that although she was willing to think of him, now, as an old man, she resisted it when he thought of himself as one. She interpreted that to mean that he was paving the way for his own death.

What she wanted from him was resistance, strength, defiance. An assurance that he would not die.

Barefoot, still wearing only Peter's shirt, Clarissa walks through the living room, stepping across the mummylike bulk of her daughter, sound asleep in her down sleeping bag, her face turned away from the flickering cartoon figures on the television screen. On Saturday mornings in winter Tara likes to wake up early, turn on the television set in the living room, and curl up to sleep again in a nest of pillows, quilts, and sleeping bag. Clarissa's attention is caught by something on the TV—an asteroid disintegrates into smoky fragments.

"Rocket Man!" a thin voice cries. "Rocket Man didn't make it out in time!"

"How can you sleep through that?" Clarissa says. Tara doesn't move. "It's the end of the world," Clarissa tells her sleeping daughter.

Clarissa is slicing scallions on the butcher-block counter when she notices the dog asleep at the foot of the leafless cottonwood tree in the back yard. The dog's tail curves snugly across its nose; there is dirty snow on the ground, and frost tips the dog's fur, but its eyes are tightly shut. She recognizes it—Barney, Sonny's malamute, who had a habit of bounding onto the bed during their lovemaking. For a moment she thinks that Barney must have run away, and somehow found his way here; then she notices an unfamiliar shape in the treehouse. The shape stretches, shifts, and settles again, and she can see that it is Sonny, sitting up and yawning, in an old, rather thin, sleeping bag. She peels a potato, coaxing the brown spiral from the cool dough-colored flesh, keeping her fingers carefully away from the knife, digging a little deeper for the eyes. It must be freezing out there. She heats an iron skillet, lets a pat of butter skate down from the rim into the basin, and throws in the handful of scallions, which hiss. What is he doing out there? Deftly, on the rim of a bowl, she breaks egg after egg.

"Mutants!" cries a voice from the television in the living room. "Half ant, half human, pure destruction!"

She beats the eggs with a whisk, places a saucer over the bowl, and pulls on her kimono over the shirt, thrusting her feet into a pair of dirty cowboy boots that Peter abandoned by the back door and never remembered to claim. As she stands in the brittle grass below the tree, Barney wags his heavy tail so that it slaps gently against her thigh, and she nudges him away and calls up into the bare branches, "What are you doing here?"

"I had to see you," Sonny says. He looks over the edge and yawns again. "Hey, Barney." Barney barks, excited.

"You could have called."

"You wouldn't have wanted to talk to me."

"You could have tried it."

"I just know you," he says.

She kicks a stone in the grass; it rolls a small distance before Barney pounces on it. "This is stupid," she says.

"So what?" he says. "Do you think I care how I look? I've got nothing left to lose."

"Horse piss, Sonny."

"What?"

"Horse piss, you've got nothing left to lose. Come down."

"What will you do?"

"What am I supposed to do?" she says. "Nothing. You've got to come down from the tree, though. I've made breakfast, and there's some coffee."

"I am hungry," he admits. "It was a cold night."

"It probably was." Barney is sniffing at the bird bath, a frozen disk of water from which twigs poke out at odd angles.

"Hey ya, Barney," Sonny says. "Hey, boy."

Barney rests his front paws on the tree trunk, barking in rapid high-pitched barks.

"Don't do that, Sonny. You're driving him crazy."

"Your house looked so safe and warm all night long. You don't know what it looks like from out here. I kept waking up and looking at your bedroom window."

"Keep it up," she says. "If I'd known you were out here, I could've called the police, you know."

"And tell them what? That I'm your ex-lover? That would really look great if you ever had to go to court for Tara."

"Nobody's going to court for Tara."

"I said 'ever.' If it 'ever' comes up."

She strikes the tree trunk with her fist. Barney, thinking she is playing some kind of a game, dashes away from the tree, rolls over in the frosty grass, dashes back to the tree again. "Don't you fucking threaten me," she says. "Don't you fucking dare."

"You know what you look like from up here?" His voice is disinterested, remote; it seems to come from farther away than ten feet above her head. "You look like a middle-aged woman screaming up into a treehouse."

She turns away from the cottonwood and walks back through the snow toward her house, Barney running in wide circles around her. She is not surprised to hear Sonny begin to climb down the ladder after her. Her toes, inside the toes of Peter's boots, have grown cold as ice.

"Your coffee was always so good," he says, at her kitchen table. "Even your *instant* coffee was good." He holds the cup with two hands. She had forgotten how his fine hair, new-washed in her shower, holds a silvery glint that vanishes as it dries. He smells of Tara's anti-acne soap, a delicious adolescent

scent, like that of a shy boy at a high-school prom, who might have to work up his nerve to ask you to dance. After all that she's been through, Clarissa isn't about to let that make any difference. Barney is curled up on the floor beneath the kitchen table, his chin resting on one of Sonny's boots. Every so often Sonny moves his foot slightly, and Barney waits for a moment until the foot is still, and then patiently replaces his chin.

Tara pads into the kitchen, a quilt drawn up around her shoulders, a corner dragging on the wooden floor. She looks sleepily from Sonny to Clarissa. "It's cold," she says. "It smells good in here."

"Food," Clarissa tells Sonny. "The only sure way to get them out of bed."

"I'm starved," Tara says.

"You're always starving," Clarissa says.

"So you're Tara," Sonny says.

"Yes," she says. There is a sudden awkwardness among the three of them that hadn't existed a moment ago. Tara sits down; beneath the quilt, she is wearing a pair of running shorts, striped leg warmers, tights, and a purple ESPRIT sweatshirt. "You know my name," she says. It is not quite a question. Clarissa is aware that the faint tone of accusation, too subtle for Sonny to catch, is directed at her, and translates: Why does he know who *I* am if I've never seen *him* before? Tara must feel that the privacy of their Saturday morning has been violated, and the fact that Sonny chose to phrase his question in that relatively smug fashion isn't helping matters any. Clarissa remembers with a surge of resentment how, often, before she and Peter had separated, Sonny had seemed determined to sabotage what was left of the marriage—making it difficult for her to get home when she'd said she would, telephoning her at odd hours of the night.

Clarissa kisses Tara on the crown of her head. "He knows

who you are because he's a friend of mine," she says. "And his name is Sonny."

Oddly, Tara extends her hand across the kitchen table. Sonny shakes it. Before them, on the table, Clarissa places red ceramic plates, a Ronald McDonald glass for Tara, a coffee cup and saucer for herself, Danish silverware. "Is this your dog?" Tara says.

"Yeah, that's Barney." At the sound of his name, the mala- mute's tail thumps the floor.

"He's got one blue eye and one brown one," Tara says to Clarissa. "Did you know that? Have we got any Cranapple left?" Clarissa takes the juice from the refrigerator and pours into Tara's glass. Tara catches her free hand and kisses it; since Peter's departure, she has been given to sudden reversals of mood and shows of affection dramatic enough to disturb and amuse Clarissa—when she was twelve, it would never have occurred to her to kiss her mother's hand. Clarissa supposes it has to do with Peter's absence, and this causes her to treat the gestures warily. Tara leans her head against Clarissa's hip, because Clarissa has paused beside her chair, and she can tell from Sonny's expression that her daughter's gleaming hair against the folds of light cloth, the fuchsia lining of the ki- mono sleeve showing as she attempts to smooth down Tara's cowlick, makes a pretty picture; she only wishes it were in a bet- ter cause. She moves away and serves them each a slice of quiche before pouring a cup of coffee for herself. She leans against the kitchen counter, sipping coffee, reluctant to sit down at the table with them.

"What are these grotesque things in the omelet?"

"Scallions," Clarissa says.

"Scallions? You mean onions?"

"Long-stemmed onions, honey," Sonny says. "They won't hurt you."

Clarissa resents it that he has called Tara "honey"; at the same time, she feels the small, improbable prick of jealousy. The coffee *is* good, scaldingly hot. She pours in cream.

"I can't eat this," Tara says.

"I thought you were so starving."

"I'd rather starve than eat this."

"Tara."

"You really shouldn't talk to your mother that way, you know," Sonny says. Tara shoots him a Who-the-hell-are-you? look as she slides from her chair, takes two pieces of bread from the plastic-wrapped loaf on the counter, and puts these in the toaster. "This toaster is always so clean," she says.

"Why wouldn't it be clean?"

"You know. Sometimes they get all disgusting. They get burned crumbs down inside."

"That's dangerous if you let that happen," Sonny says.

"Why is it dangerous?"

"It could catch on fire. Your house could burn down."

"Because of the toaster?"

Clarissa, who hasn't really been following their conversation, catches a frightened note in Tara's voice. "It's not very likely," she says.

"It can happen," Sonny says.

Tara licks blackberry jam from a knife. "He looks like he's the one who's starving," she says, about Sonny.

"Sleeping out in the cold burns off calories," he says.

"You slept outside?"

"Sure did."

"Why?"

Clarissa sends him a warning glance, which he ignores. "The moon and the stars," Sonny says. "You lie there for a while and it always seems to get very clear. When I was your age I used to pretend I was on the moon. I'd pretend I was sitting there on a stone waiting for the earth to rise. Did you know that's how it would look, from the moon? The earth would come up above the rim of the crater and you would see the seas and clouds and continents."

"I've seen the pictures that the astronauts took," Tara says. "The astronauts who were there." Somewhere in what he's been saying, she stopped listening. It can happen that fast, Clarissa thinks; perhaps Tara thought he was condescending to her. She is amused and slightly sad that he can't keep her daughter's attention any better than that. No wonder he couldn't keep hers. Tara is stroking Barney with her foot. "We could have a good time out in the snow," she tells Barney. "Does he like snow?"

"He better like it," Sonny says. "He was born and bred for snow. If you want, we could go cross-country skiing and take him with us. You should see him bounding around in snow-drifts." He illustrates with swerving motions of his hand, still holding his fork. "Sometimes he falls through the skin of the snow, in over his head, but he comes barrelling right out again. We can do that, can't we, Clar?"

Clarissa turns from the stove. She has a moment of wishing she could give up the complicated fight against him, against Peter, against all of them, and just lie down with her arms around Sonny and fall asleep. Instead she moves until she stands just behind him, rests her chin on the top of his head, inhaling a rush of fragrant newly washed hair, skin, and the sour fatigue that he is willing to disguise so that they can go skiing. She puts her fingers in front of his mouth for him to kiss, and he turns his head and rubs the back of her hand against the stubble on his chin. She feels, within the cool length of her kimono, a nostalgic surge of sexual complicity. When Tara bends down below the table, Sonny softly bites the back of Clarissa's hand. Tara is feeding bits of toast to Barney.

Clarissa watches the controlled way Barney snatches at the toast, his eyes slitted in wolfish pleasure, yet taking exquisite care not to catch her daughter's fingers in his jaws.

"I've got to teach a class at three o'clock," she says.

"You could skip teaching a class for once in your life."

"If I skip a class, all of the students show up, you see, and it's my fault that they've wasted their Saturday."

"Nobody in their right mind would waste a day like this."

"Sonny, it would be irresponsible of me."

"God forbid," he says, "that you should ever give in to an impulse."

"That's not fair."

"Well, it's not fair of *you*"—his voice rises—"to use the same automatic excuse of your fucking painting class. Why don't you ever tell the truth?"

"The truth," she echoes.

"The truth that you don't want me to come here."

"Sonny," she says. "We've been through it, haven't we? You know that I just can't see you any more."

"Look, Tara," he says, holding out his hand. "The Invisible Man."

"Sonny," Clarissa says. "Hush."

"I won't shut up."

"Don't do this," she says. "Not in front of Tara." She adds, very softly, "Okay?" but he has already bent forward in his chair, his face in his arms, and she hears a strange hoarse catch in his throat; he is beginning to cry. She feels enraged and frightened. Only rarely in her life has she seen a man cry. For her it is in a class with talking chimpanzees, telepathic dolphins —a freak of nature that is, in this instance, threatening. She looks at Tara. What will this do to her daughter, to see her mother's lover crying at the kitchen table? Tara is stroking Barney's rough coat with her bare foot. "I'm sorry," Sonny says. "I am sorry."

"It's all right," Tara says. "I'm not listening."

Clarissa leans forward to stroke his fine hair, and although with every muscle in her body she is willing him to stop, she whispers, "It's all right. You can cry. You can cry."

The old couple in the ski-rental shop on Cerrillos Road are quarrelling: the man maintains that they have skis in Tara's size; the woman objects that they do not. "We'll take anything you've got," Sonny says. He unfolds a twenty-dollar bill on the counter. "Just as long as you're within shooting range, you know." The old man retreats into a back room. After a time he emerges carrying a pair of bright blue skis. He has Tara stand on these and swing her arms. "There, Mother," he says. "You were wrong all along. These are like they were custom-made for her."

"Fine," Sonny says. "Thank you for your trouble."

"No trouble," the old man says.

"This is a business," the woman says. "Now you get the skis back in here by tomorrow morning, or it's an extra day's rent."

"We get a lot of business on Sundays," the old man says. He seems deeply grieved by his wife's attitude.

"Especially after a snow like this last," the old woman says. Sonny laboriously fills out the insurance form she slides across the counter.

"Do we really need insurance on the skis?" Clarissa says.

"You don't want to go breaking any of my skis," the man says, and winks.

"And not be able to pay for them," the old woman adds. "This is a business."

On their way out of town, Clarissa makes Sonny stop at the college so that she can tape a note to the classroom door. In the note, she's lied and said she is coming down with the flu. She walks hurriedly down the corridors, hoping that none of her students has happened to come early, thinking that even if someone does see her she looks dishevelled enough to be getting sick, but her heavy boots would be a dead giveaway. "Shit," she says, peeling Scotch tape from the door so that she can use it for her note; luckily there is a tradition of casual disappearance among the teachers here. No one will think this is extraordinary. She's never failed to meet one of her classes before. Her handwriting in the note, which she had to scrawl on the dashboard of Sonny's car, displeases her. It is crooked, slanting left and right; it doesn't even look like her handwriting. Crossing the parking lot, she stamps snow from her boots. Inside the car, Tara is leaning forward and talking into Sonny's ear. They could almost be father and daughter, from this distance. Tara has a father. As far as Clarissa is concerned, one is enough. She wouldn't have agreed to the skiing at all if Tara hadn't seemed to like the idea. As it is, she feels rueful, as if she has given in to blackmail. If she knows Sonny, once he sees it can work, he will almost certainly try it again.

"That didn't take long, did it?" Sonny says, when she climbs into his car. The bright skis look as foreign to her as a bundle of stilts; she knows she will be clumsy, a comic failure. She wonders if he will laugh if she falls. She imagines deep, soft snow—of course she can't hurt herself. For a moment she thinks wistfully of the empty classroom, the clean washed slate of blackboards that she never uses, the homely scent of turpentine and linseed oil, the high windows through which light falls on the wine bottles, ink wells, and old Noxema jars, deep indigo, varying heights and shades of glass, arranged for the still life. The truth is that she likes the students; they are company of a sort, enough so that she misses this week's installment—the ongoing flirtations among students, their gossip and teasing nicknames, their irritation with spilled paint on a ruined canvas. Most of them are predictably bad, and with these she is witty and indulgent. She thinks she gets, from them, as much almost-good work as they are capable of, although that isn't very much. Then there are one or two who are good enough to interest her, and with them she is more cutting, subtly disapproving, remote. On very rare occasions she praises a piece of work, and when that happens she knows how to do it so that the student is, for the length of an afternoon, walking on air.

Sonny drives expertly, the car skidding in the snow, which is deeper the farther into the mountains they get. When a new Willie Nelson song, "A Little Old-Fashioned Karma Coming Down," comes on the radio, Sonny sings along. Clarissa is amazed that he knows all the words. In the back seat, Tara strokes Barney's forehead with a mittened hand. She is wearing one gray mitten and one lavender one. Clarissa wonders if she did this on purpose.

Sonny stops the car near a road that is a pure white alley snaking along the mountainside between ponderosa firs whose branches are so heavily weighted with snow that they sag downward and inward, compressing the trees into steep shapes that remind Clarissa of Giacometti's figures, who always seemed to her to be suffering from some unbearable, delicate mood. Like the statues, the ponderosas seem exaggeratedly thin, but there are groves of them, hemming in the road on either side, so that each tree is deprived of its sculptural elegance and pressed into place as a further darkening of the forest. High on the snowy slopes, the separate trees resemble thorns. The peaks are sharply cut—the exposed sides are windswept dark stone, the leeward angles sheeted in snowdrifts so brilliant that they seem two-dimensional. The sky is gray and flat and it is only by looking closely that she can see that the gray is cloud, and the cloud is moving. Clarissa pulls up her hood and tucks her hair inside. She crouches by Sonny's backpack and fits in the thermos of miso soup and the sandwiches she made for them. It pleases her to think how cold and hungry they will get.

Sonny gestures at the No Trespassing sign near the entrance

to the road. "If you two are quiet, we're almost certain to see deer in there. No one ever comes up this far."

"It says no trespassing," Tara says.

"That doesn't mean us." Sonny grins.

"I want to see deer," Tara says. "Can we get close?"

"Close enough for a good look, probably."

"Really?"

"But you've got to be as quiet as if you were a deer, yourself."

Clarissa thinks, The deer will see Barney first, of course, and hide from us. At this thought, the last of her depression lifts. She looks around and breathes deeply. When she smiles, she notices that her teeth are cold. "My God," she says. "It's beautiful here."

"It is," Sonny says. "It gets more beautiful the deeper in you go."

Tara claps her mittens together, and Barney runs in a huge circle, plunging into a snowdrift and out the other side, leaping the chain that blocks the road, and loping back toward them. He falls at Sonny's feet, his fur thickened by pellets of snow, and when Sonny prods him with a boot, he yawns in delight. Steam rises from the scroll of his tongue. Tara has taken up Sonny's song and is singing it to herself while Sonny, kneeling like a suitor, fastens her skis.

13

In the renovated stable, skylights are set between the exposed beams of the ceiling so that each wall has a chipped, slanting brilliance. At dusk, the evening of the winter-solstice party, the track lights come on. At the far end of a long hallway there is a Shoshone wedding dress of beaded white buckskin hanging stiffly against a white-brick wall.

"I want that," Mia says. "Steal that for me."

"Okay," Cody says. "Wait until I'm a little drunker."

"Can't you do anything for me when you're sober?"

"Lying and cheating I can do sober," Cody says. "For stealing, drinking helps."

"I can wait, then."

Mia touches the sleeve of the dress; porcupine quills rattle against the stiff, immaculate buckskin.

"You're always so good for me," Cody says. "You know me. You have a unique perspective. Before and after, in a way."

"You make it sound like testing a dandruff shampoo."

"No," he says. "I just think it would be interesting."

"Trying to sweep me off my feet with your romanticism, aren't you?"

"Mia—"

"Does it ever occur to you that I could strike someone as more than interesting? You really think I should settle for that, just because that's the way you happen to see it?"

"Don't try to start a fight just to get out of coming home with me."

"I didn't say I would."

"You're right." He is holding her hand. "You didn't say so. We should look through the rest of the house. You've never seen it before, have you?"

"No."

"What a hick you are, really."

"Why?"

"This house was a cover story for *Architectural Digest*. It's on the walking tours. The Roadrunner bus stops out front each afternoon. You could set your watch by that bus."

"If I owned a watch," Mia says. "Who did you say lives here?"

"An old friend of mine," Cody says.

The bedrooms, each a different color, open off the hallway. In the red bedroom, lying with its paws together, there is an Afghan whose hair has been dyed to match the bedspread of quilted red satin; a crimson Japanese swordtail circles inside a wineglass on the night table. "Isn't that cruel?" Mia says. "Keeping a fish in a wineglass?" "It's a big wineglass," Cody says. "Anyway, I think that must be only temporary." In the yellow bedroom, on the honey-colored rug, a blond Afghan sleeps on its side, snoring lightly, while canaries sing. In the black bedroom, a black Afghan sits on lean haunches, gazing into a tall cage where a mynah bird taps anxiously at a cuttle-bone. The mynah bird's eye glitters like a wet watermelon seed. There is a pair of black lace panties on the floor, apparently lying where they had been dropped. "Tell me it gives you a strong sense of déjà vu," Cody says.

"Only if I had once been a New Orleans prostitute."

"Maybe you were," he says. "In a previous life. I was your favorite customer."

"You couldn't have been anyone's favorite customer. You were probably poor in that life, too."

"I'll give you ten dollars to come home with me," he says.

Behind them, the mynah bird says something in the pained, incredulous voice of a very old man just awakened from sleep.

It is still too early for many people to have come, and there is hardly anyone in the long living room. A woman spots Cody at once and comes over. There are stars pasted on her left cheekbone, the kind that Mia's music teacher used to paste in her lesson book when she'd done something well. The woman puts her arms around Cody and holds him. Backing away, she touches the thorns of a saguaro cactus in an enormous terra-cotta pot that stands against the wall. The saguaro is easily nine feet tall, with thorns like singed ivory.

"Do you have any idea what these things cost?" she asks.

"Only a rough idea," Cody says.

"Well, guess."

"I wouldn't want to guess wrong."

"I won't get offended. Guess."

"A thousand dollars."

"A thousand dollars." She laughs.

"A thousand," he says. "Was that foolish?"

"It's not so far off," she says. "It's lukewarm, in fact."

"If I offered you a thousand dollars, would you let me take it home with me?"

"It wouldn't fit into your trailer," she says.

"I could cut a hole in the roof," he says. "Like for a stove's chimney."

"Listen, Cody," she says. "It takes ten years for each foot of this saguaro to grow. Each foot. And they're very fragile, very spiritual beings. It was one of the architect's ideas, really, to have a saguaro in this corner of the living room. He has a crew that travels around the desert outside of Phoenix and searches for beautiful cacti."

"And then what?" Cody says. "They hack them out of the ground?"

"Nobody does any hacking," the woman says. "They take very good care of them. Saguaros are very valuable, after all. And for something so huge they've got incredibly fragile root systems."

"And fragile spirits," Mia says.

"I want to take it home with me," Cody says.

"You're still really in touch with your child, aren't you?" the woman says.

"My child?"

"Your inner child."

"Oh," Cody says. "My inner child."

"I should show you around the rest of the house."

"We just looked through," Cody says.

"Did you see the new *santo* by my bed? It's from a carver I've discovered near Truchas."

"He's good," Cody says. They hadn't seen it.

"You think he's good?" She seems delighted.

"Damned good."

"I thought it was a little too deliberately naïve, maybe."

"Not at all," Cody says. "It had a very natural naïveté, not at all overdone."

The woman turns to Mia and takes her hand. "I'm so sorry," she says. "I'm Carla. I didn't catch your name."

"Warren."

"Warren," Carla repeats. "What an unusual name for a woman."

"She's an unusual woman," Cody says.

"I can see that," Carla says. Mia takes back her hand.

"Actually," Cody says, "she's a member of a troubling new social class, the underemployed."

Carla clasps Cody's arm. "Come into the kitchen with me," she says. "I want you to taste the nachos." Cody glances over his shoulder at Mia, and shrugs. Mia smiles to reassure him. She looks around the long room and there is no one she knows, but she doesn't feel uneasy. She has a long history of being abandoned at parties by Cody. A passing maid offers her a glass of champagne and she takes it, grateful to have some sort of camouflage. The champagne is cold and her stomach is empty. She and Cody were supposed to have gone to dinner before the party, but he was late in picking her up.

At the end of the room a fat man in a mushroom-colored armchair is solemnly examining a Ziploc bag in which there are small thorny knobs. "Peyote buttons," he says, when he notices her looking. He spills one into his hand. It has gray mummified skin. "Want one?" he says. "All the way from Oaxaca. The Mexicans have a saying: 'Oaxaca is always far away.'"

"That's a nice saying," Mia says.

"This is genuine organic peyote," he says. "Guaranteed vision-inducing."

"Thank you," she says. "I came with someone, though, and I didn't bring any money."

"This is a party," he says. He is making an effort to control his disgust; it seems she has made a serious mistake. "*Mi casa es su casa*, you *comprende*? You think I would waste this wonderful, wonderful stuff on strangers?"

"No," she says. "I can tell you wouldn't."

He considers her again. In his eyes, she is clearly in need of the beneficial effects of a vision. "You may have one," he says.

She doesn't want it, but she's curious. The skin of the peyote button is knotted beneath her fingertips, something like the texture of a dried fig, rather wooden, hard and light. She runs her thumb across it and there are no thorns.

"Thank you," she says.

"You're welcome," he says.

She drops the peyote button into the pocket of her linen jacket.

In a corner of the room there is an African woodcarving—a woman with long skinny breasts and regal, empty eyes. Instead of hair there are rows of cuneiform nicks in her skull; inside her belly is an opening in which a fetus rests head down, its meticulously carved feet overlapping its polished buttocks.

"What sucky art," says someone beside Mia. "Don't you think?"

Mia turns. It is the girl whose father brought her to Mia's house with the painting. She's taller than Mia remembers, and her close-cropped hair seems to have been dyed at the nape—gold, indigo, and saffron, forming a sort of rainbow. Her ears stick out delicately from the thin, spiky hair.

"Jungians are famous for their bad taste, you know, but my God," the girl says. "Tara, in case you don't remember." She sticks her hand out and Mia shakes it. Her handshake is bony and cool.

"I did remember."

"You must be bored," Tara says. "Standing around looking at this."

"I am, a little."

"So am I." She touches the wooden forehead of the carving. "I was more trouble than this," she says. "Than that baby, I mean."

"Why do you say that?"

"Because I was a breech birth," she says. "That's when you try to come feet first. My mother ended up having a Caesarean. You don't have any kids?"

"None so far." But she must already know the answer to that, Mia thinks.

"Would you ever like some?"

"Ever?"

Tara, who must feel she's trespassed, gives her an engaging upward smile. "I mean, do you ever think about it?"

"Sometimes."

"Don't women your age? Clarissa thinks about it sometimes, too, but she's older than you."

"Clarissa?"

"My mother."

"She's not here?" Suddenly Mia is curious to meet the mother; she imagines a face that would be an older replica of her daughter's, with its clever, slender jaw, the black eyes, the pale eyelids.

"They don't really go to the same parties," Tara says. "They're separated."

"I know. I'm sorry."

"My father's over there," Tara says. "I wouldn't usually get caught dead doing this, you know, but he asked me to come over here and start up a conversation."

Mia feels slightly hurt. You mean they hadn't had any real rapport, it had all been because her father had asked her to come over? She realizes that she wants this girl to like her. She wants to be sought out by the daughter, not the father. Her indifference to the father is not pretended when she says, "Why did he ask you to do that?"

"I don't know," Tara says. "He just did."

"You know, you're good at it."

"Am I?"

"Why didn't he just come over himself?"

"He's shy," she says. "Or something."

The champagne glass is empty. Mia looks around for a place to put it. There is only a shining expanse of bare floor. She puts it down on the floor.

Peter is standing by the wall, watching some couples who have begun to dance. One of the women kicks off her shoes and leans closely against her partner, patting his stomach with rapid unself-conscious pats as if it were a small, friendly animal that had somehow gotten lodged between them. She wears a silver concha belt that slides and clicks across her black velvet skirt as she dances.

Peter looks at them nervously. Mia knows he is wishing he had never said anything about her to Tara. "Do you want to dance, kiddo?" he says.

"No," Tara says.

"Don't look so hostile."

"I don't look hostile."

"It was only dancing," he says. "I know it was a stupid idea." He touches the rainbow on the nape of her neck. "This will disappear in a day or two, won't it? Your mother wouldn't let you do something like that permanently, would she?"

"I really doubt it," Tara says. "She doesn't let me do anything permanently. We already talked about a tattoo."

Peter grimaces. "No tattoo," he says.

"That's what she said," Tara says. She slips away from him and wanders across the room to the grand piano. There are calla lilies in a crystal vase on the lid of the piano; the rims of the lilies are going brown. An elderly man, his suspenders making a jaunty X across his concave back, gestures for Tara to sit beside him on the piano bench, and when she does he turns up his silk shirtsleeves and begins to play a Chopin nocturne, over and against the sound of punk-rock music from hidden stereo speakers.

"Was she really going to get a tattoo?" Mia says.

"No," Peter says. "Or I don't think so. She was talking about one for a while, a small rose along the inside of her wrist. She gets some funny ideas from a friend of hers, but I think it was more a joke than anything."

"A small rose," Mia says. "That's not so bad."

"Come on," he says. "It's awful. Can't you see her in some grimy tattoo parlor? That gypsy downtown is a walking advertisement for hepatitis."

"I see what you mean."

"She's usually smarter than that, anyway."

"She looks as if she would be."

"Well, she is."

"If she wasn't," Mia says, "you probably wouldn't send her on errands for you."

He laughs. "I got scared at the last minute."

"It's all right, really," Mia says. "I'm glad you made *something* happen."

At this, he looks a little alarmed, and she is sorry she said it. Cody comes sauntering toward them through the dancers, and Mia touches Peter's arm. "Hey, I was only teasing," she says.

Cody comes over and puts his hand on Peter's shoulder. "I don't know you," he says, "but it looks as if you've taken my woman."

"Your woman?"

"That's what you get, Cody," Mia says. "For leaving me alone while you conduct your shabby tête-à-tête in the kitchen."

"It turned out to be a tête-à-tête-à-tête," Cody says. "Me and her and him. Her ex-husband."

"Don't look so disappointed."

"I try to disguise my true emotions," Cody says. "Anyway, it was business." He lifts his hand in the Boy Scout salute.

"Everything between me and that woman and her ex-husband is purely business. I've never had any dealings with Carla that weren't pure and aboveboard. She just likes me, that's all."

"She looks as if she likes you," Mia says. "She looks as if she'd like to eat you with a spoon, that's what."

"Now, darlin', what's the cause of this sudden possessiveness? You tell me who this is." Before Peter can answer, Cody pats his shoulder. "Has she thrown herself at you yet?"

"No."

"Well, it'll happen," Cody says. "She has a way of losing her head. Not like Carla, though. Carla's the kind of girl who'll trip you and be flat on her back before you hit the ground." He covers his mouth with his hand. "I said *girl*. I mean *woman*. The kind of *woman* who'll trip you—"

"He heard you, Cody," Mia says.

"Wit and restraint," Cody says. "My ex-wife. Best relationship of my entire life."

"I'm Peter," Peter says. "Wu-Barnes."

"Holding her own," Cody says. "Out in the cold, cruel world without a man."

"Maybe you could use some coffee, Cody," Mia says. "Good strong black coffee." She looks at Peter. "Would you like some coffee?"

"I don't think so," he says. "Actually, I think we're about to leave. I've got to get my daughter home before it gets too late."

"That's it," Cody says. "Break it to her gently. You have a daughter?"

"I think she already knows that."

"Oh," Cody says. "That's all right, then. But it's still early for me. I think I'll stay on a while. You know, you're leaving before they pass around the peyote. Just like Mia to walk out on a vision quest. She says she hasn't got the stomach for it, but that's not it. She just thinks it's in bad taste to have your visions in public."

"I think she's got a point," Peter says. "I could take you home, if you'd like," he says softly, to Mia. She nods.

"Thank you," she says, "I'd like that. I'll call you tomorrow, Cody."

"You know what Carla likes to tell people? 'I'll get back to you.' Even her friends. Even if you're in the same fucking room with her. Who the hell does she think she is?"

"You should know," Mia says.

Peter shakes Cody's hand. They try, and don't really manage, to smile at each other.

"You're okay, aren't you, Cody?" Mia says. "I mean, you have enough money for a taxi?"

"Taxi, hell," Cody says. "I'm staying overnight."

"You are?"

"Don't look like that, *corazón*. I don't mean *overnight* overnight. You saw all the room she has in this house," he says. "Enough room so that a man can get lost in it."

14

The Volvo is parked in front of the curb that rims the Acequia Madre. Looking down into the ice of the acequia makes Mia feel cold and charmed. Ice always gives her that feeling of childish happiness. She could stand by a frozen pond for hours. It's not because she likes to skate: on skates she is pigeon-toed and clumsy.

There is the smell of woodsmoke drifting down the narrow street from the shuttered, closely built houses, many of them with wooden bridges that span the acequia. Along some of the adobe walls and rooftops *luminarias* have been left—brown paper bags, weighted with sand, in which there are candles. None of the candles are lit, or maybe the wind has blown them out. Mia and Tara stand silently, not quite touching, while Peter searches through his pockets for the keys. Mia wonders why the men she is attracted to are always the ones who lose keys.

"I like your coat," Tara says.

"Thank you," Mia says. "It's thrift shop." It is a bulky coat of raggedy squirrel fur, and for the moment she is grateful for its generous old-fashioned warmth.

"I thought I remembered you driving a pickup," she says to Peter.

"I do," he says. "It's in the shop right now. The transmission got hit by a rock."

"A rock?"

"It bottomed out on a bad road," he says.

"He's a horrible driver," Tara says. "Half the time your teeth are on edge."

"Will you stop?" he says.

When he finally unlocks the door, Tara climbs into the back seat. Peter looks across the roof of the car at Mia, smiling. His dark hair has been raggedly cut and the collar of his jacket is turned up against the cold; his smile is very nice. "Pretty night, isn't it?"

"All the stars," she says.

"Come on, you guys. It's *cold* in here."

Peter looks upward. "Did you know that there are really only about two thousand stars visible to the naked eye?"

"I always thought there were more than that."

"No," he says.

Inside the car, Tara makes a kissing noise.

"There's Orion," he says. "And the Pleiades. The Pleiades was used as a test by certain Plains Indians. If you could count seven stars in the constellation, then you could be a warrior. I think it was seven."

"I wouldn't make it," Mia says.

"I am *freezing* to death in here."

"I'll let you in," Peter says to Mia. He starts the car. The long crack in the windshield glimmers like a flaw in mica.

"Would you look in the glove compartment and see if there are any cigarettes?" he asks Mia.

"I thought you were going to quit smoking," Tara says.

"Next week," he says.

"There aren't any in there," Tara says. "She cleaned out all your stuff."

"Would you look, please, anyway?" he says. Inside the glove compartment Mia finds a broken sand dollar, a box of crayons, and a Perrier bottle, nearly full. The cap of the Perrier bottle is gone; instead there is a cork, whittled to fit the bottle's mouth, and the water is smoky in the dim light. Strands of algae drift in a helix circumscribed by the bottle's pale green sides. Below the cork there is an inch of dirty froth. "Ganges River water," Peter says. "I didn't know she was keeping it in the car, though."

"It's a sacred river," Tara says. "Thousands of pilgrims travel all the way across India to bathe in it and pray."

"She's heard of the Ganges River, Tara."

"I can't find any cigarettes in here," Mia says.

"We can stop and get some after we let Tara off at her mother's house."

"I want to go for Häagen-Dazs ice cream downtown," Tara says.

"No way, kiddo. It's time for you to be in bed."

"It's not time. It's not even a school night."

"Your mother is probably wondering where you are."

"She never wonders where I am."

"You're crazy, kiddo. She worries about you all the time."

"I mean," Tara says, "she doesn't wonder where I am when she knows I'm with *you*."

"With me or not," he says. "She would want you home by now."

Peter stops the car on the shoulder of the road. He gets out first, digging his hands into his jacket pockets. His breath comes slowly, in a cloud. Tara climbs from the back seat. Mia looks for lit windows in the house, but it is screened by a *latilla* fence and some bushes; the house is set below the level of the road, taking advantage of the angle of the canyon's wall, and Mia can see the line of the roof and a crooked gutter. "Kiss," Peter says. Tara stands on her toes and kisses him. "You're sure your mother is home?" he says.

"Sure," Tara says. "Where would she be?"

"I'm going in with her," Peter says to Mia. "Do you mind waiting? I'll only be gone a minute." Mia shakes her head, meaning she doesn't mind. He smiles again, that quick smile. Tara skips ahead of him, down a flight of stone steps, and he closes the wooden gate behind them. Mia wishes he had left the keys in the ignition so that she could try to get the heater working. She shivers, drawing her fur collar up closer to her chin. What movie was it where Greta Garbo looked so fragile, the oval of her face sunk in fur? Mia wishes she looked like Greta Garbo, that smooth hair, the perfect profile. Greta Garbo once said, "I want to be alone." Mia doesn't believe it. How can anyone imagine they love being alone? Probably you can only feel that if you are constantly sought after. If you are obviously, irrefutably beautiful. In the house a light goes on, shining between the peeled wooden poles of the fence. Mia opens the car door, trying not to make any noise. She goes to the fence and presses her forehead against the wood; a fragment of bark digs into her cheek. She stares through a crack at the house below. In places the plaster has flaked away to show the adobe bricks underneath. The windowsills have been painted dark brown. Some of the windows are shuttered from the inside. She sees Peter pass by an unshuttered window. His jacket is off and he is carrying a can of Campbell's Soup, working the blade of a can opener around its rim; then he is gone. Light from another room falls across the floor. She looks away. On the outside of the house, high on the wall where it is partially hidden by shadow, there is a horse's skull, the bone of the nose splintered.

"Her mother wasn't there," Peter says when he returns. She is already back in the car; Mia looks at him innocently.

"She's not? What does that mean?"

"She doesn't do this very often." He sounds apologetic. "Maybe she thought I was going to keep Tara a little longer. But I'm sure she'll be back soon. You don't think I'm overly protective, do you? Do you still want to go for coffee? I know a good place."

"I don't think you're overly protective," she says. "It's nice. And coffee sounds good. I'm asleep," she lies.

He chooses a cafe that is part of a truckstop, not far from the highway to Taos, the gas pumps basking in the light of a huge neon arrow. A poster in the window advertises greyhound racing. Inside the cafe it is warm and the square linoleum tables have been placed very near each other. Mia and Peter are the only customers except for a trucker asleep in the corner, his face against his forearm. When the waitress bends to wipe his table she is careful to keep her rag from touching his outstretched hand. His hair has been heavily brilliantined and you can still see the strokes of the comb. "You want something besides coffee?" Peter says. Mia shakes her head. There is a chip in the handle of her cup that fits her thumb exactly; the coffee is black as tar. She watches while Peter eats a plate of *migas*—eggs scrambled with green chili and onions and crumbled tortilla chips. The onions have been sautéed until they are limp and translucent and there is a heap of refried beans on the side of his plate that Peter mashes with his spoon before beginning to eat. Mia can hear a distant stuttering from the parking lot, where the sleeping trucker must have left his diesel running.

"How do you like working for the museum?" she says. He has told her about that, she can't remember when.

"I love it," he says. "I can't stand it when anyone else comes around my ceramics. I'm very possessive."

"Ceramics?"

"Potsherds," he says. "When I first came to work there, it was a real mess. Drawers and drawers of sherds, and only a slip of paper with provenance for each drawer, not a catalogue or anything. It was bewildering. So what I've been doing for the last two years is the cataloguing that will eventually encompass the museum's entire collection. Otherwise no one knows what you've got, and your value to researchers is negligible. In the end all of my data goes into a computer somewhere."

"What's provenance?"

"It means the origin of the artifact," he says. "Where it was dug up."

"Where were most of them dug up?"

"Around here," he says. "New Mexico, Arizona, Colorado. Southern New Mexico has some of the most beautiful stuff in the world, the Mimbres. Collectors like it because the pots were painted with animals—minnows, quail, deer. I don't really like it. Museums have always been very aggressive in the Southwest about developing good collections. In part because they're beautiful to display, they bring people into the museum. Plus you get donations. Someone dies and leaves you a private collection." The waitress comes to take his plate, and Peter asks her whether she has a cigarette. "I probably shouldn't give this to you," she says. She hands him the cigarette. "It's not your fault if I die young," he says. She knocks on the wooden back of his chair, and leaves with his plate balanced in one hand, wiping the other hand down her stained apron. "She likes me," Peter says. He scratches a match against the table and lights the cigarette. "The last time I saw you, you talked about your work. What would happen, if you lost it?"

"I'd get desperately poor. I'd do waitressing or something. I'd only be hard up because I'm terrible with money. I spend everything I make."

"I thought women weren't supposed to say things like that any more. You sounded like Scarlett O'Hara just then. 'Figures just fly right out of mah head when I'm wearin' a new bonnet, Ashley.' "

She looks at the coffee cup.

"I've embarrassed you," he says.

"No."

"It was a stupid thing to say."

Mia's earrings are jade. He touches one of them, admiring it, or as if to admire it. She guesses he wants to touch her to ease any awkwardness she still feels. The length of jade swings against her jaw, unsettled by his fingertip. "From Chinatown," she says.

"In San Francisco?"

"Yes," she says. "It was a gift from a friend." She does not say "from Cody"; it is an asymmetry between them, though a small one, that he has seen Cody drunk and behaving badly.

"Jade is a relief," he says. "I get so tired of turquoise."

She laughs. "I wear it all the time," she says. "Only not tonight."

"Where would you go, if you could go anywhere at all?"

"I don't know, Antarctica."

"Antarctica?"

"I know it sounds odd," she says. "I think I'm attracted to places that are really cold. And there are icebergs that are tinted by the algae that's frozen in them."

"I'd go to North Africa. Or to the Galápagos Islands, or Greece again."

"Again?"

"There was an island that we went to. It hadn't even gotten

electricity yet, but the summer we were there they brought a generator over from Athens on the boat. It used to run for a couple of hours each afternoon with a sort of monotonous throbbing. You could hear it all over the island. I was tempted to throw a grenade at it. We had a house there."

"It sounds lovely."

"It was better before the generator." He exhales thoughtfully; she can smell the bitter smoke he's just breathed. "My wife wasn't as much in love with the island as I was. No electricity, therefore no hot water. She didn't like calamari, she didn't like her food cooked in oil, and all everyone ate was squid, even for breakfast, and it was always cooked in oil."

"Does she like it here?"

"Here?"

"In Santa Fe."

"Yes," he says. "She likes it here." He stubs his cigarette out. The trucker wakes and looks around. There is a peacock tattooed on his forearm; when he stretches, the bulge of the bicep causes the peacock's tail to fan. He yawns. His teeth are white and even. He brings his hands down on the linoleum table, makes fists, and says softly, "Oh, *Madre*, what a dream. Oh, Jesus, what a bad, bad dream."

"Do you want to go?" Peter says. He lifts her coat for her from the back of her chair, and slips it over her shoulders: he even lifts the mass of her thick hair so that it won't be caught under the collar. He must be used to living with a woman with long hair, she thinks. It must be a habitual gesture, second nature, yet it feels like an unprecedented tenderness. He might as well have invented the gesture, for her. As they leave the cafe he puts his arm around her shoulders and she feels very vulnerable, very foolish, in her delight.

*　*　*

Peter turns off the highway and drives through a maze of back streets, many of them no wider than alleys, that Mia doesn't recognize. Once he looks at his wristwatch, but he says nothing. She hopes it hasn't occurred to him that he should take her home. She wouldn't know how to ask to spend the night with him, and she wants to. She is a little awed with herself, that she wants to. The coffee is a faint bitter taste in the back of her throat.

He stops the car in a rutted parking lot partially surrounded by dying cottonwoods. There are lamps on aluminum poles around the lot, but all of these are dark. Ahead there is a long adobe building behind a wall with an enormous, heavily arched gate. He slams his door and comes around to hers; she climbs out, and he says, "This is my museum. I thought you might like to see it."

"In the dark?"

"There are lights inside." He unlocks the gate and she follows him down a path of slate stones in dry grass. The front door has two locks, requiring separate keys; one of them must be for the burglar alarm. In the wide lobby she feels like a thief; her boots make scuffing noises, though she's walking as quietly as she can. Peter's sneakers make no sound at all. In a tall glass case, a mannequin dressed as a Hopi dancer is teasing a coiled rattlesnake with a feathered stick. The upper half of the mannequin's face has been painted in a sharp rectangle, matte black, in which the eyes are glassy slits. She can see that it is only a regular men's-store mannequin, converted into an Indian—the arms don't bend right, and the dancer's position, crouched above the snake, is too stiff to be convincing. They pass a desk she guesses must belong to someone's secretary, maybe Peter's—there are the neat framed faces of schoolchildren peering out from a plastic cube, a coffee cup with LINDA in gold lettering on its side, and a pot containing an aloe vera. From one of the aloe vera's leaves, an *ojo de dios* dangles—red, yellow, and blue yarn in a diamond. Peter takes her hand, and leads her down a hallway to a flight of darkened stairs. There is a No Smoking sign and by its light she admires his back. She is trying very hard to make him seem familiar. "Is this too weird for you?" he says.

"No. Not yet. You mean you live down here? In the basement?"

"I guess I got stuck," he says. "After the separation I couldn't seem to find a place to live."

Near the bottom she trips, brushing his shoulder, and he steadies her. "Clumsy," she says.

"You're not clumsy," he says, and kisses her. They go the rest of the way down the stairs and the cement floor is gritty beneath her boots and she smells disinfectant and dust, and then Peter turns on a light switch somewhere and she sees the pots: rows and rows of them, each pot the shadow of one before, its upper shoulder and rim faintly polished, its mouth an ellipse of shadow. She finds the fragments of a mug on his worktable, nearly completely pieced together, though there will still be a few chinks among the sherds even when he is done. Peter loves the mug—it's one of his favorite things ever acquired by the museum. It's black on white, the black in very fine, even, neatly angled strokes, and the white with a soft pearliness, very rare. At the bottom, inside, it had had an inner space, sealed off, in which pebbles had been placed: the pebbles had rattled together whenever someone lifted the mug and drank. He explains this to her, and she laughs. "And what are these?" she says, turning to some sherds in a cardboard box. She holds one up. It is gray, very plain, and on the outer curve you can see the maker's oblong thumbprint. "It's part of an olla that would have been as high as your hip," he says. "And more or less pear-shaped. It was found in a back room of a ruin on one of the mesas above Chaco, with several others like it, about a hundred years ago."

"They found all of the pieces?"

"Not exactly," he says. "They didn't find it in pieces."

"I don't understand."

"See, it was still whole when they found it."

"You mean it somehow broke?"

"Not somehow," he says. "They put them into gunnysacks, one pot for each sack, and tied the mouths of the sacks closed and hit them with a hammer and broke the pots."

"Why?"

"Because it's easier to carry a pot down from a mesa that way. And easier to store it inside a museum drawer."

She puts the sherd back down in the box with the others.

They make love on his ratty mattress, but first they go through an awkward negotiation: Does he have a condom? Does he have to wear one? Yes, she says. She can't make love without one, not at this time of the month. He ends up searching through his things, and finally he finds a condom in the pouch of a backpack which had been, until then, tucked inside one of his paper bags of clothes. The fact that it's there embarrasses him, a little. He must have meant to make love to Clarissa on some camping trip. Hoped to, rather—certainly in the last year or so the times they'd made love with any friendliness at all had been few and far between. He hates thinking of Clarissa when Mia is so near: he's sure she can read his mind. He sits with his back to her while he dresses his cock, which softens as he tries to fit the silken cool loop over its head, and he feels desperate for a moment, until it hardens and tips upward, and he unrolls the condom.

She is agile, and she has a sweet, furtive, foxy smell, not at all familiar, not like anybody, and he worries that he isn't gentle enough, he isn't slow enough, he will either come too soon, selfishly, or too late, demandingly, he isn't intuitive enough—in fact, a little catalogue of his crimes, courtesy of Clarissa. It occurs to him that this is no way to make love, but all he wants is to get through it with her still liking him enough so that he can make love to her again, soon, without all of these things on his mind.

15

"Fellini, eat your heart out," Nat says.

She and Tara are sitting at a table in the corner of the French Pastry Shop. Their knees touch below the table, it is so small. Nat is wearing a hat with a brim wide enough to brush the sooty bricks of the wall to their left: she removes the hat and settles it on the back of her chair. It is a handsome, expensive fedora. Nat has recently cut her hair into bangs. She left them longer than her eyebrows, long enough so that strands of hair sometimes catch in her eyelashes, and now she smooths them; she's drawn zebra stripes on her long fingernails with Magic Marker.

It is a Saturday morning in March, and the tourists have already come into town. The room is noisy with them, and still others wait by the glass counter that houses baguettes, croissants, pleated paper cups of glazed strawberries, loaves of bread shaped like alligators and frogs. Tara does not know anyone who would buy a loaf of bread shaped like a frog, even one with raisins for eyes and a crust glazed with honey. Beside the pastry trays, set apart to emphasize its splendor, there is a wedding cake of many intricately iced layers. The bride and groom on top of the cake are leaning at an angle, shoulder to shoulder, like miniature mimes pretending to defy gravity.

A man lifts his arm and calls, "*Garçon*," in a Texas accent. His cufflink is a turquoise flat as a dime. The woman beside him giggles. "*Fille*," she says. "That's what you mean. *Fille*." The waitress shows her teeth and moves toward them, already drawing her pad from the pocket in her apron.

Nat tears open her croissant and spreads butter across it; the butter is shaped like a rosebud and comes in its own paper cup, like the tiny cup they used to give you to drink from at the dentist's. Lately Nat insists that they come here often for eclairs or cappuccino or Napoleons. Tara thinks she knows why. Annie has been taking classes in macrobiotic cooking; the last time Tara had dinner at their house, the meal consisted of some kind of sullen-tasting fish, flesh flaking from its translucent bones, in a bed of singed dark seaweed and brown rice. There was a tea brewed from boiled twigs, and some kind of pickled plums that were supposed to be useful in curing cancer. There wasn't anything for dessert. As soon as Tara got home, she went straight to Clarissa's private stash of Krön chocolates —the latest, most desperate gift from Sonny. Since the ski episode, his exile has been virtually complete. The chocolates were hidden in a drawer of underwear and crumpled pantyhose. Tara ate the candy in the kitchen between swallows of milk straight from the carton. She ate three of them, one after the other, wondering what they had cost.

Nat bites the end off her croissant. "I think I found the perfect slicker this morning," she says. "It was black, and had a hood that was folded into a roll at the throat. You could unroll it if you wanted it to cover your hair. It was made of that kind of parachute cloth with little rectangles all through it, like graph paper, do you know what I mean?" Tara nods, licking whipped cream from her cappuccino spoon. Whenever Nat finds something she wants, she says it is the perfect thing of its kind—the perfect hooded sweatshirt, the perfect cotton muffler, the perfect pair of tight black jeans. It is as if Nat believes in an original kingdom of things perfectly suited to her, but that kingdom was somehow destroyed, its objects scattered, and that her mission in life is to find each thing, wherever it has been hidden, and then either buy it immediately or talk about it wistfully, incessantly, until she can afford to. Nat doesn't simply want things now and then, the way other people do. She has a sense of destiny about objects. She wants what she wants with unswerving attention. If her desire can't be fulfilled in a reasonably short time, she goes through phases of absent-mindedness, sometimes not even eating, not sleeping, becoming remote and resentful, a thwarted princess. Tara has seen it before. Now, because of the necessity for chocolate and cappuccino, Nat is more broke than usual. Tara has the feeling she will be hearing about the black slicker for some time to come.

"Let's go to Collected Works and look around," she says. It's not easy to distract Nat, once she gets started on something. Sometimes the bookstore works; more often, it doesn't. Once they went in and the owner of the bookstore had a macaw on his shoulder and the macaw looked at them and bashfully plucked at the owner's collar.

"Not yet," Nat says. "It's just getting good in here."

"There are about forty people waiting for our table."

"So?" Nat says. "They're all tourists. If you feel guilty, order another croissant."

"I'll never get a waitress. Mine was burned on the bottom anyway."

"You'll never guess who I saw in here last week," Nat says. "Ms. Martin. Our very own P.E. teacher. She was with a

Chicana woman. I think she was her lover. They were eating crepes with strawberries inside of them. Don't crepes sound good? I'm still hungry." She licks flakes of croissant from her fingertips. "They looked very domestic."

"Just because they eat crepes together doesn't make them lovers," Tara says. "Maybe it was her sister or something."

"You are so naïve," Nat says.

"Well, what about you?"

"What about me?"

"Your mind is getting polluted with sex. Sex, sex, it's really all you ever think about. You deserve someone as disgusting as pimple-faced Clay Richardson."

"He's not so bad," Nat says. "He's going to be a quarterback next fall. Compared to most fourteen-year-olds, he's a god."

"I'll faint with awe the next time he passes me in the hall."

"I think he's probably slept with someone at least once," Nat says. "Maybe last summer, when he was in California. He has some cousins there. He didn't kiss like a virgin."

"You would know."

"What's that supposed to mean?"

"You've kissed about half the boys in school."

Nat shakes her head. "If it bothers you to think about me kissing boys, maybe you should see a shrink. Maybe you're gay." Her fedora, knocked from the back of her chair, falls to the floor.

"I'm not gay," Tara says. "I just think that there's nothing more disgusting than Clay Richardson's pimply face in a dark alley." Nat had told her that Clay bought her a double dip of French vanilla and then they went out into the alley behind Swenson's ice cream parlor and Clay kissed her, easing his tongue between her teeth, and asked her whether she wanted to go to the movies. He nibbled at the tendons of her throat; he was trying to give her a hickey. She told Tara it was like being eaten by Pac-Man.

"I didn't say it was a dark alley," Nat says. "I just said an alley." She bends to retrieve the fedora and as she looks up her expression changes to astonishment. She brushes the dust from the hat's brim, thoughtfully. "Your father just came in," she says. "He's with a woman."

"No," Tara says. She turns in her chair and tries to see over the heads of the people at the tables along the wall. She rises slightly on her toes. Her elbow hits her cappuccino cup and the last of the coffee runs across the wooden table and Nat begins to mop it up with a soiled napkin. Across the crowded room, the woman backs up against the panes of dirty glass that flank the open doorway. More people push in behind her. The weak spring sunlight strikes sparks from her pale red hair. Her mouth is set in an exhausted line. Peter's arm is around her shoulders. His fingers curve upward to toy with her earring. Under his other arm there is a brand-new newspaper, still folded. There is no doubt who it is. There is no doubt that they are together.

"Hey," Nat says, reaching across the tabletop for Tara's hand. She holds her by the wrist. "You got really white all of a sudden."

"I'm okay."

"You didn't know about this?" Nat says. "You didn't know," she says, more softly, to herself.

"What will my mother do?"

"Your *mother* doesn't know?" Nat says.

"No."

"Here's what you do," Nat says rapidly. "You pretend nothing's happened, okay? You don't tell your mother you saw him with somebody. We get up and leave here before he sees us. That way he's not embarrassed. Okay? Now come on." She slides a five-dollar bill beneath her cup. Tara stumbles as she pushes her chair back but she keeps going, steadied by Nat's hand, still around her wrist, steering her through the French doors that open into the hotel. Tara feels sick. Nat guides her down a tiled hallway to the women's room. By the door of the women's room there is a small lamp with a shade of perforated tin, and across the hall a man in a dirty apron is squatting, his back against the wall, smoking a cigarette. Some of the starry patterns on his apron look like bloodstains. The crumpled cigarette pack rests by his sneaker. Nat ignores him and pushes the door open for Tara, following her inside. A shawled pueblo woman is squinting at her reflection in the mirror, applying lipstick without smiling. An embroidered sash swings down the side of her long skirt, and she is wearing a man's socks. When she finishes, she puts the lipstick away and says something in a language Tara doesn't recognize, not Spanish, and thrusts out an arm draped with necklaces, coral and silver squash-blossoms and limp strands of fine heishi, necklaces of silver links joining carved birds with dots as fine as pencil points for eyes. "No thank you," Nat says. The woman moves past, out the swinging door, her deerskin moccasins making no sound at all on the tiled floor.

Tara pushes open one of the stall doors and kneels in front of the toilet. She can feel the bones of her knees against the tiles. The small of her back aches. The oval of water in the toilet basin is clear blue. She vomits.

Nat flushes the toilet and hands her a wad of paper toweling to wipe her face. She can feel Nat's hands on her back; she knows she is sweating through her shirt. Oddly, this concerns her. She doesn't want Nat to know. She doesn't even want Nat to be here. Very lightly, as if she had done it all their lives, Nat strokes Tara's hair away from her sweaty forehead. "Are you okay now?" she says. "Is that it?" Tara tries to swallow. There is a bitter taste, like rusty iron, in the back of her throat. She vomits again, harder.

"It's all right, it's all right," Nat says, still stroking. "It's going to be all right."

Tara feels light and relieved. Her shirt is sticking to her

ribs, and she shivers. She feels dizzy as soon as she stands up, but she needs to rinse her mouth. At the sink she bends and drinks directly from the faucet—cold water with bubbles in it. She spits and rinses her mouth again and again. Gradually, she can feel her heart slow down. She can't get enough of the cold water.

She washes her face. "I wanted to tell you something," Nat says. She unzips her shoulder bag and puts a lip gloss on the counter near Tara's elbow. "Your lips are all chapped," she says.

"What did you want to tell me?"

"Don't have a heart attack," she says. "Charles asked me for your address."

Tara lowers her eyes, camouflaging any trace of delight by frowning unsteadily at her reflection. She uses the lip gloss until her mouth gleams. She must have been chewing on her lips, to get them so chapped. "Why would it give me a heart attack?"

"You always bite your lower lip when you tell a lie," Nat says.

"I'm not telling a lie. I just asked a question."

"You can stop pretending, all right? I gave it to him."

Charles hadn't come home at Christmas—because, Nat said, he had gone to visit a classmate in Massachusetts, a boy so rich he has his own Arabian horse, and a sailboat he can take out alone in the summer. Charles had gone ice skating with this boy on a pond in a forest of pines and silver birches. At one end of the lake there was a brick kiln where skaters could build a fire to warm themselves or to make hot chocolate. It was only in the East, Tara guessed, that you could get a fairy-tale winter like that. She has never been to the East. Charles had sent a photograph of himself to Nat, skating backwards and grinning, his shadow falling away behind him, a thin shadow bluer than the water below the ice, which showed through in smoky patches like bruises on a peach.

"It means he's going to write to you, stupid," Nat says.

"Don't call me stupid."

"Okay, you're really brilliant," Nat says. She hands Tara a paper towel and Tara wipes her chin. Even though Nat is watching, she closes her eyes. She is skating with Charles, wearing silver skates that shave fine lines in the ice. At first, they hold hands. She can feel the bones in his hand through the thickness of his mittens, but not its warmth. When he lets go, she skates away so quickly that he is caught by surprise. He can only skate after her, calling out. In the cold air, his voice sounds hoarse. It doesn't matter how loudly he calls, she decides: he will have to catch her, and suddenly she feels almost weightless, steady, faster than a bird, winging along in swift alternate strokes of the hissing blades. The ice is strong enough to bear her weight. They have an entire frozen lake to themselves.

16

Clarissa is washing paintbrushes in the kitchen sink on a
Saturday afternoon when the telephone begins to ring. She lets
the brushes fall among the breakfast dishes, and drops of
turpentine fly up, stinging her forearm and splattering the sleeve
of her shirt. "Damn," she says. She wipes both hands on a
dishtowel and looks at the telephone, which is already stained
with paint—to answer, and risk losing the rest of the day's work,
or to disregard it, although there is a chance it could be Tara.
She scrapes a fleck of yellow from the receiver. It must be the
yellow she used for those Peruvian lilies. She had seen them
in a florist's shop and bought an armful, choosing them stem
by stem, dewy and cold from the refrigerated air behind the
sliding glass doors, not even thinking of a painting, at first,
though the lilies were two dollars apiece. She had liked the
way the vortex of dapples printed inside each flower's narrow-

ing funnel made a runway of each petal. The single dapples were smaller than rice grains and yet aligned so that the eye was drawn straight down into that waiting center. The telephone rings twice more while she stands there, considering. It would be wonderful to have a studio separate from the house, where nothing could interrupt her and she would not have to deal with these decisions, where everything would be in its place all the time; its place would be exactly where she left it. She hates for anyone to see the paintings before they are done. The Peruvian lilies are safe now in a corner of her room, the easel draped with an old shirt of Peter's and turned to the wall (in case anyone comes in who has X-ray vision, Tara said once). She wonders what Sasha would make of the fact that she always uses Peter's shirts to cover the paintings. She is still hiding behind his shirt tails? She still thinks he would give her the shirt off his back?

Peter used to wander into her room while she was working, would absent-mindedly light a cigarette and look over her shoulder, wandering out again before she had a chance to say anything. It is that gently lunatic frown of his that she misses, sharply and all at once, though it is the expression that used to irritate her most, because it meant that he had come home from the museum still thinking about his endless damned potsherds. It meant he didn't even know that she was there. Sometimes it seemed to her that for every actual day of prehistory, some man, woman, or child had broken a pot and that only Peter, thousands of years later, had elected to pick up the broken pieces. For Peter, the past had been constructed by coiling, fired in a reducing atmosphere, tempered with small amounts of very fine quartz sand, and painted in a carbon pigment that showed traces of iron; in the end, it had shattered on a stone. She resented that ancient carelessness. She resented having a husband who had chosen to spend most of his waking life mending it.

Still, a lot of cherished resentments vanish into thin air when someone packs his clothes into five brown paper bags, she thinks.

It is Sonny on the telephone. "Cimarron" is on the tape deck; she turns the volume down enough so that she can hear his voice. Emmylou Harris sings softly, "Spanish is a loving tongue."

"You don't know what this is like," Sonny says.

"You can't bully me that way, Sonny," she says. "I hate that sort of emotional intimidation. Because everyone knows exactly what it's like, everyone. Not just you."

"You could have given it some time," he says. "We might have been able to work it out."

She sighs and scratches another fleck of paint from the receiver. This is his most recent tack—that they had had something wonderful, and that she had been the careless one, the one who had thrown it away. "It lasted a whole summer," she says. "Wasn't that time?"

"You used me," he accuses. She laughs, biting it off in the middle—an instant too late.

"Oh, Sonny," she says. "You sound so Victorian sometimes. So hurt-little-boy." It is part of an apology, as much as she will give him. He knows she used to like that—the ways in which he reminded her of a little boy, with his fine sun-lightened hair and brown shoulders. In fact, when she reflects on it, all the gifts she ever gave him were gifts intended for a child—an enamelled tin horse that jumped when you wound it with a key; a plastic octopus that, when thrown, clung to the wall for a moment before wriggling its way down; a gyroscope with instructions in Japanese. He says nothing, and she sighs again, feeling her impatience signalling him invisibly, no matter how hard she tries to hold her tongue. "I'm working right now," she says. "Can you call back at a better time?" She doesn't want to acquire the responsibility of being the one to call, of taking even that much initiative; her strategy is to remain all pure, impenetrable defense.

"Don't you think you're cruel?"

"No."

"Something's missing in you," he says.

"Is it smaller than a bread box?"

"Yes."

"I think it was the right time for us to stop, Sonny. I think it was the right thing."

"Lots of cruel people thought they were doing the right thing," he says. "Hitler, for example."

Because there is no answer for this, really—she knows he doesn't expect one—she holds several brushes under the tap and turns on the water. Flakes of alizarin crimson and Prussian blue are dislodged from the wooden handles, from which the enamel coating has long since rubbed away. She has been painting apples in a bowl. Lately, whenever she begins a still life, she feels tempted to paint the empty bowl, first. "I'm tired, Sonny," she says. "I can't talk about it any more right now. I haven't got the energy to argue."

She hears the *ching* of his receiver slamming down. Her mother once told her that the three most fragile bones were in the ear; once broken, those bones could never be mended. Clarissa finishes with the brushes and decides to wash the breakfast dishes—Tara's job, often forgotten now in the last few preening moments in the coveted privacy of the bathroom. This morning she had spent fifteen minutes covering her face with some kind of gooey foundation makeup that Natalie had given her, spreading it with a sponge across her perfect skin. When Clarissa, who was watching from the doorway, said, "You don't need that, you know," Tara had shrugged.

"It's good protection," she said.

"Protection against what?"

"Against air pollution," Tara said.

"There isn't any air pollution in Santa Fe."

"Then it's good protection against atomic fallout," Tara said.

Clarissa is scraping charred crumbs of toast from a plate when the telephone begins to ring again. She imagines Sonny's chagrin and, in spite of herself, she counts—eighteen, nineteen, twenty. Just as she is about to relent, he gives up, the last ring cut off in the middle. She wonders if Sonny was counting too and decided to stop on an even number. She has tried to make it easy for him, believing that she was at least in part responsible for his grief (after all, she had been married; she had been older), but the long winter wore down her resistance—she began to see that his need to be comforted would always be greater than her willingness to comfort. Sometimes, when she tries to force herself to remember the good things about being with Sonny, she can't think of any.

She goes into her bedroom to strip her shirt off. She should have known better than to paint in one of her favorite shirts. She'd bought it in Mexico, in a dim shop that had bottles of tequila and velvet paintings of bullfighters ranged along the plank walls, from a rack jammed with hundreds of other shirts, their sleeves and dainty collars embroidered with deer, antelope, unicorns, dogs. Peter had almost ruined the shirt for her by his teasing—saying it had probably been stitched by a little girl who is slowly going blind from working in the corner of a dark hovel. The little girl, he said, had most likely gotten only pennies for all the hundreds of tiny horned and hoofed beasts she'd sewed. Clarissa had decided she wanted the shirt; she had decided she didn't believe him. She couldn't tell exactly which decision came first. He frowned at her when she paid for it, as if he had been more serious than playful, at bottom. It was true that, in the dusty street outside the shop, a small boy demanded one quarter, American, for guarding their car, and when Peter gave him not one quarter, but two, you could see his rib cage swell with pride. He had squatted by their car while they ate *chile rellenos* and *sopaipillas* soaked in honey in the courtyard of a restaurant at the end of the street; and whenever any of the other boys, who were bouncing a ball against a dusty roof, shouldering each other and laughing, had come too near the car, the boy had swatted at them with a scrap of dirty rag. They could see all of this clearly from the table where they sat, looking over a low adobe wall, drinking sangria and sucking the wine-drenched sections of oranges. They had still been enough in love then so that his hand on her bare knee, beneath the table and hidden from the waiter's professionally indulgent smile, aroused and comforted her, even in such heat and in spite of the quarrel they had narrowly avoided. When they climbed into the car the air was stuffy—they'd left the windows rolled up. Clarissa leaned her head back, damp hair sticking to her cheekbones, and smiled. Just as Peter started the engine, the boy jumped barefoot onto the hood and cleaned the windshield with the rag. "So that's what the rag was for," Peter said. "I was wondering."

Now she rubs at the stain. It isn't very big, and it will probably come out. There are small winged horses on either side of the stain. All she really wants, she tells herself, all she has ever really wanted, is clarity, and that is exactly what Sonny seems intent on denying her, and Peter, too. She is almost certain that Peter has a lover. She is as certain as she can be without actually asking him. So far she has resisted the urge to ask him straight out, because a simple question might imply that if he did have a lover, it would be legitimate. It is better to stick to the precarious balance of the status quo, which is still, however nominally, a marriage, and contained the remote possibility of reconciliation; in fact, the possibility hadn't seemed all that remote. She had counted on it being there. She had been sure that no matter what had happened between them, in the end he would propose that they try to live together again, to give it another chance. He would bring it up wistfully, ruefully, acknowledging the error of his ways, yet with an undercurrent of concerned forcefulness. After all, he would remind her, taking her hand in the old way, they had a child to think about. She had imagined herself—witty, forgiving, nodding when he said that it was human to make mistakes, admitting under the slight pressure of his hand that she still loved him, of course she loved him, she had never really stopped; they would sleep together that night and relief would be very like passion.

Instead, he seems almost unwilling to see her. When she arranges meetings, he forgets them or comes very late, just as she is about to leave, and she thinks that his sorrowing rumpled look, his expression of amused and uncomprehending regret, has more to do with post coital tristesse than the premonition of divorce. He's unfocussed in a sexual way; she finds it as hard to ignore as if he had suddenly broken out in hives or grown three inches taller. He seems more full of himself than he has in years. He's lost some weight, and even his clothes, in some not quite identifiable way, are better—they no longer look as if they've come directly out of those paper bags. When she lights a cigarette, he taps his finger patiently on the top of the table, instead of asking her for one. The last time they saw each other—in a bar near the Capitol, in a padded leather booth beneath a reproduction of a long-necked Modigliani nude, propped up on an elbow, that Clarissa always disliked—he spent the entire hour drawing his house, his imaginary house, on a napkin. He drew the highway exit into the canyon and a dotted line for the railroad tracks you had to cross and an X for the tricky part to find, the turnoff that led you the last quarter-mile to the house site; it looked like a child's treasure map in a game of pirates. Bored, Clarissa sucked her piña colada through the swizzle stick. The ink from his felt-tipped pen ran in slow blurs across the cottony paper. Clarissa said politely that she would like to see it sometime. Peter glanced at her, careful to hide his surprise. She had never wanted to see it before, he said. That hadn't meant she would never want to see it, she said. She wanted to, now. Any time, he said. The Modigliani nude seemed to be looking down on them, skepticism in every line of her attenuated body. Clarissa had wondered what his lover, if there was a lover, was like. Peter doesn't know any women. In the museum, except for his mousy secretary, there are only men, all of them with the premature dustiness of their almost endless educations and the faintly lost look that handling the artifacts of ancient cultures seemed to leave them with. So, who?

And when did Peter get so good at keeping secrets? Maybe he really is ready to divorce her, if he can keep a secret so well. Maybe that's the definition of a divorce: when one of you can finally keep a secret from the other. She knows he never could before.

She studies her reflection in the mirror in her bedroom, the hollow between the tendons of her throat, the shadow below her sharply cut rib cage, the pubic hair that she rubs with the palm of her hand until it's smooth as a cat's cheek. She can find someone sometime soon. She can find someone who will be serious, and as unlike Sonny as possible. As unlike Sonny *and* Peter. She bends forward and touches the Oriental rug, a stretch that Tara taught her, and staring down at her feet against the pattern of the rug, palms and temple roofs, she remembers counting the toes when the nurse cupped Tara's feet and moved them into her line of vision. She had counted aloud, holding onto each number briefly and firmly, as if it were the rung of a ladder she had to climb to safety. At the top of the ladder there was exultation and the milder but no less crucial recognition that she was at last released from pregnancy. She was herself again. The limits of her body contained nothing but *her.*

She straightens, takes her hairbrush from the dresser, and begins brushing her hair in rapid, fierce strokes, a ripping sound, the hair falling to her shoulders; then she chooses one of her new linen shirts and puts it on. She has two of these, pale yellow. Lately, whenever she finds something she likes, she buys two of it, in case one gets ruined: she has learned that much, at least. The car keys are lying on the dresser in the lacquered tray Peter used to empty his pockets into. That had been her suggestion—that he use the tray, which she had bought for him, instead of spilling everything, coins and keys and junk, over the dresser. He had brought home stray objects of every sort: tickets, feathers, slips from fortune cookies. He used to call his lunches in the Chinese restaurant "comfort food," and he always ordered the blandest possible combination of noodles and vegetables and pale tea. Once he brought home a fortune cookie slip that said, "MANY CHANGES OF MOOD AND MIND. DO NOT HESITATE TO LONG," and she had kept it, liking the wobbly mimeographed print, the typo, the creases where the paper had been folded to fit inside the shell. Do not hesitate to long. The bedroom is suddenly too familiar; she needs to get out. She tosses the car keys and catches them, tugs on her jeans and cowboy boots, lifts her hair, and sprays perfume on the nape of her neck. As she closes the front door and locks it, hoping Tara hasn't forgotten her key, she hears the telephone begin to ring again. Sonny, she thinks, as she climbs the steps and latches the gate behind her. That didn't take him long.

Peter had warned her that finding the house site in the canyon was tricky. Distances on dirt roads were always deceptive, as far as you could get from the shortest distance between two points. Dirt roads had quirks of their own, personas, local gods to be met and appeased. So Clarissa is pleased not to have gotten lost, as he would have expected her to. She halts the Volvo in the rutted road and climbs out to open the gate, which swings heavily on rusted hinges, the No Trespassing sign banging against the clumsily soldered bars that look as if they once belonged to someone's bedstead. The dust of the road, heated by the sun, smells pleasantly astringent. Dust in the desert has such a keen smell; she had forgotten. The walls of the canyon hold the light, and where there are clefts the shadows are very blue and cool. He had said that there were ruins above the canyon, maybe even burials in the rimrock, where no one had ever looked. From the gate it is only another quarter-mile to his house site, but she will have to watch very carefully from here on in.

It is much easier to find than she had expected, a low rise where the bank is cut away from a small level area that holds two rickety sheds, the deeply etched loops of tire tracks, and a stack of firewood beneath a fraying tarpaulin. There is a blackened coffee pot on a stump near the ring of ashy stones that serves as a cooking fire. Clarissa climbs out of the Volvo. She is disappointed at having gotten here with so little trouble. Did he really think she got lost so easily? He had made it sound so mysterious, a trip to the ends of the earth. The chiselled wall on the far side of the plain is beginning to throw a shadow across the ground below its talus slope. That shadow, she guesses, will move slowly until it touches the ground where she stands, pausing only to enfold the creased banks of the dry arroyo that divides the plain into unevenly eroding halves. There is the early cold of a swift spring evening; the crescent moon is out and it seems quite sharply white. Clarissa buries her fists in the pockets of her jacket and walks up the slope to his house site. It is very simple—stakes driven into the ground, string taut between the stakes, the skeleton of a house where she will not live.

Clarissa kneels and fiddles with the string, tentatively at first, then decisively, sliding the string from the first stake, moving to the second, string trailing behind her, until each stake in turn is loosed. She returns to the corner of the house where she started, tosses the tangled string away, and, rocking back on her heels, tugs the stake from the earth. It resists at first, then moves stiffly, like a lever weighted at the far end, and she works it back and forth, trying to be patient, gradually widening the socket, until the stake slides from the hole. She brushes dirt from the sharply cut pale wood and then lifts the stake and hurls it high into the air, listening for the flat smack it makes, landing in the brush perhaps fifty feet away. It was a good throw, and she is surprised by the lightening of her heart. She bends to the next stake and grasps it, squatting with her heels dug in, working it from the ground. The stake comes loose with a sudden dry rasp of wood against pebbles. This time, when she throws, the stake falls too close to the house site, still plainly visible, and she walks toward it, lifts and throws, the stake turning end over end and falling a good distance away, snapping twigs, bouncing and hitting again. A jack rabbit breaks from a hollow and runs uphill.

She digs each stake out in turn, working her way around the long rectangle, throwing them in different directions but always up the slope, where they will be screened by grass and chamisa. When this is finished she walks down to the larger of the two sheds and finds that it is locked and she can see no obvious way to break in. That is too bad, because he probably keeps a shovel inside. She searches until she finds a juniper branch that looks sturdy and with this she scrapes pebbles and dirt down into the first stake hole. The ground has a shallow crust; below the crust the dirt is powdery and loose and she can scoop it up in fistfuls, pouring it down the hole. She remembers her mother teaching her to make sandcastles by squeezing the dripping-wet sand from her fist into turrets and walls. Her mother had been ingenious about things like that: she had known how to mimic the dimensions of Chartres, or how, if you were not interested in Chartres, to fashion an island invulnerable to attack. One evening they had worked for hours on the Great Wall of China. Meanwhile her father would roll up his baggy trouser pants and do an excellent imitation of a sandpiper, rushing forward smoothly with his head ducked down toward his shoulders and waiting several anxious moments before retreating expertly, his dainty bare feet just ahead of the curl of the wave. That was all that ever came between us, Clarissa thinks—the Great Wall of China.

It requires some vigorous scraping with the stick and many handfuls of dirt before the stake hole is filled level with the ground. Then she smooths the place and stamps on it, scattering pebbles on top for good measure. The branch splinters on the fifth stake hole and she discards it, working steadily with her bare hands and surprised, when she looks down, to see that one of them is bleeding. She finishes the last of the holes and smooths it and walks around the perimeter, or what had been the perimeter, of the house, content that no one could reconstruct the outline except her, and she will only be able to remember it for a few minutes longer. When she is sure that no trace remains, she walks down the slope and sits on a stone in the last of the sun, brushing the dust from the knees of her jeans and examining the cut in her hand. A small triangular flap of skin screens the thorn—called a goat's-head because it resembles a miniature skull, bleached and horned. Her legs feel stiff and bruised; she stretches them before her, coughs, and begins to cry. She can feel the tears cutting sticky tracks through the dust on her face; the sliding liquid movement tickles. When tears touch the corners of her mouth she licks them away. She wipes the back of her hand across each cheekbone, knowing that the dust and wet will leave grimy streaks. She draws her feet up onto the stone and rests her chin on her knees, which causes the small of her back to ache. It isn't that she regrets doing it; it's that she hadn't known what she was going to do. She hadn't known the whole time she was driving out here; she hadn't known until she pulled the first stake from the ground. After that she doubts she could have changed her mind. She hadn't wanted to do anything that would ruin whatever chance for

getting back together is left, but she can guess how he will feel
about this: he will hate it. Still, there is a very good chance he
will not know who did it, so he won't be hurt in the extraordinary, private way of learning that she would destroy
something of his. He's probably even forgotten drawing the
map of the canyon for her on the napkin that came with his
Scotch. He wasn't all there that night in the bar. She convinces
herself gradually that drawing the map is the kind of thing Peter
is likely to forget, but even as she begins to believe this, she is
still crying, the back of her hand pressed hard against her upper
lip, just below her nose, the mucus dark with all the dust she's
inhaled. It's a relief to cry like this but she knows she can't
let it go on very long. The crying is so simple, so physical a
release that it could become addictive. Except for the hoarse
noise she makes, clearing her throat, she can't hear anything,
not a sound, as if the whole canyon has been emptied of all life
except her, until a meadowlark starts up somewhere in the
arroyo. The meadowlark rehearses several rapid, coursing notes
that have the inflection of a polite question between strangers.
Peter won't know it was her. He isn't going to accuse her. He
will come to her and tell her what happened to the house, and
she will comfort him as well as she can, because real damage
was done and she knows enough not to take that lightly. She
knows it now. He will lean against her and she'll stroke the
familiar curves of his face, pushing the hair away from his forehead the way you feel for a child's fever, touching him as
tenderly as she's ever touched anyone in her life, and she'll ask
him how it happened and he will tell her it must have been
vandals.

She prods the thorn with a fingernail, and the pain moves
nimbly from fingertips to wrist. Why do people say, why do
they ever say, "as familiar as the palm of my hand"? Her
fingerprints, limned with dust, are unpleasantly complex oval

mazes. She wedges the fingernail beneath the thorn and works it loose. The wound is clean and she doubts you can get tetanus from a thorn. Still, she lets it bleed for a moment longer before wiping it along the seam of her pants. This is an old pair of Levi's, and she can use them later for painting.

17

Tara is wearing a tuxedo. On the black satin lapel is pinned a small dragonfly of painted tin. Earlier this evening she had discovered that she did not know how to tie a bow tie. This discovery, for some reason, made her furious until Peter gently offered to teach her. She had told him the way it was supposed to look—floppy, like a boy's, not uptight. He knew that the end result of the bow tie was supposed to be that of a slight, erotic dishevelment; he was amazed that his daughter could know that much and not guess that he would intuit the rest. He found that he wasn't able to tie the bow tie either, facing her. It was impossible to reverse movements you knew so well, like trying to tie your shoe by looking in a mirror, and finally he stood behind Tara, stooping a little with his arms around her, because that way it was like tying the bow tie at his own throat.

"You're taller," he said, when he was done.

"Of course," she said warily. "Now go away, okay, so I can concentrate on warming up, okay?"

"She's lovely," Mia whispers, when he nudges her with his knee. He has already nudged her twice and each time she has whispered that Tara is lovely. Now he feels sure of it. He is nervous because it is the first occasion when he has taken Mia out formally, and because anyone who sees them will surely guess that they are lovers. They have already listened to two pianists, an oboist, and a cross-eyed boy who played the flute soberly between dazzled glances at the audience. The flutist is followed by an intermission; Peter and Mia remain seated in their uncomfortable folding chairs while, around them, couples feed slices of cheese to each other from their fingertips. Usually the couples are composed of one parent and the parent's lover. Peter cannot imagine Mia nibbling cheese from his fingers. He thinks she looks serious and far too beautiful. All evening she has been waiting for Tara to play with an air of expectation. He likes her enormously for that.

Clarissa had begun to think that the music teachers provided by the school system don't do much good, and so she sought out a teacher who gave lessons weekday evenings and Saturdays. This was a crucial time for Tara's technique, Clarissa had explained; it should be shaped by an expert hand. The music teacher could make all the difference in the world. Peter likes the house, which is handsome and old, though a little run-down. The music teacher heaped everyone's coats on the quilt in her bedroom, where some of her own things were already scattered. The implication, Peter guessed, was that only that morning she had made wonderful love with someone she barely knew: these were her friends, or if not her friends then her students' parents, and she had not felt obliged to straighten the house for their arrival. Besides, in a music teacher evidence of passion was probably good. The guests did seem flattered. Only a skeptic would have been unmoved by this evidence of haste and desire: a slip hanging from the painted frame of an antique mirror, the crumpled pillows, an ashtray ringed with cigarette butts. Peter finds that he is jealous, though he doesn't even know her. Guiltily, he takes Mia's hand and plays with her fingers.

Mia has worn a black skirt, having guessed at the solemnity of the occasion, having wanted to impress him. His own legs are too long for him to sit comfortably on the metal folding chair, so he has been twitching and shifting for the last hour. Now he has grabbed her hand and is fidgeting with her fingers. Her impulse is to jerk her hand away; instead she bites her lower lip, reminding herself that this is mostly nervousness for Tara, and absolutely natural. She had been waiting—since that evening last winter when they became lovers—for the first true instance of annoyance with him. She is a little amused to find that it comes and goes so quickly, leaving no trace. Did she think it would mean the end of the world?

He is wearing scuffed running shoes, blue jeans, and an old baseball shirt beneath his favorite tweed jacket. His sleeve is pushed up above his elbow to show the face of his digital watch. She glances down, but the watch is the kind that doesn't show any numbers unless you touch the button on its faceted side.

In front of the ranks of folding chairs, Tara seats herself, positioning the cello between her legs, pushes up her tuxedo sleeves in a gesture identical to one of Peter's, and picks at a scab on her elbow while the music teacher introduces her as an extremely promising new student who came to her last winter. The room grows silent. The bow moves across the strings in strokes parallel to the plane of the bare wooden floor, in which Mia can see the cello's reflection, upside-down, its dark mass fragmented by patches of old varnish, a Picasso cello. The spikes of the two cellos meet precisely in the grain of a warped floor-board. Rosin sifts from the moving bow and tints the legs of Tara's tuxedo a paler gray, the color of an imperfectly washed blackboard. Strands of horsehair fly from the bow. Tara's eyes are open and her expression is unvaryingly intent and self-composed, and Mia sees how lovely she is, really, how fine the bones in her face. Peter holds her hand, his grip loosening and tightening according to the music, which is nothing Mia has ever heard before.

When Tara is finished, she tips the cello away from her, stands, and looks around the room until she remembers where Peter is. Across the room of clapping people she smiles at him, and then she trips, recovering just before she loses her hold on the cello. She shakes her head, still stiffly smiling, and the parents in the room sigh with relief: it wasn't ruined for her.

Peter goes forward, Mia lagging behind, and they work their way through the crowd to where Tara is waiting. "You were beautiful," Peter says.

"Was I?"

"It was really wonderful."

"Was it okay?"

"It was more than okay. It was wonderful."

"I was so hungry before I started. But I knew that if I ate anything at all I would just throw up."

"Are you hungry now? We could take you for ice cream or something."

"It's my night to go over to Nat's."

"Are you sure?"

"It's just what I always do."

"Okay," he says doubtfully. "See you later, then?"

"Sure," Tara says.

She rises neatly on her toes and kisses him on the mouth, silencing further questions.

Peter and Mia are asleep in her bedroom, her knee tucked between his legs, his hand caught in her hair, so that when he
moves in his dream, the jerk at the nape of her neck draws her
awake. His baseball shirt is draped across the back of a chair,
his jacket crumpled on the floor, one of his running shoes is in
a corner. Pancho Villa sleeps at the foot of the bed, his nose
tucked beneath one paw.

She turns in the tangled sheets and studies Peter. Peter is the
first man whose body has ever seemed entirely right to her. He
makes her aware, in retrospect, of how clumsy she sometimes
was with Cody, freezing, she had hoped imperceptibly, before he entered her, her knees drawing up as if she needed
some measure of protection from him. With Cody, she had
closed her eyes, though he had wanted her to keep them open.
With Peter things are disconcertingly opposite. Before he comes
he nudges her face away, his chin scraping her jaw, as if he loves
her best in slightly submissive profile—as if he were the one
who needed protection. In the darkness of the rumpled bed she
admires his feet, the long slanting muscles of his thighs, the
wreath of wiry hairs around the flat brown nipples. She slides
downward in the bed, pushing at Pancho Villa's sly, settled
weight with her foot. It is still spring and the cat has already
caught two sparrows and one swallowtail butterfly that lived for
a while after he brought it into the house—an attempt, she
knew, to regain the place in her affections that has been usurped
by Peter.

She strokes one of his thighs, the cowlick of coarser hair
near the scrotum, which dips down elegantly, as if to counter-
balance the shaft of the penis, slowly becoming erect. When he
walked toward her naked for the first time in the basement, his
penis bobbled and he caught it shyly in his hand and hid it.

She loved that. Now with half-shut eyes she touches her tongue to the hood whose texture is slightly grainy, not nearly as smooth as it looks; she runs her tongue into the downy cleft, a little urgingly, to see if the first teardrop will bead the cleft, but it doesn't. She tastes the faint salt bitterness of urine and a waxy trace of Ivory soap. Above her, far above, he says her name. She rests her teeth, just the very edges of her front teeth, on the skin of the penis. Her tongue rises to the ridge of vein on the shaft, smooth as a peeled twig, ample with the blood inside that makes the vein blue or sometimes gray; if he is sufficiently aroused she can sometimes see a quickening and tightening of that vein. Farther down there are his balls and a different taste, richer and somewhat sour—she thinks of the venison Cody fed her a bite of, once, when a friend of his had shot a buck. The hair there is kinky, unlike the hair anywhere else on his body. She slips one of the balls into her mouth and the lucid floating egg shape rests on her tongue inside its pouch of coarse, pliant skin. She pushes it out very gently with her tongue and sucks on the other ball and then she rises and takes the end of the penis into her mouth, deeply, down to the scallops on either side of the hood, and she remembers being very small and scared in summer camp when someone had made her put a flashlight into her mouth and turn it on, so that the glare of the light through skin was tinted red, a monster's grimace, or a ghost's; there was, then, this metallic sliding smoothness and a feeling of helplessness. She stops, and he slips from her mouth, his penis flipping up against his belly with a soft clap. He moves down at the same instant that she moves upward, and he turns so that he is above her, and she can feel his ribs looming between her knees and she rubs her callused heels against his back to make the pleasing sandpaper friction. He says her name. It doesn't sound like her name. He says, "Clarissa."

She stares up at him, disbelieving. He stops, looking down, and her vagina tightens in close small spasms, because she is already used to him, because she couldn't have caught herself in time, because her heels rest against his back so that he holds more than half her weight, but she feels wounded; she is as coldly shocked as if he had stolen something from her, or told a lie. He is slowly growing softer within her and she concentrates sternly on this reluctant inching-out of his penis. She wants him out, but she does not move. She does not look away.

He looks down at her. "Shit," he says.

"Shit is right," she says.

"Listen, it can happen."

"I know it can happen. Of course it can happen. Do you think I'm an idiot?"

"I was with her for fourteen years."

"I know all about the fourteen years."

"It doesn't mean anything about anything. I just said her name."

"It means something," Mia says.

"It's nothing. It's one of those things."

"Oh. One of those things that don't count, that you should just ignore, because they don't really matter, even though they feel as if they matter."

He laughs.

"Don't," she says. "Don't laugh. You ass."

He laughs again. "I can't help it. I've never heard you say 'You ass' before." He lifts his hand to stroke her hair but she turns her face away sharply. "Tell the truth," he says. "Weren't you ever afraid you might slip for a second and call me Cody?"

"I've been apart from Cody for a long time."

"I know, but weren't you ever afraid?"

"It was different."

"Damn, you're stubborn," he says. "Tell me it never even occurred to you."

"It never even occurred to me," she says. "I hope you're happy."

18

Peter is in his office Monday morning, considering the telephone on his desk. Beside the telephone there is a small clay Christmas tree that Tara made him. He thinks it is supposed to be a Christmas tree. He has already tried the number of the pay telephone in the corridor outside the loft where Mia works —where she should be right now, painting the reeds that will back *Swan Lake*—but no one has answered. He would be glad to talk to anyone, even Theodore. Even Edmund, who seems to him almost pathologically depressed. Anyone, in short, who could tell him where Mia is, who could convince him he has not lost her. Who could make her come to the phone. It is an emergency. She hasn't wanted to talk to him since the night before last. He tries to reassure himself: they're not used to each other, of course they would have problems at first—it's natural. It was probably inevitable that he would say Clarissa's name; he lived with her for fourteen years. Mia should be able to understand that. She should understand. In any case she shouldn't disappear at the first sign of trouble. She shouldn't disappear.

He taps the clay tree. He probably shouldn't have had a drink at lunch. Extremely dangerous habit to get into, at his age. Especially he should not have had a martini. His calves still ache from this morning's run but he had been pleased to feel, after the second mile, only slightly winded. The last of the snow was almost gone from the foothills of the Sangres, and there was even enough sun so that, when he finished his shower, he could observe a slight paleness on his wrist that matches the band of the digital watch he wears. There is something heroic about this strip of light skin, as if he were wearing a bandage. He puts his feet up on his desk and admires his New Balance running shoes, newly broken in. He once had a professor of physical anthropology who referred to the Australopithecine fragments—a bit of phalange, the petal of bone that was the back of a small skull—as belonging to the "first runners on Earth." Peter had disapproved of this; it was ethnocentric. Deer run; horses run; jackals run. They had all been running for their lives long before *Australopithecus* came along. But now he thinks he understands something of the professor's intention: there is some purely human capacity for running, the sinewy deep effortlessness of a biological intention finally carried out. "Imagine their lives," the professor had said, in his self-dramatizing way. "They were fugitives. They had left the refuge of the rain forest for the parched savannah where all movement was visible for miles. The females were slender and feral, the males subtly conciliatory with the loss of the threatening canine." Here the professor had lifted his lip and displayed to the class his own rather blunt, yellowing incisors. "It doesn't exactly strike terror into your hearts, does it?" he said. "The loss of the malevolent canine was a concession to society, perhaps the first concession. We continue to make concessions today in the form of neckties and tight collars. We are proving, in various subtle ways, that we will not harm each other, at least not without good cause. We will be predictable. We can be relied upon. What did *Australopithecus* count on, in its newly vulnerable bands of males and females, possibly already linked by pair bonds? They relied on stealth, the extraordinary new ankle, the surprising opposition of thumb and forefinger with which one could lift, carve, chisel, butcher, sew, stroke—an infinite variety of behavior subtly meshed."

Peter scratches his ankle, considering Mia, her infinite variety of behavior, some of which she has demonstrated in bed. He rises to rummage through his bookcase for the text from the class—long since outdated, but he remembers it with fondness. W. E. LeGros Clark, *The Fossil Evidence for Human Evolution*. He reads:

> The evolutionary progress of the primates, as Simpson has well said, has been in the direction of greater adaptability rather than of greater adaptation. Thus the order can be defined only by reference to the prevailing evolutionary trends which have distinguished it from other groups—such as the progressive development of large and complicated brains, the elaboration of the visual apparatus and a corresponding reduction of the olfactory apparatus, the abbreviation of the facial skeleton, the tendency toward the elimination of the third incisor tooth and of one or two premolars, the preservation of a relatively simple pattern of the molar teeth, the replacement of sharp claws (faculae) by flattened nails (ungulae), the retention of pentadactyl limbs with an accentuation of the mobility of the digits. . . .

Well, he admires her large and complicated brain, and he has good reason to be grateful for the mobility of her digits. LeGros

Clark is describing essentially human quirks of the jaw, improvisations in the order of teeth in which certain teeth were lost in a slackening off of the powerful chewing apparatus, loss of the occipital ridge, "the abbreviation of the facial skeleton"—thus, the exquisite cheekbones and the large eyes staring up at him from the pillow. He turns several pages.

> In the Hominidae the pelvic skeletons underwent quite far-reaching changes directly related to the erect posture; in the Pongidae it retained the general shape and proportions found in lower primates generally. These divergent modifications of the limbs and pelvis are related to very different modes of life in the two families. They involve more than just those proportional differences in linear dimensions about which so much detailed and accurate information has been accumulated by the patient studies of Schultz . . .

Ah yes, dirty old Schultz with his calipers, a plumelike white mustache, Germanic and grave, edged with tobacco stains, stamping the profoundly patient curve of his upper lip as he bends to the fragments of female Australopithecine's pelvis.

> . . . for they are also accompanied by quite marked structural divergences in muscular anatomy.

"Muscular anatomy" is as close as W. E. LeGros Clark is going to come to saying "uterus." He has neatly avoided what seems to Peter a rather beautiful line of speculation. Paleontology was riddled with this sort of evasion, a covert Victorianism, tightly clasped. "Structural divergences in muscular anatomy" includes the wings of pelvic bone on either side of her mons veneris, and the silken vagina she possesses, against great evolutionary odds. Thank God for the erect posture. Peter loves her. He loves the jaw that it took millennia to narrow and lighten, he loves her abbreviated facial skeleton and elaborate visual apparatus, he loves her flattened fingernails. He loves her. When his telephone rings he almost knocks over the clay tree. He rights it, lifting the receiver. If he had more time, he would cross his fingers.

"Peter?" she says. "I'm sorry. I think I overreacted."

"Where've you been?" he says. "I've called you a dozen times today. And I called you all day yesterday."

"I didn't go in to work," she says. "I stayed home and left the phone off the hook. I just needed some time to think."

"I wish you had called me first, before you started thinking," he says. "Just so I could have known what was going on. I had a martini at lunch to punish myself."

"You shouldn't have had to feel that," she says. "It was clumsy of me to imply you did anything, even the smallest thing, wrong."

"You're not clumsy," he says. "Stop *saying* that."

"Come home then," she says. "As soon as you're off work."

"Home?"

"Here, stupid," she says. "My house."

"I won't get there until six, probably."

"Peter," she says. "Do you think we could try living together, or do you think it's too scary?"

"I think it's pretty scary."

"Could we try it anyway?"

"Do you want to so much?"

"Yes," she says.

"Well," he says. "I don't exactly have a lot of stuff. I'll pack and bring it over after work, or is that too fast?"

"Do you think it's too soon, and I shouldn't have asked you?"

"I'm a little surprised."

"Oh," she says. She sounds disappointed.

"Mia," he says. "I like the idea, you know. I was just giving you a chance to back out."

"I'm not going to," she says.

"Then neither am I," he says.

* * *

As he packs, he remembers that one of the first nights she slept
with him in the basement, she had lain beside him in the dark,
tracing his side with her fingers, and asked, "What if we were
separated, and locked up in a pitch-black room with other
people, and no one could see anything or talk or make any
sound at all, how would you find me?"

"How would I find you?"

"How, in the dark, would you know it was me?"

"Look," he said. "If a bird flew in the window carrying only
one strand of your hair, I'd know it was you."

That had seemed to be what she wanted, and she fell asleep.
They slept easily together from the beginning, for two people
on such a small mattress.

When the telephone rings Mia wakes to the feel of Peter's
shoulder below her jaw. Her mouth is open; she's been drool-
ing on his shoulder. She wipes the wet spot away. His left
knee has edged, in his sleep, between her knees; even as she
calculates how many more rings it will take her to catch the
phone, she is pleased that their positions, separately dream-
ing, should be so clearly erotic. She needs to be sure of him even
in his sleep.

She remembers her bathrobe; she had kicked it into a corner,
hours ago. As she lifts it and walks backwards into the hallway, so that she can watch the sleeping Peter and be sure he
does not wake, she is frightened: it is some Elks Club bridge
partner of her mother's, calling to warn her of a stroke, paraly-
sis, an accident; it is Theo, and Edmund has taken an overdose,
leaving only a wry, reproachful note to her, Mia, saying that
she should have understood more, seen him more often, talked

him out of it; worst of all, it is Peter's wife, calling to say something has happened to Tara and it all has to do with her, Mia, it is somehow her fault, and could she please wake Peter, her husband, up and send him home. Where he belongs. Mia answers the telephone, having lost count of its rings. It is Cody.

"Mia?" he says. She hears the radiator clank on in the other room.

"Yes?" she says. Now that she knows it is him, she can't imagine how she could have thought it would be anyone else.

"Mia, I think I've made a mistake."

"What mistake?" she says. It dawns on her. "You mean the divorce?" He knows about Peter, and jealousy has driven him mad. She wonders what time it is. "What time is it?"

"Your famous refusal to own a watch," he says.

"Even if I did own one, I wouldn't be wearing it in bed."

"The way I understand it, you're not wearing very much to bed these days, anyway."

"Who do you understand that from?"

"You always forget what a small town this is."

"You called me up at whatever time this is to interrogate me about my sex life?"

"No," he says. "I called you up because I made a mistake. I think I made a serious mistake and you're the only one I can talk to about it."

She drags the bathrobe more deeply around herself, as if it provided a kind of shelter. The floor beneath her bare feet feels dirty. She should make more of an effort in her housekeeping; Peter will get the wrong impression. "Cody, why am I the only person you can talk to about it?"

"I don't know," he says. "You just are."

They are silent. She thinks he is probably telling her the truth, about both things: however articulate he can manage to be, at other times, about antelopes and cirrus clouds, he doesn't know; and she is the only person he can talk to. She desperately wishes to be back in bed where Peter is. The wish causes her to wake up a little more, enough to ask Cody, "What's wrong, then?"

"You really want to know?"

"Cody, please tell me."

"It's the vasectomy. I think I'm really beginning to feel grief. I think I did something I shouldn't have done." He pauses. "You know what it was? It was seeing you fall in love, really fall in love, that's what made me start thinking. I think in some part of myself I really thought you never would look at another man, not seriously. Not the way you looked at me."

"It's not the way I looked at you," she says. "I *married* you."

"I know you did," he says. "But what I mean is, if you could have this other chance because you walked into that party, some-place you weren't even sure you wanted to go in the first place, and you could meet someone and fall in love and look as if you're doing fairly well—"

"We *are* doing fairly well." Yet how odd to use "we" with Cody, a "we" that does not include him.

"I know you are. I didn't mean to bad-mouth it, I can see that it's doing something good for you. But if that can happen to you, doesn't it mean that it can happen to me? What if who-ever I fell in love with wanted children?"

"Well," she says. "A million things could happen. Whoever you fell in love with could have children of her own. You might like those children. You could travel the world. You could adopt."

"I've said all of those things to myself. They don't really help."

"No," she says. "Well, is it reversible?"

"I was so sure of myself I didn't even ask."

"Oh, Cody," she says. "Ask."

"You're so reasonable tonight," he says. "I wish you'd been like this when we were together."

"I *was* like this," she says. "Sometimes I was."

19

In the plaza there are already a dozen roller-skaters moving in fast patterns down the intersecting concrete paths between the long triangles of new-mown grass. Peter has bought himself an ice-cream cone, vanilla because he wanted something plain. The day is sunny and cool and the sun strikes his shirt with the warmth of spring. He had thought that winter would never end.

He lies on his back and stares up through the shifting branches of a spruce tree. He licks the melting ice cream from his fingers and wraps the napkin more tightly around the cone. When he turns on his belly, his daughter is there, on the perimeter of the skaters, dodging and wheeling to skate backwards. She is wearing thick pads that make her knees look coltishly big, and her cropped dark hair, which has been growing out all winter, flicks upward when she turns her face into the wind created by her own momentum. Another skater rockets by him only a few feet away on the sidewalk. There is something skeptical in her hipbones that is redeemed by the innocent bulge of her belly, and she has the downy upper lip of a very young child. The skaters mark the edge of some perfect circle whose center is the monument.

Natalie spots him first and waves to him. She is wearing a Sony Walkman, skating in time to music he guesses must be punk rock. Her T-shirt strains across her small breasts, and in red lettering it says: AMERICAN PRINCESS. She certainly is, he thinks. He remembers the Texas Princess T-shirt he gave his lover at the dig—it seems a very long time ago. Natalie's hair has been braided into corn-rows, giving her head a small, fastidious, exotic look. The bare skin between the neat plaits is pink with sunburn, as is the tip of her nose. Today, if he tried, he could love Natalie Whitman. Tara skates up behind her, her hand resting on Natalie's shoulder. Tara is wearing false vampire fangs. She grins and pretends to bite Natalie's neck and Natalie looks away a little because she knows Peter is watching.

Tara skates up to him, coming to a perfectly balanced stop. Peter holds the ice-cream cone up to her and she takes it, her vampire's fangs raking long channels down the melting vanilla. She says, "Mmmm, it's good. Don't you still want it?"

"No. You finish."

"Vanilla isn't my favorite."

"Make the best of it. How come your voice is like that?"

"Like what?"

"So squeaky and high."

"Some boys brought helium balloons and I've been breathing helium."

"You've been what?"

"Don't worry," she says. "It can't hurt you."

"Why are you doing it?"

"You can sound like Mickey Mouse if you sing."

Natalie floats by backwards, her skates clashing. She flashes them a smile. One of the boys sitting at the monument's base seems to have caught the argument; he stands up, inhales deeply from a pink balloon, and sings in a tremulous voice, "We're off to see the Wizard, the wonderful Wizard of Oz."

"See?" Tara says. "Nothing wrong with that, is there?"

"For all I know, he could be brain-damaged," Peter says.

"He's not. He's in my class."

"Great," Peter says. "That's very reassuring."

"Well, it should be." She finishes the tip of his cone and licks her fingers. "Don't you have to go see Mia?"

"She's working. She doesn't get off until four. So we'll come and pick you up about four-thirty, okay?"

"Okay," she says. "What are we eating?"

"What would you like?"

"Italian," she says, with satisfaction. He laughs. She knows he hates Italian food.

"Okay," he says. "Do you need any money?"

"I have a lot of money."

"Okay, I'm going."

"Kiss," Tara says.

He kisses her forehead. In the roller skates she is surprisingly tall. "Will you do me a favor?" he says. "Just this one thing?"

"What?"

"First say you will."

"I will."

"Don't breathe any more helium," he says. "Breathe air. For me, okay?"

"It was a trick."

"That's right."

She peels away from him, indignant, and he watches her among the other skaters, and once she turns and makes a face at him.

20

"Vomitous," Nat says. She is sitting on Annie's bed, her chin on her knees, her bare feet tucked beneath the frayed hem of the quilt. "Do you believe this room? Really disgustingly vomitous. My God."

A Japanese fan, showing two women, heads inclined toward each other, mouths hidden behind a pair of daintily outspread fans, lies in a dirty saucer on the antique dressing table. Apricot stones are stuck to the bottom of the saucer, and a ball of kite string rests by the hairbrush, whose bristles seem to be matted with cat hair. Cigarettes have been crumpled into a cup still reeking of tea, and a nearby conch shell has been filled to overflowing with matchsticks, nails, thumbtacks, and a fingernail file. The telephone directory lies open on the floor, propped up by a muddy hiking boot with Wonder Woman laces, and a roadmap of New Mexico. Tara searches through the rubble on the bureau and disengages a pair of stockings marked in vertical lines of Chinese characters. "These are nice," she says.

"It's chaos," Nat says. "Pure, pure vomitous chaos. You can have them, if you want."

"I can't take something of hers when she's not here."

"Do you think she'd care? The way she's been lately she wouldn't notice if somebody robbed our whole house."

"Maybe I can wear them one time and then bring them back."

"It's all right with me, whatever you do," Nat says. "You deserve it for coming over."

Tara feels that this is right on the borderline of dishonesty, but she wants the stockings. She goes over and tucks them into the pocket of her jacket. Even the jacket isn't really hers: it's an old one of Peter's, one he stopped wearing a long time ago. She stands before the dresser and brushes her hair with the hairbrush. Nat, who is wearing only an undershirt, rises from the bed and goes to the closet and pulls a long black dress on over her head. She stands behind Tara and makes up her eyes until they seem slightly longer and fringed and then she climbs back into Annie's bed and sits in the same position as before, scratching the sole of her bare foot until her toes curl. They are waiting for Annie to come home. She has been gone all morning and all afternoon, and now it is nearly dark. Tara does her upper and lower lips in two different shades of lipstick.

"There you are," Annie says from the doorway. She shrugs off her fox coat and drops it on the quilt near Nat's knee. Then she sits down on the end of the bed and pulls the coat up to her cheek, rubbing it against her face. "When I was a little girl," she says, "my mother used to come home from somewhere and come upstairs to see whether or not I was asleep, or to see if I was really warm enough or something, and it would be really late at night and the house was quiet, so I could hear her coming, and I would close my eyes and pretend to be asleep. Now I can't remember why I did that. Why didn't I ask her where she'd been, what was there to eat, was it a nice party? But I never did." She looks at Natalie, and then she cocks her left foot over her right knee and tugs her cowboy boot off. Then she gets the other boot off. Both boots lie in the mess on the floor. Annie scoots back along the bed until she is sitting beside Nat and she puts her arm around Nat and talks into Nat's hair. "Well, baby, I'm pregnant," she says. She peels up the covers and tucks her legs down under the sheets and the blankets and the quilts above them, and then she tugs her sweater off over her head, her hair floating up through static electricity, linked to the crumpled sweater, and then she balls the sweater up and throws it across the room. It almost catches on the back of a chair but then it slides loose and falls.

"You really are?" Nat says.

Annie nods. "You and I have been really pretty close lately," she says. "I wish you could help. I wish you could help me know what to do."

"I know," Nat says.

"What?"

"Marry him," she says. "It's not so hard."

"But you haven't always seemed to want him here."

"That's nothing. That's all right now. Charles can get to like him too, after a while."

"I don't know," Annie says. "What do you say, sweet pea?"

"Go on," Tara says. "Marry him."

"Okay," Annie says. "If that's it, I guess I shouldn't wait too long. He who hesitates is lost, right?"

21

The fawn crosses the rain-wet highway first, its dished forehead and small nose dwarfed by its ears, cocked in separate directions—like a cat's ears, it occurs to Clarissa. One ear aims at the woods on the opposite side of the highway while the other ear, showing fine silvery-white hairs, slants toward her, in the Volvo. The ear flicks as she presses the accelerator with the toe of her boot, but that is the only sign the fawn gives of knowing she is there.

"Come on," she says to the fawn. "Move your pretty ass." Her breath has begun to steam the windshield glass and she rubs a clear place with her fist and watches the fawn through the opening. "You move like your legs are made of wood," she says. The fawn turns in a small circle, straddling the yellow line, its chest shining in the headlights. She rolls down the window and shouts, her breath making a cloud in the clear air. The fawn clatters across the road.

The doe follows, drawn into the open by the disappearance of the fawn, though her expression is only mildly wary. She looks toward the waiting Volvo, one retina flashing—for a moment, a watery crimson mirror shines above the doe's flat golden cheek. Light glares along the white underside of her belly and slides from her narrow rump as her hocks tuck into a leap, the hooves seeming too close together, like the knees of a knock-kneed child, and then the doe vanishes into the shadow of a piñon. The highway is empty. Clarissa accelerates. She is not paying much attention when, from the corner of her eye, she sees the buck touch down lightly, its leap ending as its hooves touch the yellow line, its haunches drawn up again just before she hits it, so that she sees the length of the belly aligned in slow motion with the hood of her car and drawn upward, toward her. One hoof kicks desperately at the windshield, spangled with blood, and the buck launches itself at a crazy angle away from the car, somersaulting as it hits the ditch; the Volvo follows a similar course, turning over once, landing on its hood, the gravel crunching curiously near the top of her skull. The world has narrowed into two tunnels carved by the headlights; she is floating in a small space, her sweat running upward, across her rib cage, into the hollow of her throat, and from her forehead into her hairline. The world within the headlights settles into place, quite perfect but upside-down. One eye is burning and she wishes to touch it; she realizes slowly that before she can touch it she must undo the latch of the seatbelt, so she does, falling and banging her head against the dented roof of the Volvo, bruising her shoulder. She crawls out through the window, feeling bits of broken glass prick her knees and the palms of her hands. Motes of dust swirl within the crooked beams of light and she can hear the buck breathing raggedly somewhere close by. Her fingertips brush something and she lifts it: it is the windshield wiper, wet with blood. She stumbles up the slope and before she has gone very far she remembers to turn off the ignition of the Volvo; she reaches inside and the keys turn with a click. More glass showers the inside of her arm. She brushes it away. The deer is making mewing sounds, coughing sounds, almost human sounds. It must be hidden by the chamisa beyond the headlights' reach. She decides to search for it. She circles down the slope, picking her way, some of the time on her hands and knees, and when she finds it the deer is lying on its side, its throat wedged in a gnarled root, its hide contracting at her touch. Now that she has found it all she wants to do is rest, lie down and rest. The buck strains to lift its head a few inches from the ground so that it can stare at her. Its lashes are dusty and there is mucus in the corner of the dark eye. It struggles to see her clearly.

She curls her arms around her knees and stares at the deer. They watch each other and gradually she can see that it is dying. It is dead before the first car stops at the edge of the highway above the slope.

Someone is making his way down the slope toward her; she realizes this when a small stone, pitched loose by the heel of a boot, hits the back of her hand. She looks up and there is a large man gazing down at her with a kind expression, then from her to the deer, its smooth side radiant as the beam of the flashlight slides across it, its head held inches above the ground by the lower antler and the thick angle of exposed root. The man's expression becomes gradually less kind as she does not move. He lifts his arm away from his side, a courtly gesture suitable for square dancing, and he waits patiently until she rises and tucks her hand through his elbow. He is wearing a plaid shirt with pearl buttons that flash gently as he turns to urge her up the slope and she trusts him, she trusts him absolutely. "You turned the ignition off?" he says. "Good girl."

She feels perhaps five years old. The man is nearly bald and the curve of his skull is flushed. Sonny would say, from his complexion, that he is a sure candidate for a coronary. Clarissa wipes her nose with the back of her hand when he isn't looking; she tries not to lean on him too hard because she doesn't want to put too much stress on him, climbing the steep slope. She is already very fond of him. She doesn't want him ever to die.

In his car he offers her a bandanna and points at his own face to show her where hers is dirtiest. "Just spit on it, honey," he says. The CB microphone on his dashboard crackles softly. He picks it up and holds it in his hand. "You're lucky," he says. "You're very lucky, you know that?"

She nods. The burning in her eye seems to have lessened and she is afraid to touch it, afraid to risk starting it up again, afraid that something is wrong. She could go blind. She is a painter and she could go blind. She shivers and tries to make herself stop thinking.

"You hurt anywhere, or just all over?" the man says.

"All over," she says. "All over, really."

"You're going to have to see about that eye."

"I know."

"I guess we should get this over with," he says. He reaches for the CB and draws it away from the dashboard on its cord, coaxing a louder sound of static from the small receiver; he clicks the button with his thumb. "Now," he says. "Who would you like me to try and get hold of?"

"Could you find my husband?" she says.

The old man in the eye doctor's waiting room is smoking. When he is done there is only a filter left, the tan paper charred down to reveal an inner button of unsinged, cottony white. In his apprehension he rubs the butt around and around in the ashtray, making rings against the glass. He rattles the Marlboro pack, and a small pyramid of cigarettes tips upward, held in place by a leaf of cellophane. He chooses one and taps it against the inside of his wrist, just above the tendon. This tapping is prolonged, gracious, as if he has somehow caught, and is delicately mimicking, his own pulse. He lights the cigarette, letting the match burn a moment too long before waving it out. The match falls into the ashtray. The matchbook, which he closes and tucks into his pocket, says ESCUDERO FOR SHERIFF.

He slides back his other shirtcuff to show Peter the face of a watch. "Timex," he says proudly. "From my son Jordan. He's in Omaha, Nebraska, now. Wife, two little girls, and a pretty place they call a duplex. I don't like the word. A house is a house, I told Jordan. If you've got a duplex, what have you got? Omaha, Nebraska, is the insurance capital of the world, they tell me. But you probably know that." He is wearing a cup-shaped eye patch, about the contour and shade of a soiled golf ball, held in place by strands of surgical tape. The old man first noticed the trouble in his eye when he was trying to feed his cat, and could not manage to fit the can opener to the rim of the can.

Peter is holding Clarissa's hand, their two hands below their seats, where the old man probably cannot see them, although he has certainly guessed from Peter's gentleness that they are holding hands. Now and then he looks at Clarissa, but she is staring straight ahead into the aquarium by the wall. A snail is clinging to glass, its body white as a rose petal. Even as Peter watches her, Clarissa's left eye unexpectedly shines, liquid filling the inner bulge of the lower lid before spilling, wetting the lashes, smudging the wing of the nostril. For a moment it is beautiful, the way that the tear, closely watched, lacquers the surface of the eye upward before gathering itself to fall. He wants to touch her cheek but he is afraid of embarrassing her, she is so clearly in pain.

"If I could have one wish," the old man says, "it would be that I could keep this eye."

"You'll keep it," Peter assures him. "I'm sure you'll keep it. They can do wonderful things now."

"The advantage of having lived so long," the old man says. "If the doctor has the touch to apply that technology just right, then you're home free." He crosses his legs and strokes the baggy cloth of his trousers; the gesture is gentlemanly and self-assured. Peter feels the man's concern for Clarissa radiating through his silence. He is a very tactful old man. Peter wonders if he can guess that they are about to be divorced. He remembers the guilty way in which Mia, naked, touched his shoulder in the darkness so that he could get up to come to the telephone. He remembers that at first he had thought she had awakened him because she wanted to make love. On the walls of the waiting room there are framed photographs of eyes, many times magnified, glossy, enormous, with ringed irises of deep bronze or malachite green. The old man nods, indicating the nearest photograph. "I wish they wouldn't put those pictures up," he says. "It only makes me nervous to be reminded of it." He sighs. "It's a very precious, precious thing, the eye."

"Yes, it is," Peter says.

A nurse comes into the waiting room and reads the old man's name from a clipboard. He rises stiffly and she directs him into one of the examining rooms that open off a central hallway. "The doctor will be with you in a moment," she says, and he nods at her. "Now, Mrs. Wu-Barnes?" she says. "Will you follow me, please?"

Clarissa's hand feels quite small and dry inside his own. "Can I come with her?" Peter says, surprising himself. Clarissa looks at him and he brings himself to look into her eye: he can see the central point of the metal fragment, so uncannily fixed within the shallow disk of the iris, held in a penumbra of rust. The rust has radiated outward from the fragment the way, in a newly halved peach, the pit seems to have stained the surrounding flesh. The corrosion is brilliant against the dark caramel-brown of the iris; the sharpness of the oxidized orange stain seems almost phosphorescent in intensity. The fragment and its surrounding stain are no larger than the head of a pin, but quite distinct.

That was how they could tell it was a metal fragment, the doctor had told Peter on the telephone: because of the orange color, which was rust. Whenever there is warmth and moisture you get rust faster, and the eye is a warm, moist place. Peter said he had never thought about it that way. The doctor said they were lucky it wasn't wood. Wood is dangerous because of splinters. "Isn't this dangerous?" "Not very," the doctor said. He also said it would be all right until morning and that Clarissa should take some aspirin for the pain. Peter had called Mia to tell her that he was spending the night—he could hardly leave Clarissa alone. Mia was wary and almost shy with him, and she did not ask him when she would see him again. He could tell she thought it would have been an inappropriate question, but somehow he wishes she had asked.

"I guess you can come with her," the nurse says. "I don't see why not. Sure."

She leads them into a neat, narrow room, indicates a chair for Clarissa, and begins to fill out a questionnaire on her clipboard. Peter answers several of the questions for Clarissa. "Husband?" she says. Peter nods. For a moment Peter thinks that he was confused and he has made a sexist slip, that this woman is really the doctor—her crooked teeth seem a sign of confidence, and the collar of her uniform shows a faint flesh-colored blur—powder? A second door opens and the doctor comes in; he is wearing a three-piece suit and dark sunglasses which he removes to study first Clarissa, then Peter. "This is the metal fragment?" he says, indicating Clarissa with the earpiece of his sunglasses.

"That's right," the nurse says. "She's all yours. I've got everything I need."

"You're the only person I know who can honestly say that," the doctor says. He washes his hands in the sink on the far side of the room and when he holds his hands up into the light Peter sees that they are very clean, the nails lustrous and short, and he feels somewhat reassured, in spite of the suit. The doctor cups Clarissa's chin and turns her face one way, then the other.

"What are you going to do?" Clarissa says.

"He's going to get the metal fragment out of your iris," the nurse says.

"I know, but how is he going to do that?"

"He's going to use a special machine," the nurse says.

They are talking as if the doctor were not there, between them, in his handsomely tailored suit. The doctor positions a hinged, cranelike machine in front of Clarissa's chair; he pushes a sort of mask into place against her face. The mask is composed of a grid of smooth curved bars and an opening through which Peter can see her eye gleaming. "Just relax," the doctor says. "You're the woman in the iron mask." He tightens some dials; it is a machine that forces Clarissa to stare straight ahead, the metal cupping her chin, cheekbones, and forehead, so that she can jerk her head neither sideways nor vertically. Her visible eye, as he watches, begins to fill, the tear again tracing the curve of the lower lid before lapping outward, wetting the lower lashes so that they shine, stiff and black, against the fold of skin that the tear now also, slowly, washes. The tear spills down along her cheekbone and disappears along skin that is now, freshly golden, reflected by the light of the machine. He feels, from his place across the room, that she is terrified and making a great effort to be still. "This won't hurt," the doctor says, softly. Perhaps he also senses that fear. "Really, I promise you." The doctor seats himself on a black leather stool with wheels and scoots himself closer to the machine.

"You promise," Clarissa echoes.

The doctor brings his face quite close to hers but on the opposite side of the mask; he peers into a dark lens and steadies himself and with one hand he makes a small, fastidious motion of adjustment, like someone focussing a microscope, and though Peter cannot quite see what he has done—the doctor's back is to him—when the doctor sighs, Peter sighs, and realizes he has been holding his breath. "That's it," the doctor says, triumphantly, but not surprised by his triumph. The nurse makes a playful motion of applause. "That was nothing," the doctor says.

"What did you do?" Peter says.

"Want to come and look?" the doctor says. Peter bends and looks over the doctor's shoulder, smelling his calm astringent scent, and Clarissa's eye seems huge and dark and there is a clear nick, unimaginably small, vertical, bare of rust and quite distinct in the iris, like a scratch in ice.

"The machine has a little lever, you see?" the doctor says. "It works just like a six iron. It popped that fragment right out." He mimes a golf swing and smiles to himself. He scoots his wheeled stool back and rearranges the machine, which seems to move stiffly on myriad noiseless hinges, so that Clarissa can stand up. "Now the nurse is going to give you a patch for that eye, so you can keep it nice and sterile, and some medication for the pain. You shouldn't drive or operate any machinery under the medication, even though it's pretty mild stuff, because it might make you drowsy."

"Thanks, doctor," Peter says.

"Yes," Clarissa says. "Thank you."

"Nothing to it," the doctor says. "You should see me play golf sometime."

22

Peter drives Clarissa home in his pickup, and for most of the way she is silent, her forehead against the glass of the window. "Pretty weird, wasn't it?" he says. "How do you feel?"

"I feel all right," she says. "It hurts more now than it did while the fragment was in."

"Give the pain stuff a chance to work," he says.

"How do you like me as Moshe Dayan?" she says. "Or who is the pirate in Peter Pan?"

"In Peter Pan he's lost an arm, not an eye."

"That's right. Captain Hook."

"Listen. You look great with an eye patch. You'll probably start a fad."

"I might look great, but I feel shitty. I wrecked my car."

"It's just a car."

"I know it's just a car. How the hell am I supposed to get anywhere? I can't live here without a car."

"You can get another car."

"*I* can get another car."

"You have the insurance money."

"I know that," she says. "It's not as if I'm broke."

"Look, I can help you."

"You can?"

"I'm hardly going to let you suffer this one through on your own."

"It was my fault."

"It was an accident," Peter says. "It wasn't anybody's fault."

"He froze in the headlights."

"I know."

"He just froze. I knew there wasn't a chance in hell that he would make it across the road, because there was that fraction of a second when he was blinded."

"You always hear that," Peter says. "Deer freezing in the light."

"Well, he did. That's exactly what he did."

"You couldn't help hitting him."

"I know, but I *hated* it. I hated the sounds he made."

"Don't talk about it."

"I keep seeing it."

"Just try to think of something else," Peter says. "Something nice."

"Like what?" she says. "Like you?"

He parks the pickup, walks around to open her door for her, and leads her along the fence to the gate, which he unlatches. She touches the horse skull on the adobe wall as she passes it, grazing the bone of its nose with her fingers, lightly. He remembers finding the skull in the mountains, at the bottom of a stream whose water was dark with tannin, and how the skull was white and polished and seemed, through some trick of depth perception, to be floating several inches above the muddy bottom. There had been water weeds growing through the eye sockets, a wreath of coppery flowers shaped like harebells, cold and slimy and fragile, and those had delighted her. She had wrapped the skull in newspapers and put it in the open oven to dry in slow, even heat. She had tried to keep the flowers intact but eventually they had dried and come loose from the supporting bone. When she opens the front door he can smell sandalwood incense and something like cooked hamburgers; Tara must have been there and gone, because he looks in her room and it's empty. Clarissa finds the note by the telephone. "She's over at Nat's house," she says. "I guess she wasn't too worried."

"No," Peter says. He watches while Clarissa takes a bottle of Perrier from the refrigerator and uncaps it, breaking the metal seal. She drinks from the bottle and shakes the pills from the packet that they had filled at the drugstore in the same office complex as the eye doctor's suite. Everything was very handy, very accessible. Peter supposes that is good. He wonders suddenly how the old man did. Maybe he should have stayed to find out. "Better?" Peter says.

"Did you ever get something into your eye?" she says. "It hurts."

"I know it hurts."

"No, it really hurts." Suddenly she strikes him on the shoulder with her hand flat, extended. "I don't think you're even capable of empathy," she says. She hits him again.

He catches her hand. "Stop it now," he says. He shakes her hand gently. Her fingers curl inside his arm.

"Peter, I was so scared," she says. "Just so scared."

"I know," he says. "Don't you want to go to bed now?"

"If I did go to bed, would you come with me?"

"With you?"

"Would you sleep with me?"

Everything about the kitchen seems familiar. He wonders how many breakfasts he ate at that table. On the wall there is

a small painting of Clarissa's, a single pear that seems to be floating in midair. It is a beautiful pear. He thinks he has probably
never before realized how good a painter she is. Scotch-
taped to the refrigerator door there are some Polaroid photographs: him with Tara; Natalie and Tara with their arms
around each other—Natalie sporting the vampire fangs;
Clarissa in a paint-stained shirt; and, for no reason at all, a
picture of his pickup. There are also two drawings Tara did so
long ago that the paper is yellowing. Peter studies the drawings,
exuberant slashes of crayon indicating clouds, a rocket, a blue
sky, white stars, green grass, one drawing labelled LOVE and
the other SPACE TRAVEL.

"I'll come," he says.

When she kisses him in bed he doesn't feel anything at first.
She is obviously tense; then her knees part more widely and he
settles along the length of her body. She cries his name and
when she comes her eyelid flutters, the eyelid that he can see,
and he touches the eye patch to test the coarseness of the bandage against her fine skin, because she really is beautiful. He
tells himself he has always known it.

Afterward they are silent for a long while and when, early
in the evening, the telephone begins to ring, she sits up and
scratches her knee. "I suppose that could be Tara," she says.

"It could be."

"I just don't want to move."

"Don't move, then," he says. "I'll get it, next time."

"You're not coming back to me, are you?" she says. "It's not
even a possibility any longer, is it?"

"No," he says. "I don't think so."

"You don't think so."

"You're annoyed by the way I said it?"

"No," she says, "this hurts"—and touches the eye patch in
the dark.

The traffic in the canyon nearly always slackens as it begins to get dark, and they can hear a truck going by on the road, its gears grinding, and once a bicycle squeaks to a halt and a child sings out, "Na na-na na na," and rides away furiously fast. Peter lies silently hoping that the medicine will work soon, and while he is waiting, he falls asleep. He hasn't been asleep very long when her weeping wakes him. He had almost forgotten how rarely she cries. He strokes her face until she falls asleep. She seems to fall asleep between one ragged breath and the next, and she is asleep for several minutes before her body relaxes against his, her face still on his chest. He is now wide-awake. He begins to wish for a cigarette. Her hair fans across his shoulder, covering it. He tries hard not to move and not to think about a cigarette. In a few minutes, he knows, the wish will alter into need.